The Puzzle Box

The Glenmere Box Mysteries

Book 1

Lisa Adair

Disclaimer

This is a work of fiction. Unless otherwise indicated, all names, characters, businesses, places, events and incidents in this book are either the product of the author's imagination or used in a fictitious manner. any resemblance to actual persons, living or dead, or events is purely coincidental.

If you can dream it, make it happen!

Prologue

Toronto, Ontario

1978

"I'm all in," Eddie declared, his voice trembling with a potent mix of anxiety and determination as he forcefully shoved his towering stack of chips into the centre of the table. His hand was a straight flush to the queen of hearts, a rare and powerful combination. This win was crucial, not just to cover his mounting expenses but to stave off the looming threat of his gambling debts, which were beginning to take a toll on his health and well-being. The potential payout for this game was staggering, promising to be in the thousands!

"Me too," Leon said, nervously looking to John for his bid as he slid the rest of his chips into the pot. "I'm all in."

It wasn't the first time Eddie and Leon had played poker together. Before the high-stakes game, their poker journey began more than a decade earlier, in high school in the small town of Glenmere, Saskatchewan. Along with John, Steve, and Gabe formed a tight-knit group that spent their time playing poker and engaging in other typical high school activities.

Every Thursday night, they'd play for pennies, which they kept in large empty margarine containers. The rules were simple, and the stakes were low. Each player initially started with five hundred pennies in their sizeable containers, but the count for each game would change depending on their wins and losses, with whatever they still had carrying over to the next night's game. Once in a while, the boys would count the pennies to see who the leader was and confirm that the total number didn't exceed 2,500, ensuring no one had added anything to their stash.

The entire group had never really stopped playing either, and even after ten years, they continued to meet once a year for their annual poker tradition. It was a time for them to reconnect, to reminisce, and to create new memories. This year, though, they'd decided to meet in the back room of a seedy bar in Green Hills, a suburb of Toronto, and join the high-stakes poker game the dealer held there on Friday nights. Leon had insisted that knowing each other's playing strategies as they did, they would have an obvious advantage over the others at the table.

Eddie ran his hand over his blond hair and looked at Gabe, who was busily trying to read the room. Gabe raised his brown eyebrows before shifting his eyes to John. Eddie followed Gabe's gaze, noting that John's overgrown black moustache was twitching ever so slightly, a tell-tale sign that he was agitated. John's blue eyes turned dark as he stared at Eddie's cards.

"You're cheating!" John growled.

"Shut your mouth," Eddie said dismissively. "You're just jealous that I'm winning." Eddie tapped his cards on the table in front of him. "Are you in or out?"

"I saw you!" John cursed and slammed his hand down. "You palmed an extra card!"

"You didn't see shit! You're just pissed because you still suck at cards, and you're losing! Just like you always—"

John didn't let him finish. With a decade's worth of frustration with Eddie's bullshit condescension finally bubbling over, he leapt to his feet and flipped the table, sending poker chips flying everywhere. "You lying, son of a bitch!"

Unfortunately, in the heat of the moment, he'd forgotten that this wasn't just a small-town game between old friends. Everyone was jumping up now, friends and strangers alike, yelling and shoving each other as chaos broke out in the smoke-filled room. John leapt at Eddie while Leon, Gabe, and Steve struggled to hold the two of them apart.

"HEY!!" The dealer was now on his feet, his face red with anger. "Everyone back against the walls! NOW!" When no one listened, he reached into his jacket, produced a handgun, and fired two quick shots into the ceiling, stopping everyone in their tracks. "This game is over! There are no refunds on the buy-in! And you five, consider yourselves banned from my poker room! Don't ever show your faces here again!"

Eddie couldn't believe it. He'd been so close! That pot had been his, and it would have fixed everything! John had ruined it! He'd ruined everything! How the hell was he supposed to pay back all the money he owed now? Hell, he was worse off now than he'd been before! Not only had he taken another significant loss, but he'd also been banned from the one game in town rich enough to cash in on!

Kicking his chair against the wall in a rage, he stormed out, practically flying through the back door and inadvertently knocking into some guy in the back alley who happened to be standing in the wrong place. With a cry of fury, frustration, and uncontrolled anguish, he lost all control, throwing the young stranger to the ground and going off, hammering him with his fists. After Eddie spent his wrath and came back to awareness, he found himself kneeling over his unfortunate victim, breathing hard through clenched teeth, his fists dripping with blood that shone bright red in twin beams of light, as two police officers approached him with their guns and flashlights out, silhouetted against the blue and red flashing lights of their cruiser, which parked at the end of the alley.

Eddie slowly raised his bloodied hands into the air and stood up, not taking his eyes off the young man he had just brutally beaten for no apparent reason. He was only vaguely aware of the officer cuffing his hands behind his back. Almost numb with shock and horror, he watched as the club's back door opened and other players started filing out of the poker room, each blinking in silent shock and confusion at the scene before them.

Only one of them moved, rushing to the fallen man and dropping to his knees beside him. "CRAIG!!"

Eddie watched as the man struggled with where to put his hands amidst all the blood, then pulled his victim into his lap with tears flowing down his cheeks before looking up at him, asking him why he'd done it and cursing him through his tears.

One of the officers looked down at him. "Sir, the ambulance is on its way."

Eddie's head was shaking slowly from side to side. *It's not my fault,* he thought desperately. *I didn't mean to.* At that moment, he spotted John among the stunned onlookers, and his face twisted into a sneer.

"You! This mess is all your fault!"

His long-time friend had no idea what it was like to struggle, having never experienced it himself. Not with his happy family supporting him, ensuring he'd never know what it was like to fight for every crumb to survive. At that moment, Eddie found it amazing that he'd never realized how much he hated John.

"You ruined everything! You always ruin everything! THIS MESS IS YOUR FAULT!!"

As he was led away and loaded into the back of the cop car, he replayed every moment of their so-called friendship, all the way back to high school. Every time he'd willingly taken a back seat to John over the years, and every time he'd let things that bothered him slide, out of some stupid sense of loyalty and friendship, when he should have known better than to think John had ever given a crap about him.

Well, no more! That fucker's gonna pay!

Chapter 1

August 13, 1985

Tuesday

The radio alarm jolted Amy Young awake at 6:55 a.m., playing the number-one hit song from last year's Billboard Charts: "Thriller" by Michael Jackson. She tried to reach for the snooze button but was tangled in her bedding, so she just laid still and listened to it play with closed eyes. She was exhausted, having spent the night being plagued once again by a recurring nightmare, which had kept her from sleeping very well. As usual, she vaguely remembered what she was dreaming, but it was somewhat foggy. Someone had been chasing her down a dark hallway or narrow street while she frantically tried to get away.

She must have dozed off again because the next thing she heard was a radio announcer's deep voice reading the seven o'clock news. "—Charles Simmons escaped police custody last Wednesday in Ontario but is believed to be moving west into Manitoba or Saskatchewan. He is considered armed and dangerous. Police caution the public not to approach him but to call the local police immediately—"

After fighting with the blankets for several long moments, Amy managed to wriggle one arm free enough to turn off the alarm. Yawning, she worked her arms and legs until she could unravel the blankets. Finally, she sat up, rubbing her hands over her face and gritty eyes, even as she worked her tongue around in her dry mouth. *I guess I should get up and face the day. It's going to be a long one,* she thought.

After pulling on a pair of blue uniform slacks and a checkered blue shirt, Amy padded across the hall to brush her teeth and wash up. Her hair looked like she'd combed it with a tornado. "Must have been some dream," Amy said, smirking at herself in the mirror, grabbing a yellow scrunchie off the countertop, and pulling all her shoulder-length brown hair into a high ponytail at the top of her head. She splashed cold water onto her face to rinse away the remnants of yesterday's makeup before reapplying heavy blue eye shadow, pink blush, black mascara, and bright pink lipstick to complete her look. Taking a good look at her appearance in the water-splattered mirror, she went back into her room to get the blue vest with the Family Grocers logo and name tag, then did a quick check of the floor to find her jean jacket and searched the pockets for her house key. The alarm clock was already flashing, and it was past the time for her to be out the door. She pulled on the vest and jean jacket as she ran out the front door.

Looking up at the sky, Amy decided the clouds didn't look dark enough for rain. At least, she hoped it wouldn't rain because she had to ride her beloved flashy orange ten-speed bike with yellow handlebars to work to get there before her shift started. Amy cherished her bike. It was the first thing she'd bought with the money she earned as a cashier at the Family Grocers.

The job wasn't glamorous, but it was one that a sixteen-year-old could handle and would give her the money she desperately needed to survive in the world. Amy was determined to save her earnings to buy a car, her ticket out of Glenmere, this boring, little Northern Saskatchewan town. She wasn't sure how long it would take to save up enough to buy a car, so she was confined to riding a bicycle to her $4.25 per hour part-time job. The only thing she especially liked about the cashier job was the knowledge that she was earning slightly more than minimum wage. Even so, she still found her finances tight, even with the occasional shifts she picked up at Frankie's Diner, washing dishes and busing tables. She was only paid $3.50 an hour (in cash) and complimentary hot meals for that job.

Amy currently lives in a little house with her aunt Jeannie. Though not a blood relation, Jeannie Young was sadly all Amy had. The two barely survived financially, even though Jeannie also worked two jobs to afford the small house, which meant she was hardly ever home. When Jeannie's husband, Amy's uncle John, abandoned her several years earlier, he left her to deal with his gambling debts. As such, Amy did not doubt that her aunt had been barely making ends meet even before she'd arrived on her doorstep, but still, Jeannie had opened her home in the middle of the night to provide Amy with food and lodging. Sometimes, that food was in the form of groceries, and sometimes, it was leftovers from Frankie's Diner, where Jeannie worked night shifts as a waitress. Amy didn't complain, though, knowing that even leftovers were better than starving. Frank, the diner's owner, knew that Amy was willing to cover a shift or two when the restaurant was short-staffed, which seemed to be more often than not.

During the day, Jeannie worked as the part-time receptionist at the town's only doctor's office but didn't talk much about it, as she didn't enjoy it. Jeannie had been living on her own until last spring, when the police had dropped Amy off at her doorstep in the middle of the night in April after her grandmother had died, saying that Jeannie could either take temporary custody of her or Amy would be put into foster care because social services couldn't locate any other living relatives. Jeannie hadn't said much but moved out of the doorway and showed Amy to the first of the three bedrooms. When Jeannie married Amy's uncle, John, she'd envisioned a life filled with their children. Little did she know she would be shouldering the responsibility of supporting a teenager who was only connected to her through her estranged husband, John. This unexpected turn of events had placed a heavy emotional burden on her.

With their four combined jobs, Amy's interactions with her aunt, Jeannie, were limited. She had to fend for herself, buying clothes, toiletries, and sometimes even food. However, a glimmer of hope still burned within her. The recent death of her grandmother, Dorothy Young, had left her yearning for an inheritance that could ease her life and provide a brighter future beyond their pint-sized town.

Jeannie and Amy had been speculating about who would inherit Dorothy's farmhouse and whether or not that person would sell it. Jeannie thought that her estranged husband John would be the benefactor and that he would likely sell it and spend all the money gambling, leaving them both in their current situation unless she sued him for half of it in a divorce. Amy agreed that this was likely since he was Dorothy's only living child, but until the reading of the last will, neither of them would be sure of anything.

A few months had passed since Dorothy's death. Still, her lawyer had since retired, leaving the paperwork in the hands of a new lawyer, who was waiting for some documents to clear up certain matters before the estate could be settled and he could proceed with the reading of the will. Jeannie thought that maybe the lawyer was still trying to locate Uncle John, but like she had tried to tell him, he would likely have returned to Glenmere if he had wanted to. Jeannie didn't know what documents he was waiting for. The paperwork seemed to be taking a lot of time, and Jeannie had already accused the new lawyer of drawing things out to pad his fees.

Amy locked the front door behind herself, putting the key around her neck, where she always kept it, and the farmhouse key on a blue shoelace for safekeeping. Sometimes, the keys jingled against her chest when she moved.

She reached for the combination lock on her orange and yellow bicycle when she heard her next-door neighbour, Beatrice Petersen, yell out from her front step, "Aren't you running a little late for your shift, Amy? You better hurry up, girl! And watch out! There seems to be a shady character hanging around town. Did you listen to the news? I bet he's behind all the break-ins we're hearing about on the radio!"

Amy was sure that her neighbour said a few other things, but she wasn't really in the mood to listen and had no time to let Beatrice talk her ear off with town gossip. It was a little town, so it didn't take long for gossip to spread through the usual channels, but if you could stay away from the drama and those spreading the gossip, you could stay out of it.

"Thank you, Mrs. Petersen. I'm on my way!" Amy called out, cutting off whatever she was saying but still trying to be polite as she concentrated on unlocking her bike and getting to work on time. She twirled the combination numbers again, trying to free her bicycle from where she had chained it to the gas meter. Finally, she hopped on her bike and started pedaling, giving her neighbour a little wave, trying to remind herself to be kind to people trying to be helpful in their way, even while hoping that Beatrice wouldn't start spreading gossip about her being late and irresponsible.

Amy glanced at her watch and then put it up to her ear to check if she'd remembered to wind it. It was still ticking out what Amy hoped was the correct time. The grocery store was a ten-minute ride from Jeannie's house, so Amy figured that if she pedaled faster, she should make it there with five minutes to spare.

Out of breath, she coasted her bike to the grocery store parking lot and jumped off her bicycle by the bike rack in the corner. Glenmere was a little town, but petty theft was its main crime, followed by family violence and vandalism. Lately, everyone talked about a rash of thefts and small items going missing all over town. After securing her prized possession with the combination lock, Amy entered through the main doors at 7:57 a.m., just in time for her eight o'clock shift, silently congratulating herself as she stepped across the threshold of the Family Grocers.

Amy could hear talking near the three registers and looked over. Her boss, Dan Fisher, was already manning one of them. Dan was average height, with round features, wire-rimmed glasses, a moustache, and a ruddy complexion. He looked over his shoulder at Amy as she entered before turning back to the early-morning customer. He wore his uniform: a blue dress shirt with a matching blue plaid tie and matching blue dress pants. It was what all the men in the store wore. Only the women had to wear vests, but Amy was happy with the uniforms, so she didn't have to struggle with what to wear to work every day. The customer was an old gentleman in a dark sports coat, talking Dan's ear off and complaining that he used to be able to buy bread for less than a dollar. *What year does this guy think it is? It's 1985! Get over it!* Amy thought, rolling her eyes.

Amy headed straight to the staff room and hung her jacket on an empty peg. A few other employees were doing the same, and then they stowed their lunch kits under the little shelf against the wall before heading out onto the sales floor. Amy didn't have a lunch kit to stash away. Her stomach growled, reminding her that she hadn't eaten breakfast or remembered to pack a lunch.

The staffroom was already a haze of cigarette smoke, which made her stomach feel queasy.

Why would you come to work early to sit and smoke a cigarette in the staffroom? She was dreading what seemed likely to be another long and miserable day. She quickly left the staff room to go to her usual position on register three, but Dan motioned her over to his.

"Come take over for me at this one, Amy," he said as he backed away from the register.

Amy looked around for Anna Labrash, who usually ran the first register. Not seeing her, she took Dan's spot, picking up the last item the old man had placed on the belt. The can didn't have a price tag on it.

Of course not! Amy thought, reaching for the microphone to call for a price check over the sound system, hoping that one of the stock boys was already on the sales floor. "Price check for store-brand canned tuna, please." Silence met her request as Amy looked awkwardly at the older man standing beside her, who was craning his neck to look down the rows of aisles. Amy patiently waited for what seemed like an eternity for the price. She smiled awkwardly at the man standing with her and sighed, wondering if she should abandon her post and find the price sticker for the tuna herself. It seemed preferable to make small talk with this old grumpy man first thing in the morning, for which she didn't have the energy. Silence hung awkwardly between them.

Finally, the price was called out to her from the canned goods aisle: "A dollar three!" The stock boys were supposed to come to the registers to tell the cashiers the prices, but whoever had called it out hadn't followed store policy. Amy rolled her eyes, punched it in, finished the sale, and then moved to her regular station on register number three.

Amy continued her work day as usual, but nothing exciting happened. It rarely did in this boring little town or her job. She kept reminding herself she was there for the paycheck to buy a car, not for a lifetime career. Customers talked to Amy about the weather, farming, weather affecting farming, the latest rash of break-ins, and *The Farmer's Almanac* predictions about the weather. It didn't matter. Amy would rather talk about the weather than answer people's questions about what she would do with her life after she finished high school, how Amy was surviving as an orphan, or whether or not she had a boyfriend. She felt like she was always standing in the same place, having the same conversation repeatedly.

Luckily, things got slightly more exciting mid-afternoon when an older, heavy-set woman with a floral dress came through Amy's cash lane.

"Whatever you do, don't squish my bread," the old woman huffed. Amy recognized her as Beatrice Petersen's friend, Denise Schneider. I want paper bags—not those plastic ones!"

"Did she say paper?" asked Shane, the stock boy, from behind Amy, making her jump slightly before turning and nodding to him. He smiled back at her, pulling the paper sacks out from the end of the counter to start packing. Denise was the only other person in town with more gossip than Beatrice Petersen. Amy thought that if you wanted everyone in the town to know what was happening in your life, you just needed to tell one of the two women to guard your deepest, darkest secret, and you would hear your news come back to you in less than an hour—two at the most.

Denise rambled on about a friend whose house had been broken into last week, with small items stolen and a big mess left behind for her to clean up. Amy was only half listening to her stories, but she nodded as she tried to punch in each price quickly so she wouldn't have to endure Denise for too long. Suddenly, Amy stopped what she was doing, realizing Denise was asking her a direct question. Amy blinked a few times. "Pardon me?"

"You're that girl—Amy, aren't you?" she asked, pointing at her.

"Yes, I'm Amy. What did you say?" Amy's eyebrows furrowed in confusion.

Denise sighed, taking a big breath. "I said, 'I heard you had to move in with your aunt Jeannie after your grandma Dorothy mysteriously died last spring. How do you like living there?' Is she back together with that no-good husband of hers? I thought I saw your uncle down the street yesterday. He was a block away so I couldn't be sure. Is it him? Is he back together with Jeannie? You should hide your valuables if you have any, or they'll surely go missing!" The woman's eyes were bugging out as she punctuated each question by pointing a chubby finger at Amy.

"I-It's fine... No, I-I wouldn't know where he is," Amy stammered, stepping back a little, hating the bombardment of these unexpected questions. "I haven't seen him since I was small, when my mother was still alive."

Amy wiped her sweaty palms on her pant legs, wondering if she should address her weird comment about Dorothy's death being mysterious and the whereabouts of her estranged uncle or ignore Denise Schneider's need to dig for more gossip altogether. Finally, she asked, "Why would you think Aunt Jeannie and Uncle John were back together? I haven't seen him around, but I'd think Aunt Jeannie would have mentioned seeing her husband since he owes her a lot of money."

Amy shook her head to clear her thoughts. She wished she hadn't responded at all and ignored Denise Schneider's attempt to fish for more information.

"I knew your grandmother Dorothy. She was healthy until her sudden death. It was so shocking! I just wondered what happened to her." She raised an eyebrow and nodded while waiting for Amy to share the gossip she craved.

Amy, deciding not to give in to her probing looks or strange questions, dismissed the whole thing. "I have no idea what you're talking about. She died of natural causes." Amy turned toward the register to read off her total and finish the transaction. "That will be $58.53. Are you paying by cash or cheque?"

Denise pursed her lips like she'd eaten something sour and handed over three crisp, green, twenty-dollar bills. Smiling sarcastically, Amy gave her the change and the dollar bill, saying, "That's fifty-nine and sixty. Shane will take your groceries out for you, Denise." Denise stood there momentarily, staring silently back at Amy before turning and marching out the door with Shane following closely behind with her bags.

Amy rolled her eyes, hoping Denise wouldn't tell her boss she'd been rude. Everyone in this town knew everything and everyone in it. Unable to shake the sick, hollow feeling in her stomach after that conversation, Amy's confusing thoughts were consuming. *What would cause someone to question the cause of my grandmother's death as mysterious? Is Uncle John back in town after all these years to take possession of the farmhouse? Why didn't Aunt Jeannie say something to me? Where does this leave me?*

Amy's palms were still sweating, and she was starting to feel a bit light-headed. She put her hands on her temples, closing her eyes for a moment. She didn't even want to think about her financial welfare or her future chances for a better life with the help of a little inheritance.

One thing Amy knew for sure was that she wouldn't stay in small-time little Glenmere, operating the register at the Family Grocers for the rest of her life. When she opened her eyes, she didn't see anyone else standing in line, so she slid the "please use other registers" sign to the end of her cash lane, needing to take advantage of this lull in the day to get away from other people for a while.

She called over to the cashier next to her on register two. "Gloria, I'm just going to go clean the washrooms." Gloria nodded without looking up, filing her nails and waiting for her next customer.

The washrooms were accessible by walking through the staff room, which is why they were technically called the "staff washrooms." However, as in any little town with no secrets, customers came in through the staff room to use the washrooms on a regular basis, just as though they were intended for public use.

As the part-time student cashier and the last hired, Dan gave Amy the additional task of cleaning the two washrooms on her shift days. She'd negotiated a nice raise based on the argument that she would be cleaning them in addition to her regular cashier responsibilities. It was a good task because it gave Amy a break from standing behind the register and didn't involve handling heavy stock items. Today, she figured she could take time to clean the washrooms while calming down after interacting with Denise.

She stopped at the little counter against the staff room wall to grab a coffee mug to fill with water from the sink. She hoped a little water would stop her stomach from gurgling and growling. She wished she'd remembered to eat breakfast as she felt light-headed, shaky, and irritated. After taking a few gulps of tepid water and setting the mug in the sink, Amy noticed an opened box of oatmeal cookies on the counter. Irresistible to a starving teenager. She eagerly shoved one in her mouth and started to chew as she headed to the cleaning closet. She was startled by shuffling feet behind her as she dug around in it, looking for the cleaners and yellow rubber gloves. She jumped and almost choked on her cookie.

"I'm sorry. I didn't mean to scare you. I'm checking to see if you were okay after that last customer."

From her crouching position before the open closet, Amy looked up, her eyes watering from coughing, to see the tall, skinny stock boy, Shane O'Conner, towering over her. *He has to be over six feet.* "Yes, ... I'm fine."

He reached up and pushed up his glasses with his index finger. "Okay. I was checking because I thought you looked upset after Denise left."

Amy shook her head and stood up, straightening to her five-foot-tall stature as she finished the rest of her cookie. Swallowing, she looked up at him and nodded with more self-assurance. "I'm fine. Really. I just came in here to clean the staff washrooms." They looked at each other awkwardly before he stepped away and left the area. She returned, picking up the rubber gloves and cleaner to begin her task.

Amy was only finishing the ladies' washroom when she heard her name being called over the sound system, instructing her to return to the registers. "I guess I'll do the other one later," she said, pulling off the yellow rubber gloves to wash her hands before returning. On her way out, she grabbed three oatmeal cookies and shoved them into her vest pocket in case they were all gone before the end of her shift.

All three registers had a line at least two customers long, so Amy hurried back to her station. The afternoon stayed busy until the end of her shift, not allowing Amy the chance to clean the men's washroom, but as she was pretty tired and starving, she left without doing it. Amy retrieved a partially crumbled cookie from her pocket, pushed open the main doors, and headed across the parking lot. She noticed that her boss, Dan, was talking to a short, skinny man who had his back to her, but Dan gave Amy a nod of acknowledgement over his shoulder. Amy waved, continued to the bike rack and twirled the combination on her lock: *Two-three-six.*

Climbing onto her bike, she started pedaling towards home with her thoughts clouded by the day's events. Her feet hurt. Her legs hurt. She pulled the last cookie out of her pocket and ate it while slowly going home. She looked forward to returning to working weekends and short after-school shifts this fall. Summertime work was great for a student like her because another employee always wanted time off, leaving full-time shifts for her to take from them. The money was good, but the shifts seemed endlessly long. Just another reminder that, after Amy's last year in high school, she just had to get out of this little town, go to university, get a better job, and make some decent money. The only problem was that she didn't have enough money to attend university. Still, she hoped to be able to get a student loan based on her current financial situation, which would keep her continuing education within reach.

When Amy was little, her mother, Sandy, had moved them in with Dorothy, her mother. Amy was too young to remember what the situation was that had brought them to live at her grandma's farmhouse, but when her mom had died from cancer, her grandma had been there to finish raising her—well, until she'd suddenly died too.

Amy stopped pedaling and thought, *Wait, maybe it was mysterious. No, what am I thinking? It was a heart attack. That old busybody has me all worked up for nothing! I'm probably just hungry.*

She shook her head to clear it, steering her bike into her aunt's driveway and almost hitting the back of Jeannie's rusty old green Ford truck. *If she's home, food just might have come home with her!* Amy quickly locked up her bike in its usual spot and went to the front door, her stomach growling in anticipation of a hot meal.

Just as Amy reached for the doorknob, the door swung open. Jeannie wore her Frankie's Diner uniform: an orange striped shirt, black dress pants, and a blue apron with matching orange ruffles. She had tied a bright orange ribbon in her hair to hold it back from her face. "Hi, honey; I brought home leftovers from the diner last night. It's in the fridge for you. There's a bit of a selection this time, which you can thank Bob for!"

Amy smiled. Bob Crookedneck was one of the cooks at the diner. Amy suspected he was either taking pity on them or was in love with Jeannie. Unfortunately for Bob, Jeannie only dated men with flashy cars, fat wallets, and leather jackets if it was the latter.

"Did you pick up groceries too?" Amy asked, crossing her fingers.

"No. I didn't pick up my paycheck from the doctor's office in time to get to the bank. I'll do it tomorrow on my lunch break if I have time. Are you working tomorrow?" she called back to her niece over her shoulder as she brushed past her and into her old green truck. The engine groaned as she attempted to start it. After pumping the gas pedal twice, it came to life with a cloud of black smoke. Not waiting for her question answered, she called, "See you later, kid! I work until close again tonight." She slammed the door shut and ground the gear shift into the drive as she headed toward the Main Street diner.

Amy felt disappointed that she hadn't had the time to ask about her uncle John and his whereabouts. She sighed and turned towards the open doorway of the little house, kicking off her shoes onto the little mat by the front door as she walked over to the fridge. There wasn't a lot in it except the five new Styrofoam containers full of promise (and diner leftovers)—at least, they were promising for a starving teenager ready to eat just about anything. Amy took out all the containers and set them on the kitchen counter to view her options for tonight's meal.

The first two containers were the same: meatloaf, gravy, mashed potatoes, and corn; the other three offered roast chicken dinner with peas, carrots, and potatoes or chicken stir fry. Amy wasn't expecting so many options, but a salad or some fruit once in a while would be nice. Her stomach growled, reminding her that she hadn't eaten anything today other than the oatmeal cookies from the staff room. Amy chose the chicken dinner container and returned the rest to the fridge. After a quick look in the pots-and-pans cupboard, she grabbed the last clean pan to heat her feast. Dumping everything into the pan, Amy turned the burner to medium. Thankfully, Bob had once told Amy the best way to reheat the dinner leftovers, and she'd been able to enjoy hot meals ever since.

It would be ten or fifteen minutes before her meal would be hot, so she placed a lid over the pan and hurried down the hallway to her room. She grabbed clean underwear, pajama bottoms, and a well-worn Family Grocers Sale Days t-shirt from her room and headed for a quick shower. The water was hot and felt good on her aching shoulders and back. She washed her hair and scrubbed her face clean before turning off the water.

After a quick towel off, she climbed into her pajamas and walked into the kitchen with a towel still wrapped around her head. She inhaled the heavenly smell of the warmed-up leftovers on the stove, lifting the lid to reveal bubbling gravy through a cloud of steam. She smiled, taking it as a sure sign that it was hot enough to eat. There weren't any clean dishes in the cupboard, so Amy folded a tea towel, put it on the table, and placed the hot pan on top. She burned her mouth a little on the food, too quick in her hunger, and then blew on each subsequent mouthful while trying to figure out what she would do on her day off tomorrow, finally deciding it was time to hang out with one of her friends.

Just as she shoved the last bite of food into her mouth, a knock sounded at the door. Glancing at the clock on her way to answer it, she noted that it was only seven-thirty. She looked down at her pajamas, deciding that she was decent enough to answer the door, even with the gravy she had spilled on her shirt. As she opened the door, she realized her mouth was still full, but the man at the door spoke before she could say anything.

"Good evening. I'm Officer Gerard, Staff Sergeant. Is Jeannie or—" He looked down and checked his notebook. "Amy Young home?"

She swallowed hard. "I ... I'm Amy." She cleared her throat. "My aunt Jeannie is at work at Frankie's Diner until later. What's happening?" Her mind started racing, wondering what this could be about and willing him to blurt it out.

"Do you take care of the farmhouse owned by the late Dorothy Young, about thirty-five kilometres west of town?" he asked, his pencil poised over his notebook, ready to write down whatever Amy was about to say. She simply nodded, so he continued: "Who owns the house now that she has died?"

"We don't know yet. Maybe my uncle John?" She took a deep breath, not pleased with her answer. "That's to say... the estate of my grandmother hasn't been finalized yet. The new lawyer, Donald ... Donald Tracker, says he can't finalize anything and read the will until he can locate all the people referenced in it and find some more documents, or something like that, I-I guess." She shrugged, and the towel around her head slipped off, falling across her shoulders. She ran her fingers through her hair to tame the wet mess.

"That sounds a bit complicated," he said as he peered over her head into the kitchen. Amy turned around to see what he found so interesting, but there wasn't anything to see but a little kitchen wallpapered with a fruit-bowl pattern, a white table with three orange chairs, a sink full of dirty dishes, and a yellow fridge with a matching yellow stove.

Amy turned back to face him. "What can I help you with?"

"I received a phone call yesterday from one of your grandmother's neighbours that the farmhouse belonging to your grandmother, Dorothy, has been broken into. I went out to the farmhouse but saw no evidence of a break-in. From what I can see from the windows, there were a few lights on, but no sign of anyone there. The doors are still locked, but I wanted to advise you and your aunt to go to the farmhouse to determine whether a break-in has occurred. Here is my card. Call me at the station if you find anything suspicious."

He handed Amy his card and turned to leave, but then he turned back. "Do you know where I can find your uncle John? I need to speak to him, too. Please have him come see me when he returns." He turned, stepping off the stoop and saying, "Goodnight" over his shoulder.

Amy stood in the open doorway, looking at the card she was holding and feeling shocked over what she'd just heard. All kinds of questions were going through her mind. *Was there a break-in? What was stolen? Was anything of mine taken? Most importantly, when can I go to the farmhouse to find out?* Amy was about to return to the kitchen to call her aunt at the diner when she saw Beatrice Petersen heading briskly across the gravel driveway towards her at the front door.

"Was he here because you had a break-in? I can't imagine your aunt would have much to steal after having to sell most of her stuff to pay her bills when your uncle disappeared years ago." She frowned and looked genuinely concerned. "Although, you never know what someone might be looking for! It seems your aunt works hard not to have any money to buy nice things ..."

Amy stood silent, feeling like her neighbour was fishing for information and trying to lead her into revealing something juicy to gossip about. She couldn't figure out any other reason for her to be questioning her like this.

"No, we didn't have a break-in here," Amy finally answered, skirting the whole truth to avoid giving her too much information.

"Oooh! Did they arrest your uncle for fraud? Theft? Drunk and disorderliness? Or did they find your father at long last!" She clapped her hands at this thought, excited at all the possibilities.

Amy took a deep breath and tried to grind out each answer as clearly as possible, "No, the police didn't arrest my uncle John. No, we don't know where he went. As far as we know, he hasn't done anything but leave my aunt in a whole lot of gambling debt! And as for my dad ..." She paused long enough to take another deep breath. "Really? Mrs. Petersen, you already know he left before I was born. I've never seen him, and I'm not looking for him either. You can't miss something you've never had, and anyway, what if I got sent to live with him? It would be like moving in with a stranger! Not interested." Amy turned to go back inside, hoping this would end the conversation.

"Really?" Beatrice said. "I heard that the lawyer needs to find both of them to settle Dorothy's estate." She left that information dangling in front of her like a carrot.

Amy stopped and stared at her incredulously. "How could you possibly know that? You couldn't! The lawyer didn't indicate whom he was trying to contact or what he was still waiting for to read the will, settle Grandma's estate, and determine the fate of her farmhouse. It makes sense that her son, John, would be included in the will, but why would my father? Goodness! Grandma better not have appointed *him* as my legal guardian!"

She panicked a little at the thought; her heart beat rapidly. Dorothy Young had been Amy's maternal grandmother, and she had to admit that at least part of Mrs. Petersen's statement was likely the truth: Her uncle John almost certainly stood to inherit everything. Sighing and taking a deep breath, Amy tried to speak more calmly. "I have had a long day and have to go. Goodnight, Mrs. Petersen." Slowly, she turned, closing the door and leaving Beatrice gawking on the front porch.

One thing was clear to Amy: She had to get to the farmhouse to find out what, if anything, was missing. While there, she wanted to look for her birth certificate again. She needed it to get a driver's licence before she could buy herself a car, which she would need to leave this miserable little town!

Chapter 2

August 14, 1985

Wednesday

Amy picked up the phone receiver from its base, inserted her index finger into the dial plate, and began rotating it for the first number of the five-digit telephone number. When her finger reached the stopper plate, she withdrew her finger, listening to the clicking noises through the receiver as it reset for the following number. She finally finished dialing, and after a brief pause, Amy could hear the call connected and a ringing tone began. Amy tapped her fingers against her lips, waiting as it rang four or five times before someone finally answered.

"Hello?" answered a soft-spoken female voice.

"Hi, this is Amy. Can I speak to Sarah?" She expected her to be home since Sarah didn't have a job, but she hoped she would apply soon.

"Yes, just a moment."

The noises on the other end were muffled, but Amy could still hear Sarah's voice as she took the receiver just before she came on the line. "Hey!"

"Hey, can you hang out with me today? My life has gotten weirder than usual lately, and I need to talk to you about it."

"Oh? What's goin' on?"

"A police officer came here to tell me that someone broke into the farmhouse, and I need to go check it out. Auntie Jeannie said she was too busy to drive me out there for at least two weeks. I'm considering riding my bike to the farmhouse to do it myself. What do you think?"

"I don't know. Maybe you need to give me more details. What crazy idea do you have?"

"Aunt Jeannie told me I would have to wait unless I could find someone willing to ride their bike out there with me to check for damage and missing items. I thought I could convince you to make that trip with me. It would make the two-hour bike ride to the farmhouse more interesting to have someone to talk to. Come on! It would be fun! I need to check my work schedule for my next days off."

Amy was confident that the idea would intrigue Sarah's sense of adventure. After the brief conversation, she slung a messenger bag across her shoulder and rode her bike to Main Street to meet Sarah at their usual meeting place, on the bench in front of the brick post office building. While downtown, Amy planned to pick up the mail and check her work schedule at the grocery store.

Sarah wasn't out front when Amy got to the post office, so she locked her bike on the bike rack and went inside to get her aunt's mail and anything in her grandmother's post box. There were bills and letters addressed to Jeannie in her box, most stamped "past due". Amy stuffed those into her bag, discarding the flyers into the trash can. She moved across the little hallway to open her grandmother's mailbox. Taking a deep breath, Amy inserted the key to open it, preparing herself to see envelopes with Dorothy's name on them. She hoped that there wouldn't be another letter from one of her many pen pals who still didn't know that her grandmother had died last spring. She hated writing the bad news responses. Amy pulled out all the envelopes, put them into her bag without looking at them, and decided they could wait until later. Right now, Amy is focusing on her need to meet with Sarah to start planning her ride to the farmhouse.

Sarah was sitting on the bench in front of the post office when Amy came out of the building. She wore Kmart brand dark blue jeans, a pink crop top, white slouch socks, and white tennis shoes. Her big, pink hoop earrings jangled when Sarah turned, watching Amy walking on the sidewalk towards her. She shook her blonde head with a smirk. "I can't believe you're wearing that baggy old shirt downtown."

Caught off guard, Amy looked down at what she was wearing: the worn-out old Family Grocers t-shirt with the gravy stain. At least she had changed into faded jeans, discarding the pajama bottoms. Amy ran her hand over her face and through her straight brown hair. She hadn't put on any makeup or jewelry before leaving the house.

"I'm pretty sure I brushed my teeth and combed my hair, but I was too distracted to do a great job of things." She shrugged. "I have bigger things on my mind than what I look like right now." Amy started retelling the story of the day's events and continued to summarize everything that had happened yesterday, too. Sarah asked her to repeat a few things with more detail as Amy talked about her irritating day. "—And that's why I need to go to the farmhouse. Wanna come?"

"When do you want to go?" she asked without hesitation. Sarah could be a very impulsive, free spirit, unlike Amy, who needed to curb her anxiety with well-laid plans.

"As soon as possible, but I have to check my work schedule at the store for my days off. We'll need to ride out one day and return the next. It's too much pedaling to do all in one day. Remember when we rode our bikes from the farmhouse to your place last summer? We had to stay overnight at your place because we were so tired, and the next day, I called my grandma to come pick me up!"

Because Sarah had walked down to meet her at the post office, Amy left her bike locked up where it was as they headed towards the grocery store to check her schedule. They paused to look into a few shop windows along the street. The drugstore displayed jewelry, perfumes, and little gifts in their window. "Oh, look! They have the Sony Walkman now!" Amy frowned as she leaned closer to the window, trying to see the price tag. She cupped her hands on the glass and pressed her face between them. "I can't see the price." She pulled away, disappointed. "I probably couldn't afford it anyway. I don't think I have enough in my plastic piggy bank."

They continued past the little radio station with speakers set up to broadcast to people walking out the front of the building. It was just the news reported by one of the male radio announcers: "A rash of robberies still plagues our little town. The robbery victims report missing jewelry, televisions, and small household appliances. Local police are reminding citizens, again, to lock their doors when they are not home—" Uninterested in what was being said, the teenagers ignored the noise as they rounded the corner into the grocery store parking lot.

There were only a few cars there. "It doesn't look like it's very busy. Hopefully, I can sneak into the staff room to review the schedule and get out again without talking to anyone."

"Who is that creepy man watching us?" Sarah asked in a hushed whisper as she grabbed onto the sleeve of Amy's baggy t-shirt.

"What man?" she whispered back as she turned to check behind them, not seeing anyone on the sidewalk behind them.

"There was a freaky skinny man with a black moustache. He's all dirty and gross-looking. I think he's following us!" Her eyes grew almost comically wide. "Do you think he's the criminal everyone is looking for?"

"I didn't see anyone following us, but I saw someone like that talking to Dan at the store yesterday. He stinks, too! He's been in the store to buy cigarettes. He stares and doesn't say anything!" I reached for the handle of the store's entrance door. "Are you coming in or waiting out here for the creep to show up?"

"I'll, like, wait here. I want to make sure the creep isn't still following us." Sarah squinted and scanned the area. "Oh, look! There's your auntie across the street."

Turning to look, Amy watched Jeannie walking briskly towards Frankie's Diner with her frilly orange and blue apron tucked under one arm. "She must be on her way to the diner. Funny, I thought she was already there, working her shift." Amy wondered if her aunt had said anything about when her shift started, but couldn't recall anything.

"What do you think of the new blue and orange ruffles Frank picked out?" Sarah continued to watch Jeannie walking farther down the street.

In a non-committal response, Amy rolled her eyes at her and went inside to avoid the fashion discussion that was likely to follow. The store wasn't very busy for this time of day. Amy waved at Anna, who was standing behind her register restocking the cigarette rack, and then went to the staff room to check the schedule. The staff room was a little less hazy with smoke than usual, but lunch breaks probably hadn't started yet. Amy searched through her messenger bag to find something to write her schedule on, finally deciding to write it on the back of one of the envelopes she'd retrieved from the post office. Scanning the posted schedule, she smiled to herself. She was scheduled to work the next day, but then Amy had two days off, followed by a late shift on the fourth day. "Perfect!" she muttered as she wrote down her schedule for the week.

"What are you doing here today? Aren't you off?"

She jumped and turned to see Shane standing close behind her again, leaning over her shoulder to look at the posted schedule.

"I'm just checking my schedule," Amy answered with a frown. She bustled past him and out the door, annoyed at him for sneaking up on her to stick his nose in her business.

Amy found Sarah standing just outside the main doors where she had left her. "I can go to the farmhouse the day after tomorrow. How does that sound to you?"

Sarah smiled. "I'll ask my mom for permission, but I'm sure it's okay. I already mentioned it to her." They decided to walk on the opposite side of the street to look into the shop windows while returning to the post office.

The girls stopped in front of Ace's Pawnshop & Used Goods. The windows were dusty and smeared from people trying to look in. The shop proudly displayed used jewelry, clocks, a VCR, and other assorted trinkets at "the best prices in town"—at least if the old, crinkled signs were believable. Amy's eyes glanced around the cluttered window display until they finally stopped on something familiar.

"I can't believe it!" she gasped, putting both hands on the dusty window pane. "That's my grandma's puzzle box from the farmhouse!" She pointed at the brown wooden box with the intricately checkered square design and black-lined pattern that was unmistakable in its uniqueness. Amy had never seen anything else like it. When she was little, her grandma told her it held secrets but that she had to solve the puzzle to get them.

"What?!" Sarah moved closer to her to figure out what had gotten her attention.

"Her puzzle box! It's that smooth, dark wood box with intricate patterns on the top and sides! It must have been stolen and pawned!!" Amy's heart raced in her chest, her breaths coming in short gasps. The realization hit her like a punch to the gut. "Do you see anything else that belongs to her?"

Amy stepped back from the window, realizing that she was just standing in front of the window like an idiot when she could be going inside and demanding the return of the stolen puzzle box. Shyness forgotten, she marched through the door, Sarah hot on her heels, and approached the counter to speak to the man behind it. Pushing a rising sense of panic deep down, she blurted, "I was just walking by the window … and … um … I spotted an item that was stolen from my grandmother's farmhouse." She swallowed hard, her voice trembling. "I want it back, now!"

"We're a pawnshop, missy. That means that people bring in their possessions in exchange for cash, and when they don't return for the items, we sell them for profit." His condescension was just as off-putting as the smug look on his face, apparently unfazed by the accusation that pawning stolen items might be a regular occurrence at his shop. "Do you have a receipt for the purchase or a claim ticket?"

Amy crossed her arms across her chest and stood up straighter. "No, I don't, but I know it doesn't belong here. It was stolen!"

"Well, it will cost you … a hundred bucks to repurchase it." He laughed then, revealing his yellow nicotine-stained teeth as he moved his toothpick from one corner of his mouth to the other, not even bothering to look for the item or its price tag. He seemed so sinister that it gave Amy the creeps.

"Did you just make that price up in your head just now because I asked for it back?" Amy rubbed her hand across her forehead, squeezing her eyes shut. "This is all starting to give me a headache." Sarah tugged at her sleeve, nodding towards the door, clarifying that she didn't think they would get anywhere with this man or his shady business. The two friends left the store with heavy hearts.

"What should I do? My grandma said that the puzzle box was something extraordinary. She said that if I could open it, I would have everything I ever wanted." Amy tried to clear her dry, constricting throat, but her emotions were getting the best of her. She blinked rapidly, trying to prevent tears.

"Did you ever open it? What was inside?" Sarah asked. "More importantly, what is it that you 'want?' What's the big secret?"

"No, I don't think it's anything too special. It was just another puzzle she wanted me to solve. Grandma wanted me to go to the library to research how to open it or maybe even solve it on my own, but then she died, and I never got around to it. I think maybe it was just to test my research skills. It was just a lesson for me, something as simple as 'knowledge gives you everything you want' or something corny like that."

She shrugged, mentally kicking herself for not taking the time to solve it. *Was there something inside of it? Or was it simply some life lesson? If it was important, then why hadn't her grandma just told her?* Amy was so occupied with her own thoughts that she didn't even notice that they had arrived back at the post office.

"Okay," Sarah said. "I'll devise a plan to get the puzzle box thingy back while you plan our bike ride to the farmhouse. I'll call you later."

They said goodbye, going their separate ways, promising to discuss their plans after Amy's shift at the store the next day. As Amy walked over to her bike, she wondered how she would repurchase the puzzle box with her limited funds. If she couldn't afford a Walkman, she was pretty sure she couldn't afford the hundred dollars to buy the puzzle box.

Amy knew her aunt Jeannie wouldn't have the money to lend her even if she asked—not that she ever would anyway.

It was a nice day, so Amy thought that while she was downtown, she could make a trip over to the library to see if she could find a book to help her open the puzzle box as soon as she could get her hands on it. Because the library was just around the corner from the post office, she decided to leave her bicycle, which was locked up, and walk over. Amy hadn't been back to the library since her grandmother died. She'd felt it would be a bit weird going there without her.

Instead of riding the bus to school, Dorothy would drive Amy to school and then spend the day volunteering at the library, running errands, or visiting friends. In the afternoons, Dorothy loved to read to the little kids for story time. Amy smiled as more memories of her grandma at the library came flooding back to her. She could still hear her grandma saying, "What better way to spend the day than in a building stacked to the rafters with books!" The library, with its familiar scent of old books and the comforting sound of pages turning, was a place of solace for Amy.

The library was a large red brick building with large windows full of posters announcing new book arrivals and reading programs. The shelves were crowded with old dusty books with faded covers, vibrant new books, flashy magazines, and newspapers from nearby cities. You could find anything you needed if you looked in the right place. It was a good bet that she would have to start with the card catalogue to get a general idea about where she would find information on solving puzzle boxes in the library. Amy walked through the main doors and turned right, heading past the front desk and over to the card catalogue cabinets. The librarian, Lena Merasty, had her back turned to her as she worked to wrap an old, worn-out book with thick brown paper to cover its front, back, and spine. "Hello, Lena," Amy said quietly over her shoulder.

Lena turned around to see her walking past the front desk. "Amy! Did you think you could just breeze past me without giving me a hug? It's been almost four months since I saw you at Dorothy's funeral. Come here, my girl! I have a hug for you!" She removed her black-framed glasses from the tip of her nose and let them hang on the metal chain around her neck. Amy moved into her warm, soft hug. The fuzzy pink sweater she wore tickled Amy's nose as her eyes filled with unshed tears.

The library felt like a second home that she hadn't realized she'd been missing. When Lena stepped back, Amy could see tears running down her cheeks. "It's so good to see you, Amy," she said as she retrieved a tissue from the sleeve of her sweater to blot her eyes. "I know you love books just as much as your grandma. I knew you would need a good book to read eventually," she said, tossing her long black braid over her shoulder.

"I'm here to do a little research, not to get a book for reading. I don't have time to read with my schedule at the grocery store... and stuff." Amy's voice was shaking, and her palms were damp. "To be honest, I'd hoped I could be in here without being reminded of Grandma. I was fooling myself, though. If I didn't need to search the card catalogue drawers, I think I would have turned right around and left." She swallowed hard, taking a deep breath.

"I can imagine," Lena said with an understanding smile. "I'm sure you'll find what you need, but if you need help, just let me know. It's so good to see you again. And to see you here has made my day!"

Amy nodded with a smile of her own and walked over to the three large card catalogue cabinets that took up most of the far wall of the library. The cabinets had many small wooden drawers, each with a brass knob and a tag, organizing its paper cards into alphabetical order according to either the author, subject, or title of the book. Every book was cross-referenced under these three headings with pertinent information, including its call number, so you could find where it was located on the shelves. Since Amy didn't know the name of any author who might have written a book about puzzle boxes, she had to do a general search under the keywords describing the research subject.

Amy located the drawer marked "Ph-Pz" and pulled it open. The first card started with *Phases of the Moon, The, by Dr. A. Hubert, 1964*. Pulling the narrow little drawer out further, she read the cards nearer to the middle, thumbing through each card until she found the section of cards that started with the word "Puzzle." She read each card, trying to find one related to opening puzzle boxes. From the cards she found, it was clear that the library also loaned out actual puzzles, not just books about them.

"Interesting," Amy mumbled to herself. *There are so many different kinds of puzzles,* she thought. *Some I've never even heard of before.* Unfortunately, she couldn't find anything related to puzzle boxes. She closed that drawer and opened the "Ga-Gn" to see what was listed under "Games," finding several books listed under the subjects "795: Games of Chance" and "794: Games of Skill" but nothing specifically about puzzle boxes. There were slips of paper and several pencils on the top of the cabinets. Taking a slip of paper and writing down the beginning of some of the call numbers, Amy thought she could browse for a few books.

She stopped writing down numbers when she remembered being told by her grandma that her grandfather had made all sorts of wooden boxes and crafts! Amy decided she would also look under "W" for woodworking directions for building wooden puzzle boxes, just in case. She found one called *Small Woodworking Projects*, by James Jones, and excitedly wrote down the call number: "690.9124.25." *Perhaps woodworking projects would be the answer!* She took the slips of paper and searched for a book or two that would give her some ideas to help her open the puzzle box.

Chapter 3

He stood casually leaning against the corner of the post office, partially obscured by the bushes. His long, skinny fingers held the smoking cigarette. He flicked ash onto the grass, hoping no one would remember him. It had been a long time since he'd left this little town. Who would have thought he'd ever be so desperate for money that he'd want to return to his hometown? He doubted anyone would recognize him with his recent weight loss, moustache, and artificially blackened hair. He barely recognized himself sometimes when he caught a reflection. He was no longer the clean-cut geeky kid from high school.

These days, he was going by the name Bobby Wilham. After so many years, the fake name rolled off his tongue quite easily whenever he had to introduce himself. So far, no one in town had asked him his name except the owner of the Family Grocers. The man didn't seem to like him hanging around his store, browsing the merchandise or watching the cashiers. He was told he could shop for what he needed but then needed to leave the store. Bobby apologized to Dan because he hadn't even realized he was standing in the aisle, staring at one of the young cashiers. He'd just been startled by her appearance when he'd come around the corner and laid eyes on her.

There was something very familiar about how that brown-haired teenage girl moved, talked, and laughed. Looking at this young girl transported Bobby back in time to an easier, more carefree time. Her smile was similar to her mother's, except this girl's didn't quite reach her eyes or light up her face. There was a bit of sadness lurking under all of that makeup. Bobby planned to return after he could get some money to pretend to buy things. He needed to get a closer look at the girl. He was confident she wouldn't know who he was, even if, by chance, she had seen photos of him as a teenager. His disguise was perfect. Bobby needed to ask the girl some casual questions about her family that could help him with his big plan.

Sandy's girl wasn't working that day, so Bobby left the parking lot disappointed when he couldn't find her. He was walking down Main Street when he spotted two teenage girls window-shopping on the other side of the street. It had been hard to tell definitively with all the makeup she had on, but after seeing her today with a clean, fresh face, he was sure she was Sandy's daughter. The family resemblance was remarkable. She looked just like Sandy had at that age. He followed them from the other side of the street, trying to keep his distance. The last thing Bobby needed was another arrest, although living on the streets wasn't exactly keeping his belly full and cigarettes in his pocket. He shrugged. At least in a jail cell, a man could get a hot meal or two.

Bobby watched the girl enter the grocery store, leaving her friend standing guard outside. Then he turned around and walked a little way in the opposite direction to hide in the shadow of a doorway where he wouldn't be seen but could still see the edge of the parking lot. The two girls were not at the store very long before they exited the parking lot and crossed the street, talking and not paying much attention to other people. Bobby moved out of the doorway and started walking down that side of the street, back towards the park beside the post office. He didn't want the girls to catch on to the fact that he was watching them. They were looking into another store window when Bobby noticed a police car approaching him. *Shit, that's my cue!*

He continued to walk at an easy pace down the street away from the girls. Although Bobby was looking straight ahead, he was trying to use his peripheral vision to watch for the police car that slowly drove by and then parked at the end of the block in front of the post office. The officer didn't leave the vehicle or even shut off the engine. *Well,* Bobby thought, *He can watch me if he wants. I'll slowly walk by and act like I don't even notice the cop watching me ... Stay calm ... Minding my own business ...* Bobby began to whistle softly to himself, trying to look like he belonged on the sleepy streets of Glenmere.

Bobby continued past the post office to the corner of the block, pausing on the corner and wondering which way he should go before noticing that the church across the street had a few cars in its parking lot. He looked both ways and crossed the street again, heading straight towards the church's front steps, which was just as he remembered it: a small community church that seemed to hold some type of gathering every day. It didn't look like today was any different. Since he had never attended church when he'd lived here, he was confident that no one inside would recognize him. He planned to sneak in and blend into the background while waiting for the cop to drive away.

He climbed the cement steps to the big wooden main doors and pulled one open. The doors were on a heavy spring, making him push one door with his left hand as he pulled open the other with his right. After the blinding light of the sun, the interior lobby of the church seemed dark, making Bobby blink a few times while his eyes adjusted. As the door slammed closed behind him, a large balding man dressed in tan dress pants, a white dress shirt, and a wide plaid tie (circa 1970-something) smiled broadly at him.

"Are you here for the meetin'?" The man's voice boomed, his hands clapping together in anticipation.

Bobby was caught off guard but managed a hesitant nod. "Yes," he replied, drawing his features into a slow, friendly smile, pretending like he knew what meeting this man was talking about.

The man stepped forward and offered his hand. "I'm Pastor Bill. Welcome to our little church! What's your first name?"

Bobby reached out and shook Pastor Bill's hand. "Thanks, I'm Bobby ... Where is the ... um ... meeting?"

"I'm sorry. It's in the basement. Go to the right, and you'll find the door leading downstairs. My wife set out some cookies and made the coffee. The cookies are delicious, and the coffee is strong, so help yourself."

Bobby thanked him and followed the directions to the church basement. He could hear laughter and talking as he turned on the landing to the last flight of stairs, which opened into a one-room basement with a little kitchen off to one side. There were tables and chairs set up in a circle in the middle of the room. Bobby made his way to the kitchen counter and poured some hot, aromatic black coffee into a Styrofoam cup. He noticed several different kinds of delicious cookies near the coffee and picked up a few to enjoy. He didn't know what kind of meeting this would be or how long it would take, but he worried it might be hard to blend in. He'd counted only nine other people in attendance. *Hopefully, I won't have to talk if I'm chewing cookies.* He settled into the chair closest to the exit just in case he had to make a quick getaway.

A large man with suspenders stood up and asked everyone to take a seat so the meeting could start. "Welcome, everyone," he said. "My name is Gary, and I'm an alcoholic. I'm leading this week. Let us start with the Serenity Prayer, and then we'll begin our discussions."

Together, the group monotonously chanted, "God grant me the serenity to accept the things I cannot change, the courage to accept the things I can, and the wisdom to know the difference—"

"Oh, boy," Bobby sarcastically mumbled as he slumped down a little more in his seat. He had just joined an AA meeting for recovering alcoholics, a situation he hadn't anticipated! He wasn't interested in being a participant in this meeting, but he thought he would enjoy a few cups of coffee and cookies while he waited for the police cruiser to be on its way. Bobby looked around, thinking that this could give him just the chance he needed to hear what was happening in town without having to talk to too many people. If he was patient and waited, he could learn some helpful information.

He looked around the room at the men and women in attendance, his eyes scanning their faces. Each person who spoke started by stating their name and how long they'd been sober before making a comment or telling their story. Thankfully, Bobby didn't recognize anyone and assumed no one would know who he was. It was good that not everyone volunteered information or introduced themselves because it allowed Bobby to sit back and listen while he enjoyed the deliciously moist cookies.

The meeting lasted just over an hour, and everyone exchanged pleasantries at the end. It was enough time for Bobby to drink three cups of black coffee and eat almost a dozen cookies. Bobby hung around, wondering whether he should make his exit now or if the police would still be outside waiting for him. While contemplating his next move, the big guy, Gary, came up beside him. "I noticed that you're new here. I want to let you know that we meet every Monday, Wednesday, and Friday at the same time and place. Please come back and join us. All are welcome."

"Thanks. I might do that, especially if there are always cookies," Bobby said, shaking Gary's hand.

"Yes, well ... er ... sometimes, Missy makes cakes or pies." Gary furrowed his brow. I haven't noticed you around our little town. Are you new to the area?"

Bobby forced a smile, his heart pounding as he tried to keep his voice even. "Yes, I'm new. I was passing just through town and heard that I could stop in here for a meeting." He pulled at the soiled cuffs of his shirt, trying not to look as nervous as he felt about all the questions. He started to regret not leaving sooner with the others.

The man eyed the state of his clothing and unshaven face, then reached into his pocket and put four quarters on the table in front of Bobby. "Missy also runs a soup and sandwich church fundraiser for a dollar once a week. It's today and starts at five. You can get yourself a good meal for a buck and fill your stomach with more than just her cookies." With a nod, Gary turned and exited up the stairs without another word.

Bobby stared down at the four quarters. He hadn't thought it was so obvious that he was living on the street. Inspecting the state of his dirty clothing, Bobby had to agree that he could use a shower and some new clothes. It was time to see if he could make use of someone's unoccupied or vacant home for a shower and a change of outfit. Most people who went away in the summer were gone for at least a week at a time, so Bobby was confident that it would be easy enough to find a place to hide out and take advantage of the food in the pantry, clothes in the closets, and small objects he could pawn for cash. Bobby had done it a few times before when he was down on his luck. It was time to scope out the surrounding neighbourhoods. He stepped forward, scooped up the quarters, slid them into his pocket, and then headed up the stairs and back out onto the street.

The police cruiser seemed to have moved on, but he did not want to take the chance that the officer would return, so he headed away from Main Street and into the residential area. He started searching for a vacant house or a home that looked like the family was away on vacation so that he could seize his chance to take refuge there. The coffee sloshed around in his stomach as he walked, making him regret having that last one. He didn't regret the cookies because they were the best he had ever tasted. If the soups at the fundraiser were made by the same person who baked the cookies, he would happily spend his money on it.

After walking seven or eight blocks, Bobby changed direction and turned down 5th Street West. The houses on it were average in size and well maintained, with little white picket fences and flowerbeds. He could see that the green lawns were all freshly cut except one down away on the left side, which had flowerbeds full of weeds and shaggy grass out front. He smiled in relief. *This house looks promising.*

He walked over to the house and stared at it from the sidewalk. Two neglected newspapers were sitting on the front step. Bobby walked up the empty driveway and around to the back door. Everything was quiet, but just in case, Bobby knocked on the door. As his knock went unanswered, he strained to hear any noises inside, but all was silent. He jiggled the doorknob, finding it locked.

Bobby looked around. The window just to the left of the door didn't have a curtain on it. He stepped closer to the window, cupping his hands against the glass to peer inside. The family was not home. He checked the latch on the window and found it unlocked! He sighed in relief that this would be a quiet break-in without needing to break any glass and risk alerting the neighbours. Bobby put both palms on the top of the bottom panel and tried to slide the window up. It was a bit sticky, but with a little force, it eventually gave way and opened for him. Once he had room to crawl through, he slid inside, across the sink, and onto the kitchen floor.

He stood up and looked around at the open boxes stacked in the corner of the kitchen. He needed to find clues as to when the homeowners would be returning. It wouldn't be good if they were just out for a quick trip to the grocery store and returned unexpectedly.

"Aha! The family calendar! That should be filled with their plans," he mumbled to himself. "Let's see ... vacation from the twelfth to the twenty-fifth of this month ... What's today? Wednesday ... the fourteenth!" He shrugged. "I guess they didn't mow the grass before they left. And I have almost a week and a half to enjoy this little hideaway before the family returns."

There were opened letters on the kitchen counter addressed to Darren and Tanya Howards, forwarded from another town. That and the stacked boxes in the kitchen told him they were new to town, making this hideout much more manageable. Bobby carried the letters over to the table, sitting down to rest before exploring the rest of the house. He chuckled at his good fortune while he fingered the envelopes. His luck had been changing lately.

When he'd stumbled upon Dorothy Young's obituary while he was in prison, just before he'd finished serving his time for aggravated assault, he could barely believe it. That obituary brought him back to this little town after all these years. If it was accurate, he had information the family didn't seem to know about, which he would use to change his financial situation.

"Well," he said with a happy sigh. "After I shave and shower, there should be some of Darren's clothes for me to wear. Then, I can read one of the papers from the front doorstep while I plan my next move."

Chapter 4

August 15, 1985

Thursday

Amy was sitting in the smoky staff room on a break, sipping on a mug of warm tap water and thinking about her life and where it was going. Nowhere. That's what it felt like anyway, which made it hard not to dwell in despair. She used to be filled with hopes and dreams of adventure, school, career, and family. She wanted to go to college to get a good job—though she had yet to decide what career that might be. Still, Amy was going to do ... something. Her grandmother had not been in a rush for her to move away to attend college, saying that Amy still had time to figure it all out. She'd also said she would take care of everything when Amy was ready.

Amy's whole life changed the night when her grandmother died. She remembered it like it was yesterday. Dorothy had been baking cookies in the kitchen when the phone rang. After a short discussion on the phone, Dorothy left Amy with a few rushed instructions to finish the baking while she ran into town. Amy didn't know where her grandma was going or why; she had just "forgotten something."

Amy had been waiting contently at home until the police officer showed up on the farmhouse doorstep that night to deliver the bad news. She would never forget the hollow drop in her stomach and the noise of her heartbeat rushing to her ears after opening the door to a police officer with a panicked look in his eyes. He urgently explained to Amy that her grandmother was in serious condition at the hospital after suddenly collapsing.

She couldn't remember what the young officer had said next, but Amy remembered rushing out the door with him to ride in his cruiser, with lights and sirens blazing, speeding along the highway to bring her to her grandmother's bedside. When she'd arrived, Dorothy had been weak, struggling to stay awake and coherent. There had been wires and cords attached to her grandmother, winding in and out of the hospital gown. A machine was slowly beeping along with her heartbeat, and Dorothy reached for Amy with a shaky hand.

Tears had streamed down Amy's face as she'd grabbed her grandma's hand, just trying to comprehend what was happening and desperately trying to swallow the lump in her throat, thinking, *What's happening? What was so important that she had to rush to town?* She'd had so many questions, but the words would not come! Dorothy motioned Amy closer with her dying breath and whispered, "All your dreams will still come true ... You need to open the ... puzzle box ... your grandpa. Look in ... the box."

From the hospital, the police took Amy and dumped her unceremoniously on Jeannie's doorstep in the early hours of a grey morning, the last words her grandmother had said to her echoing in her head. Amy had not seen much of her aunt before that day, though she'd never really questioned why she didn't visit her much. Her best guess had been that there were hurt feelings between Jeannie and Dorothy since her uncle John had left town.

Jeannie had gone to the farmhouse soon after Amy had arrived to bring her some clothes and a few things from her room because Amy had been unable to bear doing it herself. She'd also brought back all of the refrigerator contents so the food wouldn't go bad. Jeannie must have had a key, or Amy had forgotten to lock the door in her rush to leave for the hospital.

Shaking her head, Amy returned to the present, thinking it had been four months since Grandma's death. *I should have returned to get the puzzle box right away, but I didn't think I needed to since her estate still wasn't settled.* Amy had been waiting to discover what would happen with the estate, hoping to have some inheritance to help her plan a better future. In any case, Jeannie had told her that she couldn't take things from the house until the lawyers finalized the estate in case everything had been inherited by John. Jeannie also wasn't always available to drive Amy anywhere, but when they did go to the farmhouse together, it was always a rush to grab things and then leave quickly. Jeannie would occasionally go out to the farmhouse without Amy, leaving things she brought back for her on the kitchen table.

Amy certainly hadn't been expecting a police officer to tell her that they needed to check whether the farmhouse had been broken into. Still, after seeing the puzzle box in the pawnshop window, Amy feared that many other items might be missing as well, but she wasn't going to wait to coordinate her days off with her aunt. Amy almost didn't want her there anyway because Jeannie had rarely ever come to the farmhouse before Grandma died, and Amy wasn't sure Jeannie could identify what was missing anyway. It was in Amy's best interest to take the two- or three-hour bike ride thirty-five kilometres out of town to the farmhouse as soon as possible.

Amy heard her name over the sound system, paging her to return to her register. She shook her head to clear it and left her seat in the staff room. There was a lineup of three customers at her cash lane, waiting to ring through their purchases. Amy took her place behind register three, turning to the first customer but quickly realizing that he wasn't putting any items on the counter. "Do you have groceries to purchase today?" she asked, looking at the short, skinny man with the dark moustache.

"No," he said. "I just need a pack of smokes. The red king-size." He pointed to his brand with one of his nicotine-stained fingers.

Amy turned and pulled a pack of smokes from the little shelf behind her and held them up. "These?"

"Yep." Nodding, he rummaged around in his baggy brown pant pockets, not taking his eyes off of Amy while he looked for his wallet.

"I need four dollars and twenty-five cents, please," Amy told him as she tried to figure out why he looked so familiar. She was sure that she'd seen him somewhere before. It was unsettling how he kept looking at her like he was sizing her up for something. Amy glanced nervously at the other customers waiting in line as she held onto the cigarettes. Finally, the short man seemed to produce enough change from his pockets to cover the cost of the pack.

Amy quickly slapped her hand over a quarter that was about to roll off the edge of the counter and began to count the change. Finally, she pushed a nickel back towards him. "I don't need this. Thank you, and have a great day." Setting the cigarette pack next to the nickel, she turned and smiled at the next customer in line.

She kept serving customers, planning to phone her outgoing, adventure-seeking, free-spirited friend, Sarah, once she finished working to tell her that they should leave very early tomorrow for the farmhouse. She also wanted to listen to Sarah's plan to get the puzzle box. Hopefully, she would be free to call in a few favours and gather enough money together to satisfy the man at the pawnshop.

When Amy finally finished her shift, she returned home to her aunt's house on her bike. Reminding herself that she should let her aunt Jeannie know that she would go to the farmhouse on her own, Amy rehearsed what she was going to say as she pedaled home. "I can't wait for you to have a day off, so I am going to the farmhouse on my own... I'll be gone one night. The farmhouse was my home from the time I was three years old, so I want to check to ensure everything is safe." Amy practiced this over and over with determination. The bike's hand brakes screeched as she stopped in front of the little house. Jeannie's rusty old Ford truck was parked in the driveway. Everything seemed to be going according to Amy's plan so far. She smiled as she locked her bike to the gas meter and went inside to speak to her aunt.

Jeannie was talking on the phone when Amy entered the kitchen, but she abruptly ended the call when she saw her.

"Okay ... okay ... Got to go!" Jeannie's voice, filled with excitement, abruptly cut through the air, startling Amy. She slammed the phone receiver down, her smile widening as she turned to Amy. "I brought some groceries home. Please put them away. I have a date tonight to get ready for!" Her eyes twinkled with anticipation as she delivered this unexpected news. Without giving Amy a chance to respond, she rushed down the hallway and into her room, the door slamming shut behind her. Amy was left standing in the kitchen, her voice trapped in stunned silence.

There were two paper bags of groceries on the kitchen counter. Amy started to unpack everything and put it away. Just as she finished with the groceries, her aunt came back down the hallway, wearing a new blue and white polka-dot dress and smelling of strong floral perfume.

"Who are you going out with?" Amy coughed, trying to clear her throat of the perfume in the air.

"Hmmm? Probably no one you know," she cooed. "He dresses nice and drives a sports car! I'll be out late, so don't wait for me." The plastic bracelets around her wrists clacked together when she pointed at Amy, and her large, white-plastic hoop earrings swayed when she moved her head.

Amy struggled to breathe in the heavy scent of her aunt's perfume, trying to suppress a cough and calling after her aunt as she moved towards the door, "Auntie, I want to go with Sarah to—"

"Yes, yes! Whatever! He's late," she said impatiently, looking at her watch and not listening to Amy's pleas. A long blast of a car horn sounded outside. "Ooh, that'll be him! Wish me luck!" Jeannie waved her fingers as she sailed through the front door, leaving it to slam shut.

Amy shook her head in disgust. "She is so weird sometimes! I have never waited up for her." It was so difficult to have any conversation with her aunt. She was always so distracted and rushed to get out the door to go to work or out with friends. She supposed she couldn't blame her aunt for the limited attention she got from her. They weren't directly related, after all. Still, she had married Amy's uncle, John, making them family. *The fact that she doesn't know where he went doesn't change that*, she thought. Neither did the fact that he'd left her in heaps of financial debt, and she felt they shouldn't worry about him.

Jeannie clarified to Amy that those debts were why she had no spare money to provide. That was why she'd needed her job at the Family Grocers. Even most of the food Jeannie brought home was stuff she hadn't paid for, getting it free from the diner.

With unwavering determination but no goals, Amy decided to transform her life by figuring out a way out of her financial problems and taking action in her best interests! "The only person that can change me is me!" Amy said to herself as she folded the paper grocery bags and stowed them under the sink. She walked over to the telephone and started dialing Sarah's number, ready to discuss their plans for tomorrow.

Sarah answered the phone breathlessly after the third or fourth ring. "Hello?"

"Sarah, it's me, Amy. We have to leave for the farmhouse tomorrow morning. Are you coming?" Anxiously, Amy swirled the phone cord around her fingers as she waited for Sarah's response. She wanted to fire all kinds of questions at her but bit her tongue, waiting instead.

"Yes, of course! But we have to go early. The earlier, the better." She paused. "I've worked out how to get the puzzle box, but you might not like my plan. Were you able to come up with something?"

"No, I've been thinking about the farmhouse and our plans," Amy confessed, her anxiety palpable. "Do you have some money you could lend me to buy it?" she blurted out, unable to contain her worry. Without waiting for a response, she continued, "Probably not. What's your plan?"

Amy scribbled details on a piece of paper near the telephone as she listened to Sarah explain her plan, though she seemed hesitant to go into too many specifics. Still, what did they have to lose? She sighed, thinking, *Everything I have.* But, considering how little she had, she thought the payoff would likely be worth it. In the end, Amy agreed to meet Sarah late that night on Main Street and then hung up the phone. Amy trusted Sarah to help her out of any problems that might come up and be there for her no matter what.

To execute their plans, Amy had to shower before getting a few things ready. She went to the bedroom to get her messenger bag. It still had all the mail and two library books in it. Amy set the books on the dresser and started sorting the mail, making a stack of bills that had come for Aunt Jeannie and separating it from her grandmother's mail.

Some farmhouse bills were marked "past due," just like her aunt's. Tossing those on the pile of unopened bills from the last four months, Amy frowned. She'd thought the estate lawyer would handle the bills until the lawyers named the primary inheritor. *What was taking the lawyer so long to get things sorted out?*

Amy then held up a manila envelope with a return address from a city in Ontario, from "Morgan, P.I." Curious as to who this person could be and whether or not they were aware of her grandma's death, Amy opened the letter to read its contents out loud to herself.

"Dear Mrs. Young, I haven't been able to reach you by phone since our last conversation in April. I have discovered that your son, John Jr., filed for bankruptcy on Dec. 9, 1978. He was later charged with mischief and intoxication in a public place and sentenced to a rehabilitation center here in Ontario. I'll continue my investigation as to his whereabouts after his arrival there. Please call me at your convenience, and I'll apprise you of my findings. Sincerely, Alister Morgan, Private Investigator."

Amy took a deep breath, letting it out in a long sigh. She realized that her grandma must have talked to the private investigator before she died, though Dorothy hadn't told Amy that she was looking for her son. Amy wondered what other secrets her grandma might have been hiding.

It occurred to Amy that her aunt Jeannie might not know that she'd been looking for her son, John. She tucked the envelope back into her messenger bag for safekeeping from her aunt, deciding that she would call this investigator from the farmhouse tomorrow unless the phone company had disconnected service. If it had, it would have to wait until Amy returned home. She didn't know why, exactly, but she didn't think letting her aunt Jeannie overhear that conversation would be a good idea.

Chapter 5

Bobby laid the newspaper he had finished reading on the table. He noticed the law firm stopped running the classified searching for John Young and his whereabouts. "That little mystery was solved, wasn't it?" He chuckled to himself over the secret he knew about John's whereabouts. He knew John had disappeared into the pit of alcohol and drug addiction, forcing him to live on the streets. They would never find him, which was perfect for Bobby, who was well on his way to taking everything from him now, just as John had done to him.

He'd dyed his hair and grown a moustache to look like his old friend before returning to Glenmere, where he would pose as John Young to steal the hefty inheritance and finally stop worrying about the people who were after him for debt repayment. As far as he was concerned, John owed him at least that much after what he'd done to him.

The idea had come to him a few months ago in prison. He'd been reading the newspaper during outside time in the yard. Since he had all the time in the world to read while finishing up the final days of his prison sentence, he would read every word of the news from the first page to the last and then start over again until he could barter for another paper. They were usually a month or two old when they reached him, but they gave him something to do while the other inmates played basketball. He wasn't tall enough to be a very effective team member, nor was he interested. His small, skinny frame excluded him from many sports, especially those played without referees behind prison walls.

Bobby reached into his wallet, pulling out two classified articles he'd saved in prison. The first was the obituary for Dorothy Young: "Young, Dorothy. 1910-1985. With great sadness, the Young family announces Dorothy Mary Young's sudden passing at the age of 75. She is survived by her son, John, Jr. (Jeannie) and her granddaughter, Amy. She is predeceased by her husband, John, Sr., and daughter, Sandra. A funeral will be held on April 5th at the Community Church at 1 p.m. In place of flowers, please donate to the local Public Library." The second was the classified ad, which had appeared in a later issue and said, "Seeking John Young, Jr. Contact 1-800-555-8432."

Now that Bobby had grown out his hair, moustache, and sideburns, dying everything black, the next step in his grand revenge scheme would allow him to pay off his debts and make a better life for himself at John's expense! He'd called the number in the classified ad just before he exited prison, speaking to the new big-shot lawyer in his hometown who'd told him he was looking for John to settle his late mother's estate. That's when Bobby seized the opportunity, introducing himself as John and setting his plan into motion. He was betting that John was the sole beneficiary of his mother's estate, even though he had once told Bobby that he'd cut all family ties in 1975.

It would take a little work to make himself presentable and look even more like John Young, Junior than he already had. Luckily, he still had some time because his appointment with the lawyer was scheduled for Monday. The new lawyer who had taken over the estate said he was a bit behind in his cases, but Bobby figured that since he'd waited this long, he could wait a few more days to do what he'd come to do. Bobby planned to sell everything of John's by auction by the end of next week and be on his way to start his new life somewhere that no one has ever heard of him. Meanwhile, he decided to bide his time, pawning worthy items from this house that he'd "borrowed" for smokes and other essentials.

Chapter 6

It was dark and later in the evening, but Sarah wanted Amy to meet her in front of the pawnshop at 11:30 p.m. She told Amy to walk because her orange and yellow bicycle would attract too much attention from people who might recognize it. Sarah also instructed Amy to wear dark clothing so that they could hide in the shadows a little easier.

Amy wasn't sure what Sarah was planning, but she was extremely suspicious of any plan involving sneaking around at night in dark clothing. Her stomach dropped, and the hair on her neck stood on end. "Oh … no!" What Sarah planned to do suddenly hit her like a ton of bricks. She was going to steal the puzzle box! Amy mentally kicked herself for her stupidity and failed to recognize that immediately! Rubbing her shaky hands over her face and hair, she sighed. "This can't be good."

In the past, Amy and Sarah had gotten into trouble for staying up too late or forgetting to tell their parents or grandmother where they were going, but they had never done anything illegal. *But is it illegal? The puzzle box belonged to my grandmother, and she wanted me to have it after she died. The will hasn't been read yet. Is it mine? And does it even matter? She told me she wanted me to solve the mystery of the puzzle box. That was the last thought on her mind before she died! Okay, the puzzle box is mine. I need to get it back!* Amy nodded in agreement with herself, determined to do what she had to do to get what was rightfully hers.

Amy finished changing into dark pants and a dark hooded sweatshirt, referred to as a bunnyhug in Saskatchewan, hoping that the hood would keep her warm while further disguising her if needed. Putting the house key around her neck and tucking it beneath her hooded sweatshirt, Amy turned off the kitchen lights and stepped outside into the cover of darkness, locking the door behind her. The street was eerily quiet. She had to get a move on if she wanted to make it to Main Street on time to meet Sarah. The air was a bit chilly, but with her quick pace and the added adrenaline rushing through her veins, her muscles seemed to warm up fast.

Amy jumped when she thought she heard glass breaking as she passed one of the back alleyways. A dog barked, then a male voice yelled, "Shut up, already!" The dog and man continued to argue back and forth. That gave Amy all the motivation she needed to continue to her destination. She didn't think the man noticed her or cared that she was walking around at night, but just in case, she increased her stride to a light jog, putting some distance between herself and the alley.

Amy didn't like walking around town in the dark because her active imagination kept her jumpy about what was hiding down every darkened street and narrow alley. She envisioned the kind of disrespectful people that might be hiding in the shadows, just waiting to assault her. She was only five feet tall with a tiny frame, which certainly wouldn't intimidate any would-be attacker, even though it allowed her to easily pass for a twelve-year-old whenever she wanted to get into the movie theatre for $2.50 rather than the adult price.

Amy stopped under the streetlight to catch her breath and check her watch. It was a quarter after eleven. Pleased that she would be early instead of late, she slowed her pace a little to prepare to run if needed.

Main Street was so quiet that voices spilling out from Frankie's Diner two blocks down reached Amy's ears. Most businesses on this block were closed by six o'clock during the week, leaving shadows near the darkened storefronts. The large maple trees blocked most of the streetlights, giving the block an unfamiliar feeling. Amy shivered as she hesitantly crossed the street. Realizing that her sneakers made a slight scraping noise with each step, she stopped and tied her laces tighter so her shoes wouldn't drag as much. She reached up to nervously twirl a strand of her hair, but when her fingers met only the cotton hood of her bunny hug, she let her hand drop back down to her side.

"There you are!"

"Ahhh!" Amy tried to cover her scream, but it escaped through her fingers as she turned to Sarah, who had just whispered this from behind her. Her heart was beating loudly in her chest, and her breathing was heavy. "You scared the crap out of me!"

"Shhh! You're making too much noise," Sarah whispered again. "We need to make sure that we don't get caught. I brought a brick so that we could smash the window and, like … make a grab."

Amy stood up straighter, putting her hood back up over her head. Then, with conviction, she looked up at Sarah and nodded. "Okay. I'm with you on this. There is nothing more important to me than doing what my grandmother wanted. I have to get the puzzle box back, open it, and then… then I think I have to see what the big mystery is all about. One thing is for sure: something weird is going on. I can't say for sure, but I think it could be related to the farmhouse and the puzzle box. All I know is that it has something special for me inside it, so I will do whatever it takes to learn what that is."

They quietly walked away from the post office towards the pawnshop, their heads swiveling to ensure no one was around. Amy would have to think about how she would prove that the puzzle box belonged to her grandmother if this went sideways, the police got involved, and she had to justify her actions. She also prepared to ask Sarah for help earning the money necessary to repair the window.

The girls stopped in front of the dusty pawnshop window. The lights were off, and the shop was deep in the shadows of the large maple trees that partially blocked the streetlight, further hiding the girls' identities. They stood still for a long time, carefully listening for noises nearby. Amy also looked around for any noticeable security cameras, wishing she'd thought to do so in daylight, given how dark everything was. She realized Sarah's plan wasn't particularly well-thought-out.

Pressing her face closer to the window, Amy could barely make out the dark wooden box still displayed in the front window. Relief washed over her. She'd been worried that someone might have already purchased the beautiful box. Deciding that she needed it more than anything, Amy pulled her hood further down over her face as she turned to look at her friend. "Okay, Sarah, smash the window with your brick, hard ... so we only have to hit it once."

Sarah raised the brick above her head, but just before she brought it down to break the window, she grabbed Amy's sleeve and pulled her into the shadow of the recessed doorway. Amy tripped over her feet and fell to the sidewalk just as the lights of a passing car temporarily lit up her sprawling form. As it continued along the street, Sarah released the breath she'd been holding and whispered, "They didn't seem to notice. The black clothing must have made you look like a shadow. Are you sure this is a good idea? I didn't think this through."

"Yes!" Amy whispered back with urgency through gritted teeth. "It's the only way!"

Sarah took a deep breath and nodded; then, with speed and force, she spun out of the doorway and around to the front window, jumped up, raised the brick over her head, and sent it crashing through the window. As things settled, Amy stepped out of the doorway and stood beside her. Sarah's hard breathing, and the crunching of glass under their shoes were all Amy could hear. They both turned and looked at each other, listening for any alarm, but there was nothing to hear but a dog that barked a few times over on the next block. They struggled to quiet their breathing and loud heartbeats.

Still searching the street for signs of other people, neither one moved to grab the box. Amy hesitated, thinking they would only get in trouble for breaking the window if they just left now. Then Sarah suddenly moved as if to turn and run, but Amy instinctively reached out and grabbed her sleeve to stop her, desperately whispering, "Wait!" She slowly released her grip on Sarah's sleeve. "I'm still doing this! Don't leave me."

"No—" Sara said in a wavering voice. "Let's bolt."

"We already smashed the window!" Amy argued. She couldn't believe they stood arguing about how many laws they would break. "What are you going to do? Just come back tomorrow, offer to pay for the window, and tell the sleazy guy that we changed our minds about robbing the place?"

Sarah chewed her lip as she considered this. "Um... Okay, let's just do it and get outta here!" She looked both ways down the block. No one was watching. Now was the time to move and retrieve the wooden box. They both moved towards the opening of the broken window at the same time.

"Ouch!" they cried out simultaneously.

"What are you doing?" Scowling, Amy snatched the wooden puzzle box and pulled it in close to her body. She looked at Sarah, noticing she had something white in her hands. Looking back at the window display, trying to visualize what it looked like in the daytime, Amy realized that her friend had stolen a satin display case holding an antique silver necklace with matching earrings and shiny yellow stones set into a sunflower pattern.

Sarah scowled at her scrutinizing look. "We'll talk about it tomorrow when I come by to pick you up from your place," she muttered angrily at Amy, taking a few steps back before turning and walking briskly away, leaving Amy standing at the scene of the crime in stunned silence, wondering what Sarah's motives could have been to take the jewelry.

Amy's heart was thundering in her chest. When she shifted, the broken glass crunched again under her sneakers. She looked at the opening the brick had made in the window. It looked like there was blood running down the glass remnants still being held in place by the window frame. Looking down at herself and checking her arms, shoulders, and then her hands, she noticed that her right hand was wet with blood. It was throbbing. Amy grimaced, hoping she didn't have any glass stuck in her wounds.

She let out a ragged breath, shaking her head to clear it. It was time to leave. She hugged the wooden box closer to her body and started to walk briskly away, picking up the pace as she went until she was running in a full sprint towards home. The sound of her sneakers hitting the pavement echoed around her. She took a different route home, using back alleyways and doubling back on herself a few times. She didn't want anyone to be able to guess who she was or where she might be going.

The streets were dark and empty, with only the occasional porch light or streetlight on the corners, but she wasn't thinking of miscreants lurking in the shadows this time. Sometimes, she would hear faint rustling noises, a dog bark, or a cat screech, but she didn't stop to check it out. She purposely tried to stick to the shadows as much as possible. This time, she was the delinquent in the darkness.

Finally, Amy approached the house, relieved that her aunt Jeannie's green Ford wasn't in the driveway and hadn't returned from her date. If Jeannie's evening had gone the way most of her dates had recently, she probably wouldn't be back until morning. Amy doubted her aunt would even realize that she had left the house that night and certainly wouldn't suspect her of breaking any laws.

She pulled on the string with her house key on it out from under her hooded sweatshirt. Still, instead of taking it off from around her head, she just bent over to nudge the key into the lock, mentally kicking herself for not leaving the outside light on to make it easier to get back inside. Then again, maybe it was best that no one saw her coming home late at night. It took her a few attempts, but she finally got the door unlocked, and once inside, Amy let out a deep breath that she hadn't realized she'd been holding as she walked around the kitchen table towards her room in the dark.

"Safe!" Amy still felt like adrenaline was rushing through her veins, although her lungs burned from their exertions, and her legs felt wobbly. She pushed her bedroom door open and flicked on the light. Squinting and blinking against the harshness of the overhead illumination, she haphazardly tossed the puzzle box on the bed and looked closer at the cuts on her hand. Luckily, they didn't look too serious, though it was hard to tell with the blood running up and down her arm. She didn't think that she would need stitches, just some Band-Aids.

Amy washed her hands and inspected the cuts again before applying clean Band-Aids from the medicine cabinet, brushing her teeth, and taking a big drink from the tap. Then, she headed back to her room, feeling exhausted. Although she remembered to set the alarm for 6:30 the next morning for the bike trip, she didn't bother changing out of her clothes before she climbed into bed.

Chapter 7

August 16, 1985

Friday

Amy put her messenger bag across her shoulders and swung her leg over the bike seat. Her muscles were stiff from her late-night run home. This morning, the street seemed quiet and deserted except for the birds singing in the trees. It was very early, with the sun only just above the horizon. Though she wasn't genuinely energetic, she was determined to ride to the farmhouse today. She put her left foot on the pedal, took a deep breath, and headed out. As she turned onto the street, Amy was surprised to see her neighbour, Beatrice Petersen, sitting on her front step and sipping her morning coffee in her housecoat and fuzzy pink slippers.

"I noticed your aunt Jeannie didn't come home last night," Mrs. Petersen said, her voice just loud enough for Amy to hear it from the street. "She isn't taking very good care of you. I have to say that, though she seems nice enough, she isn't very motherly."

Amy stopped, putting her foot down to prevent herself from falling over, and called back as quietly as she could manage and still be heard: "I know... but with no other family until I'm old enough, I have no choice over where I live."

As she pedaled away, her mind wandered to her grandmother's friends and acquaintances, many of whom Amy would have preferred to have as her guardians. Sadly, it hadn't been up to her. Aunt Jeanie had been the only relative she'd been able to come up with when the police officer had asked her, other than her Uncle John, of course, but he had disappeared from town years earlier. She didn't know who her father was, let alone his side of the family, and doubted they knew about her at all. Dorothy never seemed to want to talk about that side of things, so she eventually stopped asking.

Amy pulled her bike up to the sidewalk curb by the post office to wait for Sarah to appear. Her watch said that she was on time. Sarah was late, but that wasn't unusual. Amy was always waiting for her. It didn't usually bother her, but she didn't want to hang around when people started arriving on Main Street to open up the stores and check for the morning mail. The minutes seemed to tick by very slowly as Amy tried to curb her anxiety, taking slow, deep breaths. Finally, she spotted Sarah pedaling her bicycle towards her. Amy was so relieved to see her that she forgot to ask about the necklace and earring set Sarah had stolen from the pawnshop.

"Let's start heading out of town," Amy said. "We'll follow the old highway because it's shorter. The pavement will be a little rougher, but with less traffic. My grandma used to come into town on that road to avoid traffic when we were hurrying to get to the school."

Sarah nodded in agreement, and they were on their way in no time. They didn't talk too much at first, but Amy supposed it was because neither had gotten much sleep the previous night. Sarah broke the silence after about a half hour when she awkwardly started talking. "I guess you're wondering why I ... like ... stole the jewelry?"

Amy looked at her but didn't say anything. She wanted Sarah to continue without interruption if it would derail her train of thought. Amy had been so surprised at her actions that she didn't truly know what to think.

"I saw the set in the window that day when we were in front of the pawnshop," Sarah explained. "It was my mom's. I couldn't figure out what it was doing there in the first place. When I asked my mom about it, she said she hadn't even noticed it was missing, but she had looked all over the house. She discovered that several other small items were missing, too. No one seems to know when this happened, but the only day that there wasn't anyone at home in the last few weeks was, like ... on Wednesday of this week, when our family all went to Frankie's Diner to eat."

After considering this in silence for about five minutes, Amy asked, "What did you do with it? Like ... what are you going to do now?"

She was aware that there had been many break-ins lately, with items going missing from people's homes, but she was surprised that such a thing could have gone unnoticed. It would appear that the thieves had gotten better at their jobs.

Sneakier. Amy realized that if the same thing had happened at the farmhouse, it might be challenging to figure out if there'd been a break-in.

"I gave it to my mom this morning before I left. I told her not to tell anyone but that I'd broken the window at the pawnshop and stolen it," Sarah explained as she stared down at the road beneath her feet. "She wasn't too upset but said she had to talk to my dad before they decided what to do. I'm sure we'll have to pay for the window or maybe even apologize... or something."

Amy was shocked. Had Sarah mentioned her as well? That she had also taken something? Countless scenarios started rushing through Amy's mind, most ending with her in a jail cell.

Sarah continued to explain her reasons for telling her mom what they had done and why it felt justified. "Face it, Amy, you would have told your grandma everything, too. She would have understood, just like my mom. She said we would discuss it tomorrow when I returned from the farmhouse. I told her all about you wanting to figure out what your grandma had meant about the importance of the puzzle box and what might happen to you and her farmhouse."

Sarah's complete trust in her mom's support left Amy feeling a great sense of loss. Amy used to have that kind of support and trust from her grandmother. And though her mom, Sandy, had died of cancer when Amy was six years old, she could remember how loving and supportive she had been as well.

Chapter 8

Bobby opened dresser drawers, bedside tables, and the cabinets under the bathroom sink, looking for any loose change, watches, prescription drugs, or painkillers. Thoroughly searching through some of the unpacked boxes, looking for anything he thought he could sell or use for himself, and piling everything of value on the kitchen table on top of the newspaper he'd just finished reading. Jewelry was easier to pawn than most items because he could hide smaller items in his pockets or wear them into the pawn shop. Carrying a television or VCR into a pawnshop could draw unwanted attention to himself. He knew from experience that household and kitchen items were a waste of time because you couldn't get anything but garage sale prices for them anyway. The prescription drugs and painkillers were a little trickier to sell on the streets, but he had managed it many times before. It was just a matter of finding out who needed the drugs you had to sell.

Satisfied that he had found enough items to warrant a trip to the pawnshop, Bobby began to search the kitchen for the stash of keys everyone always had close at hand. He spotted a white ceramic bowl on the counter with a few single keys and a leather key ring with four or five keys on it. He first wanted to find the spare house key for this place so he could trespass more easily. *What were these people's names?* he thought, feeling too lazy to recheck the mail. *Darryl? ... No ... Darren! And Tanya!* Bobby snapped his fingers, pleased with himself. He'd stayed in many different houses while people were away, and it was always easier to explain your presence to nosy neighbours if you had the key to unlock the door and knew the owners' names. Bobby didn't want to have to give up this new scheme and the chance to sleep indoors. He opened the back door to try a few keys that looked like house keys.

With a careful eye, Bobby tried each of the loose keys on the back door. None of them worked. He figured they might fit into the locks of some of the neighbours' houses or might have been left by whoever had sold the house to the new owners. He decided that he could try his luck with the neighbours' houses later. Finally, he tried one of the keys on the key ring on the front door, and it worked. Relieved, he put the keys into his baggy trouser pocket, ready to make his next move.

Next, he dug a coat out of the closet by the back door and put it on. He put the money he had found in his wallet, filled the coat pockets with some of the jewelry, and put the man's gold watch on his wrist. It was time to walk down to the pawnshop to trade some of these pieces for cash. There was a brown hat hanging on a peg at the back door. As he headed out that way, Bobby took the hat off the peg and positioned it on his head, hoping it would help him maintain his disguise.

He walked towards Main Street and the pawnshop with purpose. As he rounded the corner in front of the Family Grocers, he thought, *Maybe, that sleaze-bag owner would be there. I bet he'd be interested in the painkillers.*

He almost ran into two middle-aged women standing on the sidewalk and having a chat. The older, heavy-set woman in the wild-print dress sneered at him. Her friend was gawking down the street and didn't notice him. Bobby followed the woman's gaze to Ace's Pawnshop & Used Goods, where an employee was hammering up a sheet of plywood over the front window.

He paused and turned towards the two women. "Excuse me, ladies, but what's happening at the pawnshop?"

The woman in the wild print dress said, "Someone has broken into the pawnshop sometime last night." She narrowed her eyes and looked down her nose at Bobby. "Who are you? I've seen you in the grocery store, and you look familiar, but I can't seem to place you—"

Caught off guard, he stammered a bit in his answer. "I-I'm Bobby. I'm just in town, visiting friends." With that, he tipped his hat in mocking respect and turned to walk away. As he cut across the street, he could hear the two women chattering about where else they might have seen him before. Bobby chastised himself for not being more careful, vowing to avoid those two women in the future. If he didn't need the money for groceries and other things, he would have just laid low at the house, watching daytime soaps and *The Price Is Right*.

As he approached the pawnshop, he had to step around a pile of swept-up glass in the middle of the sidewalk. A middle-aged man in a dirty white t-shirt, with a cigar hanging out of one corner of his mouth, was struggling to hold up the plywood board while he hammered it in place. Bobby realized he was the man he'd thought was the owner. *Maybe this is a chance to get on this guy's good side. I might get better deals.*

He strode up to the storefront and put his hands on the plywood to help hold it up. "Here, let me give you a hand so you can get this done," he said, smiling reassuringly at the man with the cigar.

"Hey, thanks," the man said, mumbling around his cigar. "I just got here this mornin' and saw that someone broke my window."

Bobby noticed that he'd said, *my window* and thought, Yup. Definitely the owner. "Yeah, I see the broken glass. Is there a lot missing?" He thought he might as well fish for information while he buttered up the owner, hoping that pretending to be a concerned citizen would help him get a good cash deal on his items.

"I don't know yet," the man said, as he kept hammering. "My only guy, Curt, didn't show up this morning, and I haven't had a chance to take a look around. My name's Fred Lavallee. This is my shop."

Bobby almost offered his name in return but decided not to, figuring it was probably best not to introduce himself to everyone on the street, even though it was only an alias. If his larger scheme was going to work in his favour, people knowing him as Bobby would be no more helpful than them knowing his real name. "I'm just in town for a few days visiting. Have the police already been called?" He glanced around the street, nervously wondering what he would do if they showed up.

"No," Fred sighed, shaking his head. "I don't need the police messing around my shop. I think some kids were just messing around and throwing a brick through the window." When he finally finished hammering in the last nail, he turned to his helper with a nod of thanks. "I've got so much junk that I can't keep track of what comes in and goes out, let alone where it all comes from."

"I can imagine," Bobby offered sympathetically. "Are you opening up today? I was actually on my way here this morning on business. But I could maybe come back later if you'd rather finish with this mess."

Fred looked at Bobby long and close and then grinned. "I think I could make an exception for you. You know, as a thank you for the help this morning."

Bobby smiled shyly back and followed him inside. "So, why's your shop called 'Ace's' if your name is Fred?" Bobby smiled, knowing it was always good to ease into the business part of any pawnshop dealing with small talk. When you don't rush them or look like you're in too big of a hurry to get out of the place, it gives the staff more trust in your items as being legitimate. Bobby laid on the charm to avoid arousing any suspicion.

Fred seemed to fall for Bobby's phony interest Bobby in the polite small talk, but when he started explaining in great detail how he'd won the shop in a poker hand with a pair of Aces, Bobby's interest became genuine. Bobby raised his eyebrows, thinking about how things could get really interesting fast if there were a chance of getting in on a poker game. He was sure he could beat most players in this sleepy little nothing of a town.

"I like poker," Bobby said, trying to sound casual, even though his hands were itching to play a high-stakes card game or two. He could triple his money and get back on track in no time!

The pawnshop owner made a big show of trying to remember something, scratching his head and looking up at the ceiling before answering. "I have a regular card game with some friends tomorrow night if you're interested in a few stakes. What's your name?" Fred leaned both of his hands on the counter and smiled at him.

Bobby didn't hesitate this time, eagerly replying, "John." With that, he pulled out a few pieces of jewelry from his jacket pocket. He would save the gold watch for the poker game if the stakes were piled high on a good hand. "But I'll need a little cash for the buy-in. I don't have a paycheck this week."

Fred nodded as he inspected the items one by one. After a few minutes, they agreed on a price for them all. Bobby suspected he got a little more cash than usual because Fred wanted him to lose it all at the poker game.

As he left the shop a short while later, eager to swindle the other players out of as much money as he could, he was already settling on a strategy. He would play it easy on the first few hands until he could figure out each of the other player's tells and then raise the stakes. Bobby was so happy with how well everything was working out that he didn't notice the same two older women from earlier, who were still nearby on the other side of the street, watching him leave the pawnshop.

Chapter 9

Amy burst through the farmhouse door and ducked into the pantry to her left. She knew what she wanted and exactly where to find it. Her mouth was already watering in anticipation of the sweetness as she reached the higher shelf and took a jar of her grandma's homemade peaches, canned with syrup and a touch of cinnamon. Amy's adrenaline was pumping through her veins, giving her the strength to twist the metal ring off with her two thumbs, quickly releasing the vacuum seal with a loud, satisfying pop. Tipping the jar up to her mouth, Amy greedily drank the syrup straight from the jar. It was so good! The syrup dribbled down her chin, but she used the back of her hand to wipe away its stickiness as she licked her lips. Movement near the door caught Amy's attention then, and she noticed that Sarah had followed her into the pantry.

With her hands on her hips and eyebrows raised. Sarah asked, "What? Are. You. Doing?"

Amy attempted to wipe more of the mess away from her chin with the back of her hand, then reached into the jar with two fingers, shrugging. "I can't help it. Grandma's canned peaches are totally awesome! They're all that kept me going the last ten kilometres." Grinning with contentment, she licked the syrup off her fingers before reaching up to get Sarah a jar for herself and handing it to her. "Hit that light switch behind you. I want to check and see if the power is still working." Relieved that the power company had not yet cut the power, even though the bills were marked past due, Amy carried her half-eaten jar of peaches into the large farmhouse kitchen to look around.

Typical of many farmhouses, the kitchen and dining area was one big room that ran from the front to the back of the house. The kitchen area, stove, and refrigerator were on the wall at the back. The builder installed a little window situated above the double sink so you could look out at the yard while you washed your dishes. The cupboards were flat, stained dark brown, and had little brass knobs. The large chest-deep freezer was off to the side along one wall for easy access to frozen items.

Amy walked across the room to the sink and turned on the faucet with her free hand. The pumps were still on, though they groaned and released some pockets of air from the faucet before the water began to sputter out. Amy wrinkled her nose as she let it run until it flowed freely. "It smells bad. I'll leave the water on to get rid of the bad stuff. Please don't drink it, though. It may not be safe. Grandma used to bring in town water in five-gallon pails for drinking. I don't think we have any drinking water here now, but luckily, we have peach juice." Amy held up her jar of peaches, clinking it against Sarah's before taking another drink. "I'm going to have to remember to turn the hot water tank on so we can shower."

"Maybe we should open a few windows and air the place out, too. It stinks a little, like ... I don't know

... something gross." Now, Sarah wrinkled her nose, sniffing the air.

Setting her jar of peaches on the counter, Amy licked her fingers before running them under the flowing water. Finally, she shut off the tap and opened the window above the sink. Turning to her right to walk out of the kitchen and through the living room, Amy turned left into the hallway towards the two bedrooms. She walked past her grandmother's closed bedroom door and opened the door to her old bedroom. Bunk beds stood against one wall, and a little dresser and closet were opposite the beds. She glanced around the room; nothing seemed different from the last time she'd been there.

She walked across the room to the window. When she pushed the curtains aside to open them, she noticed that someone had turned the latch. Amy tapped the unlocked latch, thinking, Strange. She couldn't remember if the window had been unlocked the last time, but since she had apparently closed it, or perhaps Aunt Jeannie had, it seemed odd that it was left unlocked. Doing so helped the window seal tight on the old frame, which would have allowed for a draft otherwise. She shrugged finally. She had so much stuff in front of the window that it seemed unlikely anyone could have gained entry through it in any case.

After turning on the water heater, she returned to the living room. Sarah was already in there, sitting in the big armchair with one leg draped over one of its arms and the other on the floor. Amy made her way over to the couch, collapsing onto it. "I think I could have a nap now. My legs feel rubbery," she said with a yawn.

"Where's the TV?" Sarah mumbled.

Amy jolted upright then, looking at the spot where the television and VCR used to sit. "Right," she said, blinking rapidly. "S-So ... we need to add that to the puzzle box as something missing from here."

In their haste to get to the farmhouse, Amy had almost forgotten why they had come. Sheepishly, she admitted, "I think I left my bedroom window unlocked. I'm so stupid! I guess someone could have got in through there to steal stuff." Her heart sank. If that was how someone had gotten in, it was her fault that the farmhouse had been burglarized!

She pulled herself off the couch and picked up a scrap of paper and a pencil off the coffee table. It was time to start listing all of the missing items. Looking around the living room, Amy began mumbling as she looked around the room and jotted things down: "TV, VCR ... vase ... stereo ... puzzle box." She walked into the kitchen, wondering if anyone would steal anything in that room.

"The toaster?! Who would steal a toaster? So... weird." Scribbling it down, Amy turned back towards the bedrooms, going into her own first. Satisfied that nothing seemed to be missing from her room beyond what her or Jeannie already brought back to her aunt's house, she walked back into the hallway.

"The door into Grandma Dorothy's room is locked," Sarah said while she jiggled the doorknob.

"That's not unusual. The lock seems to do that all on its own sometimes. Grandma kept a key for it in the linen closet under the towels for whenever that happened." Amy walked around Sarah to open the closet at the end of the hall and fished out the little brass key hidden under a stack of towels.

Holding it up, she sighed. "I don't know how long it's been locked this time. I haven't been in this room since ... well ... since Grandma died."

"Do you want to go in by yourself? I can give you some privacy if you need it."

"No," she reassured her. "I think I'll need you close for this one." They exchanged weary smiles as Amy inserted the key into the lock. It took a little bit of jiggling, both of the knob and the key, to gain entry into the room. Then, Amy's senses were assaulted by a mixture of dust and the familiar fragrance she had always associated with her grandma. She inhaled deeply, blinking back tears, then straightened her shoulders. "Help me search her room to see if anything is missing. Jewelry, I guess, would be the most likely."

Sarah nodded, feeling nostalgic. "I feel like when we were kids, sneaking into your grandma's room to play dress up." She sighed. "I miss her too." The girls worked quietly, searching the drawers for all of her jewelry and valuables, laying each item on the ruffled purple bedspread as they found them.

Amy was pulling out drawers and searching for hidden items mixed in with the clothing when she found a large manila envelope near the back of her sweater drawer. Curious about its contents, she opened it, pulling out pieces of paper one at a time. There was a newspaper clipping of her grandfather's obituary, two copies of his death certificate, and a copy of his will, all of which Amy placed on top of the dresser. Then, she pulled out the last item, a wallet-sized document that Amy needed: her birth certificate. Smiling to herself, she tucked all the documents back into the envelope.

"Hey, Sarah, I found my birth certificate! Now, I can apply to get my learner's permit and learn to drive! It would be so much more fun if I could drive myself everywhere I needed to go. I'd have to figure out what kind of vehicle I could afford to buy. Aunt Jeannie is always gone with her truck, so I really need my own wheels."

Then something occurred to her: "I wonder if whoever inherits the farmhouse would let me keep Grandma's blue car. It would sure be nice if I didn't have to buy one. We could go on a road trip!"

"Oooh! That would be awesome. Where is her car, anyway?"

"I think my aunt said she put it in the barn for storage. Or maybe the workshop. I don't remember which one." Amy tossed the envelope onto the bed and then continued to search the room. When Amy thought they had gone through everything, she inspected the items on the bed: several pieces of jewelry, a small stack of money, and the manila envelope with the documents. "I don't think anything is missing. I guess whoever took everything else couldn't get into this room without breaking it down and decided against it or will return later."

Amy stood there for a long moment, studying the assorted items, unsure of what to do next.

"I think you need to take this stuff back to town with you, just for safekeeping. What if, like, someone breaks in again while the place is empty? It'll be safer with you."

She had a good point, and Amy couldn't disagree with her logic. Remembering that Grandma kept assorted bags in her closet, Amy rummaged around until she grabbed one big enough for everything but small enough that she could still manage it on her bike. It even had a zipper—since her grandma had made it out of scraps of denim from an old jacket—she shouldn't have to worry about anything falling out. Luckily, it also had a long enough strap that Amy could sling it over one shoulder across her body. It shouldn't get in the way while riding her bike. It's much better than juggling a big purse or a suitcase.

Unzipping the bag, Amy started putting all the jewelry, the envelope, and the money inside while Sarah closed all the drawers. Together, they left the room, closed the door behind them, and walked back into the living room. As Amy put the denim bag down beside her messenger bag, she nodded to Sarah and collapsed onto the couch. "I feel sweaty and dusty. The water should be hot enough to shower by now. You can take the first one but save some for me."

While Sarah showered, Amy rummaged around in her room for clean clothes and random items she could put in her messenger bag to take back to town the next day. She wanted to leave as soon as they woke up in the morning and wanted to be prepared ahead of time. Although Amy was pretty sure that she would sleep soundly tonight after all the exercise and fresh air she'd had, she didn't want to leave and forget anything.

Amy was standing in front of the bookcase in the living room, scanning the book titles, when Sarah emerged from the bathroom with a towel wrapped around her head and a big smile on her face. "The shower is all yours. And you were right; the water is nice and hot. There's even still more hot water for you, I think."

"Thanks, I think," Amy said, rolling her eyes slightly. "I'm going to use up however much is left, for sure." Snatching up her change of clothes and the towel from the living room chair, she quickly made her way into the steamy bathroom, calling out a suggestion to Sarah. "Maybe you should call to let your mom know we made it here safely! I think the phone's still working."

"Oh, right. I forgot! I'll go check and see if the party line is free," Sarah said as she made her way to the kitchen. Amy smirked, knowing that if it weren't, Sarah would boldly ask whoever was on the shared line to get off so she could get a quick call home.

The hot shower felt terrific on Amy's body. She needed it to wash away the dusty grime and sweat. When she turned off the shower, Amy could hear voices from the living room. *Who is she talking to?* Amy strained to listen while she rushed to get dressed, pausing when she recognized the other voice belonging to her aunt Jeannie. *What's she doing here? Weird.* Amy hadn't told Jeannie they would be at the farmhouse because she hadn't gotten the chance. Amy hung the wet towel on the rack to dry, gathered her dirty clothes in her arms, and left the bathroom.

"So, I'll drive you both home," Jeannie was saying to Sarah when Amy entered the living room. Then she turned and smiled at her niece.

"Aunt Jeannie," Amy said, plastering on a smile of her own, trying to disguise the confusion over her aunt's sudden appearance. "We weren't expecting you. I thought you had to work today. How did you know we were here?"

"Well—" she said as she fluffed up her hair with her fingers, "As it turns out, I didn't have to work.

So, I decided to come to the farmhouse to check on things! Now that I'm here, I can give you both a ride back to town. Your bicycles will fit easily in the back of my truck."

Jeannie raised her eyebrows innocently as she looked around the living room. She was hiding something, but Amy couldn't put her finger on what it was just yet. Maybe Jeannie's intentions would be clear once Amy found a private time to ask Sarah about their conversation. *She definitely didn't come to offer us a lift since she didn't know we'd be at the farmhouse. So why did she?*

"Do you want to leave right away?" Amy asked, looking up at the living room ceiling as if she could see through it to the boxes stored upstairs. "I still wanted to check up in the attic."

"What would you look for up there? I thought that was just storage." Jeannie squinted a bit, tilting her head upwards and trying to envision what Amy saw. "You'll just get all dusty."

Unsure of what she should say to her aunt, who seemed to be in a hurry to leave, she decided to remind her of what the police officer had said. "I need to check for signs of a break-in ... like the officer told me to do. I also want to make sure all the windows are properly latched before we leave. We wouldn't want another break-in. We've already spotted a few missing things."

Jeannie looked at her watch and then at Amy, considering her request and the time it would take. "I guess I can give you a little bit of time before we leave. Say fifteen to twenty minutes. I don't want to spend too much time here, though. It just reminds me of coming here with John and all the promises he made to me. If this place were mine, I'd sell it and move far away from everything that reminds me of him. I'd leave this boring town forever!"

Picking up the denim bag as discretely as she could manage, Amy turned to Sarah, trying to signal her with her eyes to keep an eye on Jeannie. "No problem. You can hang out here with Sarah while I run up to the attic and check on things."

Jeannie nodded with a frown and moved slowly over to the couch to wait for her.

The narrow stairs to the attic were at the end of the hall behind a little narrow door. As Amy climbed the stairs, she could hear Sarah making a polite but strained conversation with her aunt Jeannie. When she reached the top, she switched on the light. The attic, a treasure trove of family history, was waiting to be explored if only she had the time. Typical of most attic spaces, the ceilings were sloped on the sides, and the best place to walk was right down the middle. Christmas decorations lined one side of the attic, and boxes of books, photo albums, old toys, and outdated clothes lined the other. Every box was labeled with a black permanent marker, describing its contents. She scanned each label as she walked by, looking for a box that might contain important documents. She wasn't sure if Grandma had kept any up here, but she figured it was worth a look for any information that might help her figure out where her uncle John was and what her own future with the farmhouse might be.

As she reached the far end of the room, she spotted a box with the word "papers" written on it. Her heart skipped a beat. Could this be it? The key to all the answers she was seeking? She lifted the dusty lid to see what kind of papers they were, flipping through several pages before finding one that looked like the deed to the farmhouse property. She set those papers on the floor with plans to take them with her to read later. The same box also contained more correspondence from the private investigator Dorothy had hired, printed on the same stationery with the same letterhead. It seemed she had hired him quite a while ago. Not wanting to waste time reading anything, she added them to her growing pile of important paperwork. When she was satisfied that there wasn't anything else that she needed from the box, she replaced any papers she wasn't taking with her and shoved the lid back on.

"Are you just about done up there?" Jeannie's voice called up from the bottom of the stairs.

Amy looked at her watch and rolled her eyes. It had only been ten minutes. Standing up, she called out, "Hold on. I'm coming." She carefully put the paperwork into the denim bag. Brushing her hands over the back of her pants and walking briskly to the window to check the latch, she rushed down the stairs and into her old room to secure its window.

When she returned to the living room, it was empty, so she proceeded into the kitchen and found Sarah leaning against the deep freezer, holding Amy's other bag, which she handed her. "I locked the kitchen window already," Sarah said. "Your aunt is foraging for food in the pantry." Amy nodded just as her aunt returned with a few paper grocery bags heavy with food.

"We may as well take a few canned goods back to town while we're at it," she said as she nodded for them to get going. "Groceries are too expensive to waste. We shouldn't leave any here."

Sarah and Amy exchanged glances before following Jeannie out the door. Amy shrugged, deciding that her aunt had probably just driven out to the farmhouse to grab a few groceries. It would be good to have some wholesome food back at the house in town. She felt a bit sheepish that she'd begun to suspect that her aunt had come to the farmhouse to steal its valuables.

The sun was setting behind them as Jeannie drove back to town. There wasn't very much conversation among the three of them. The local country station crackled through the truck's radio while Jeannie focused on the road ahead, seemingly lost in thought and ignoring the speedometer. It had been a very long day for Amy, with many questions still left unanswered. And a new one that had popped up to pique her interest. Shortly after they'd gotten into the truck, her aunt had casually said that she'd gotten a call from the new lawyer in charge of Grandma's estate to set up a meeting at his office early next week. They both had to attend. Though she hadn't been any more specific than that, her casual aloofness had left Amy wondering what had finally changed to trigger a call for a meeting after so much time waiting. Had the lawyer finally managed to contact her uncle? Amy also wondered if the lawyer was in contact with the private investigator her grandmother had hired. She looked at Sarah, who raised her eyebrows in return, wordlessly acknowledging these questions, though she had no answers to share.

Chapter 10

August 17, 1985

Saturday

Amy woke up mid-morning, feeling dehydrated and achy all over. When she stumbled into the kitchen, her aunt Jeannie was just leaving, dressed in her frilly orange and blue uniform for her job at the diner. "See you later," Jeannie grumbled as she left the house.

Aunt Jeannie clearly hadn't woken up very cheerfully before she left today, but with her gone all day, Amy would have the opportunity to sort through all the papers and browse the library books about woodworking all day without interruption. She had to figure out what was missing from the estate, why the puzzle box was so important, and the whereabouts of her elusive uncle John. Something just wasn't adding up about any of it. When she tried to look at the bigger picture, there were clearly some pieces missing.

Opening the cupboard, Amy got a tall glass to fill with tap water to quench her thirst. The cans and jars from her grandma's pantry were still sitting on the counter where Jeannie had dropped them yesterday before they'd retreated to their bedrooms for the night. Amy decided that nothing would be better than another jar of canned peaches.

Feeling a sense of urgency, Amy rummaged through the bags until she found one. Taking the last clean spoon out of the cutlery drawer, she hurried back to her room with her breakfast. Setting the glass of water on her nightstand, she popped the lid off the jar and ate half of its contents while considering what to do first.

Amy decided to read and organize the papers. She smoothed the covers on her bed, emptied the papers and the letter onto it, and then put the small stack of household bills on the dresser. "I should probably open and sort those too," she muttered. "I need to ask the lawyer who needs to pay them. I hope it is not me."

She shook her head, thinking it was probably the executor's responsibility, whoever that was, and wondered why the lawyer hadn't informed them of the mounting bills.

Settling down on the bed beside the stack of papers, she began to read through the deed for the farmhouse and the land, along with the included description. The morning sunlight filtered through the curtains, casting a warm glow on the dusty pages. Nothing seemed out of the ordinary, so Amy started a pile that would include all of the information related directly to the farmhouse. Then it occurred to her that maybe the bills should go into that pile, too.

With a sigh, she looked at the pile of bills on the dresser and, deciding they needed to be opened, went to retrieve them before settling back down. Among them, she also found a letter from the municipality, reminding her grandma to pay the land and property taxes by September 30th, as well as several monthly bank statements, which she left unopened, adding them to the growing pile of information for the farmhouse.

Each bill had unpaid charges carried over from the previous month. She arranged them so that the most recent of each bill would be at the top of the pile. She was surprised to note that the telephone bills were thick envelopes containing many pages. In the sections titled "Long Distance Charges," there were lists of each long-distance phone number that her grandma had called, accompanied by the date, the time of day, and the number of minutes the call had taken. The most recent telephone bill listed nothing in this section, but the others had several. The bill for May had a list of long-distance calls her grandmother had made in April before she died.

Amy looked at the last entry, realizing that there had been a long-distance phone call that was called from the farmhouse just before her grandma had suddenly left to go into town, later dying at the hospital. Something seemed familiar about the out-of-province phone number, but she couldn't place it.

Gathering all of the manila envelopes postmarked from "Morgan, P.I.," Amy started emptying all their contents into a pile and began reading each letter. Some letters were just requests for Dorothy to call him at her earliest convenience. Others had pertinent information he had uncovered, from which Amy learned that her grandma had hired him to look for her son, John Young, in Ontario. The P.I. had tracked John through towns across two provinces, using police records with minor charges and offences, a bankruptcy, and drug rehabilitation periods. One letter indicated that "the documentation you requested is enclosed," but nothing else in the envelope.

Suddenly, Amy's eyes widened as she skimmed the letterhead, and she quickly picked up the phone bill to compare P.I. Morgan's phone number to the one her grandma had called the night she died. It matched! What had the investigator told her that had made her drop everything while baking cookies to rush into town? And what was she doing in town that night that had ended up putting her in the hospital? Who had she gone to see? Although the private investigator's letters seemed to pose more questions than they answered, Amy put them all into a pile by themselves, figuring they were essential puzzle pieces that she likely needed to assemble.

Deciding to empty the envelope with the documents she'd found at the farmhouse and sort them along with the other papers spread across the bed, Amy read through the last will and testament of her grandfather, John William Young, Senior. His sole beneficiary had been Dorothy Mary Young. He had died in 1970 when Amy was only a baby. His death certificate listed his cause of death as "kidney failure."

Amy frowned a bit, unsure if she'd ever known that this was his cause of death. She had never asked and didn't think anyone had ever thought to mention it. Apparently, when Amy was growing up, there had been quite a lot she'd never known about her family. She started a separate pile for all the information relating to her grandfather, putting the death certificate, along with a second copy of it, on top of the pile without giving it much thought.

Lastly, Amy's wallet-sized birth certificate was placed by itself since it didn't belong with the other piles of papers. It listed only her full name, birth date, and birthplace, but that was all she needed to apply for a driver's licence. She felt giddy just thinking about one day being able to drive a vehicle of her own.

Amy zipped the denim bag closed, leaving all of her grandma's jewelry and cash inside. She decided that it would be best to hide the bag under her bed for safekeeping. She knelt beside her bed, lifting the quilt out of the way, and then paused. The puzzle box was under there, begging her to open it. She'd forgotten she had tucked it under her bed before falling into it, exhausted, after they'd stolen it from the shop.

"Right, I need to get that box open, too." She promised herself she'd do it as soon as she could, then moved it aside and shoved the denim bag under the bed beside it.

Deciding to reuse the art folder she had completed for school the previous year, she crawled over to the end of the bed to reach for it, pulled out her drawings, and put them in a pile on the floor at the foot of the bed. She then carefully placed each pile of sorted papers into the folder, gathered all the empty envelopes into a plastic bag and tied it shut so that she could put it out with the trash later.

Sighing with satisfaction that she'd accomplished at least part of her list of things to do today, Amy brushed the dust from her hands onto her pajama pants and thought about having a hot shower as her reward for her productivity. Deciding it was a good idea, she quickly jotted down a few things on a scrap of paper so she wouldn't forget what needed to be done.

"Let's see," she said as she looked around the room, mumbling as she started scribbling things down. "Give the list from the farmhouse to the police. Call that Alister Morgan guy. Read woodworking books. Clean my room. Work on Sunday. Lawyer?" She tapped the pencil against her lips and re-read the list. She couldn't think of anything else, so she gathered some clean clothes to put on after her shower.

Amy's hair was still wet from the shower, but she didn't feel like blow-drying it. She wasn't sure that she wanted to leave the house today anyway. Instead, she decided to call Alistair Morgan, the private investigator her grandmother had been using to find her Uncle John. A one-eight-hundred number was on his letterhead, so Amy could call him long-distance for free. It took two tries at dialing the number correctly before the call could be connected. When it finally was, Amy pressed the handset to her ear while she fiddled with the telephone cord with her other hand.

After several rings, the call was finally answered. Amy rolled her eyes as an answering machine clicked on just before the recorded male voice began: "You have reached 1-800-555-4141, office of Private Investigator Alister Morgan. Please leave your name, number, and message after the tone, and I'll return your call within a few days. Thank you." There was a slight pause, followed by three loud beeps.

"Hi ... My name is Amy. I'm Dorothy Young's granddaughter. Um, I found your letters in her things ... She died." She cleared her throat, swallowing hard. "In April. The estate still hasn't been settled yet. I think we will meet with the lawyer early this week. I don't know ... Was there something you needed or information you want to pass on to me? You can still use the same mailing address because I still pick up her mail—or call me at my aunt's house. Aunt Jeannie's number here is six—Sorry, I mean, area code three—" Amy was cut off by another loud beep of the machine before the call disconnected, leaving her with a dial tone buzzing in her ear. Amy realized that she hadn't gotten to finish her message because she'd been too long-winded. Looking at the handset, she rolled her eyes, deciding that she should have started with her name and number before telling him her whole miserable life story. She didn't want to call back to continue her message, so she hung up the handset, assuming he would just mail out whatever information he wanted to give her.

Next, Amy thumbed through the phone book to find the phone number for the police station. She congratulated herself on her progress, thinking she would get a lot done today if she made good use of the telephone. She dialed the five numbers needed to connect to the local police station. After one ring, a cheery woman's voice answered. "Police station, this is Gladys. How may I direct your call?"

"Hi. My name's Amy Young. I had ... um, Officer Gerard, he told me to talk to him about a break-in at our farmhouse."

"Just hold on a minute, please." The woman must have set the receiver on the desk because the noise of papers shuffling and people talking in the background came through over the line. After a few minutes, Gladys came back on. "He'll be in on Monday. Can you come into the station and talk to him in person then?"

"Okay. I can do ... Oh! Wait! Does it have to be at a specific time, or will any time be good?"

"Any time is fine," Gladys said, and Amy could hear the smile in her voice. "If he's not here, you can leave him a note. Have a nice day!"

"Goodbye," Amy responded and hung up the handset, not waiting for Gladys to say anything else.

Deciding she'd had enough of calling around, Amy retreated to her bedroom to browse through the library books she had not yet read. She hoped she would find something resembling her puzzle box to figure out how to open it to find the secret her grandma hid inside. *What makes a wooden box into a puzzle box, anyway?*

Lying on her stomach across the bed, Amy was reading one of the library books about woodworking, which was open in front of her. The book had all sorts of projects, but so far, nothing related to wooden boxes with secret drawers, compartments, or puzzles.

She heard the front door open and then her aunt calling, "Amy! Are you here? Are you dressed? Amy?"

Amy turned over the open book, laying it flat on her bedspread, and turned to look over her shoulder at her open bedroom door. "I'm in here! Yes! Why?"

Aunt Jeannie appeared in the doorway, wearing her uniform from the Diner. "We're swamped at the restaurant today. Two people called in sick! We need someone to bus tables and wash dishes to help us keep up!" She tossed Amy a blue apron with orange frills, hitting her square in the face. "They'll pay you in cash, as always, but you have to hurry! I've got to work a double shift. We'll get fed in between rushes. Hurry!"

Amy couldn't argue because she knew the money would come in handy. "I'll just be five minutes," she told Jeannie as she brushed past her to go across the hall to look into the bathroom mirror. Quickly, she combed her still-damp hair into a high ponytail and put on a bit of makeup. The bathroom door was open, and she could hear Jeannie carefully dialing the telephone.

"Frank, yeah, it's me, Jeannie ... Yes, Amy's coming to bus tables and be our dishwasher. We'll be there in about ten minutes ... Yup. See you in a bit." She slammed down the receiver then and called, "Hurry up! Let's go! He's waiting on us!"

Frankie's Diner was on Main Street, just two blocks from the Family Grocers. Jeannie drove down the back alley behind the restaurant and into the staff parking area. Frank Demmans, the owner, didn't want his staff taking up valuable parking spaces out front. Many of Amy's fellow employees from the grocery store would walk over to the Diner on their lunch breaks, as did many people working on Main Street, but since Amy ate food from there all the time, it wasn't something she would do as a lunch treat for herself. She thought a treat should be something she didn't get very often, like a nice cold, crisp, green salad with fresh vegetables.

The back door opened into a bit of a mudroom where the employees could hang up their coats. There were also random pieces of orange and blue uniforms on many of the hooks left by other staff members. Amy followed her aunt through the noisy kitchen. Today's cook was Bob Crookedneck, a large man with brown skin and black hair dressed in a blue shirt with orange trim. He nodded at Jeannie and Amy as he handed plates up to the window for the servers to grab from the other side. "Order up!" he called. "Well, put that apron on, my girl! Grab that grey bin behind you and start cleaning tables. Hurry it up! People need a clean table so we can feed them already!"

"Okay." She nodded as she slipped on the apron, crossing the ties from the back and then wrapping them around in the front to tie them. The big apron reached past her knees, too large for her small, skinny frame. This was just as well since Amy knew that it would keep her covered and clean, which was ideal as she was wearing her own clothes and not having a proper uniform of her own. She didn't think anyone would notice, though.

Bob's dark eyes twinkled as he looked at her and started to laugh. "I need to send home more meals for you, so maybe you can grow a little more."

"I don't think I'm going to grow much more. I was almost the same height as my grandma, and she said my mom was the same height as me." Amy picked up the grey tub and headed into the dining area, walking around the counter and heading for the orange tables in the far corner. She planned to start at the front of the diner and work her way back so the tub would be at its heaviest when she was the closest to the kitchen.

The first few tables filled with new customers as soon as Amy finished wiping them down. People liked the tables by the window to watch people walk by on Main Street while they ate. As she cleared and wiped the tables, she occasionally would find dollar bills or loose change left behind for tips. When she walked by the waitress counter, she would add it to the tip jar. The Diner staff put all the tips into the jar, splitting them at the end of each shift, so that waitresses could help all the tables instead of focusing on one area of the Diner. Amy's aunt had told her that everyone at work, including the cooks and dishwasher, got a share of the tips.

After a few trips back and forth from the dining area to the kitchen, Amy almost had the tables all caught up. As she looked around, she spotted one last dirty table she needed to clear before starting with the dishes in the kitchen. When she set the grey tub on the bench seat, Amy noticed her neighbour, Beatrice Petersen, and her friend, Denise Schneider, seated at the table right beside where Amy needed to clean. Beatrice caught Amy's eye and smiled. "I see you're working hard here, too."

"Yeah. Aunt Jeannie told me they needed extra help today busing tables, and I needed the money." She smiled at her then, making a grandiose motion with her arms to show off her dirty blue apron as though she were modeling it. "What do you think, Mrs. Petersen? Is it my colour or what?"

"You're a beautiful young lady in any colour." Beatrice winked. "You better watch out for the boys. My son, Gabe, says he met the love of his life in this diner." Denise and Beatrice both pointed and looked over to the table to their left.

Amy's eyes followed their pointing fingers to where some stock boys from the Family Grocers were sitting. She felt the heat of embarrassment creep up her neck and wished she could crawl under the table. Why did I even look?

"I work with those boys. They've all seen me before at work and school," Amy told the ladies as she picked up the tub of dirty dishes to carry to the kitchen.

Beatrice reached out, grabbed Amy's arm on her way past, and whispered, "Watch out if you're working late tonight, dear. There has been talk of a few shady characters in town. Please, don't walk home alone in the dark. There's been a lot of crime lately. Who knows what might happen to you?"

Denise leaned her buxom body forward to add to the conversation. "There's this one guy—" She looked around to see if anyone was listening before she continued, though she didn't make any attempts to keep her voice down. "I've spotted him on Main Street, in the park, and at my church. This short, skinny man with a dangerous look about him. He told us his name was 'Bobby,' but Fred Lavallee at the pawnshop says it's 'John.' I know because I went into Ace's to find out what I could about him. Something is fishy about the whole situation. I suggest you stay away from him. Please!"

"I don't remember seeing anyone like that," Beatrice said, frowning slightly. "When was this?"

Thinking this might take a while, Amy raised her eyebrows and set the corner of the grey tub of dishes on the table to take some weight off her arm. "And what does he look like? This Bobby, or whatever his name was?"

As Denise started describing the mysterious stranger, the hair on the back of Amy's neck stood up. "Short, skinny, big moustache, smells like stale whiskey and cigarettes." Amy inhaled sharply at the familiar description that made her shiver involuntarily.

"Oh yes!" Beatrice almost shouted at Denise, adding a little bit of excitement by sharing in the gossip. "Shifty eyes, leather jacket, and slicked-back hair, at least from what I've heard!" Thoughtfully, she looked over at her companion. "Though I heard that he was tall, not short. But whatever. I don't like the thought of random, no-good hoodlums coming here from the city to cause trouble in our town."

Taking this as a change of subject, Amy also took it as her cue to leave the two ladies arguing about the descriptions of this new lousy character in town. "Have a good day, ladies." Amy headed into the kitchen towards the row of grey tubs full of the dirty dishes she had lined up. Opening the two large, square industrial dishwashers on the counter to let out the steam, she had to empty the hot, clean plates and trays of mugs from the morning rush before she could begin the next two loads.

It seemed to take forever to get all caught up on the dishes; Amy was putting the last load into the dishwasher when her aunt Jeannie came into the kitchen with another tub of dirty dishes. "Why don't you take a short break before the mid-afternoon coffee rush starts?" she said. "That'll be mostly coffee mugs, so you can do this bin later."

"Thanks," Amy said. "Did you know our neighbours, George and Beatrice Petersen, have a son named Gabe?"

Jeannie blinked a few times before answering. "Yes, Gabe and John were in the same group of friends in high school."

"Oh! You know her son, then?"

Jeannie smiled, thinking back fondly to an earlier time. "Yeah. Gabe was around a lot when I started dating John. They hung out with Leon and... what's his name? Some red-headed kid who became a lawyer, and then even the mayor once. He was a nice boy. Rich, too. Maybe I should have dated him instead of your uncle." With a grimace, Jeannie turned and left the kitchen.

Amy looked over at Bob, who had been listening to their exchange. He shook his head and adjusted his hair net. "Mayor Steve was not a nice guy in high school. And she wouldn't have been any happier living with an adulterer. John was a good guy, though, at least until he started running with that Eddie character. I'll never figure out why he began hanging out with that loser." He waved his brown hand in front of his face as if to shoo his ideas away. "Don't listen to her anyway. She hasn't figured out what happiness is yet. She still thinks that money buys happiness. It's a shame when women can't see the road to happiness when it is right in front of them." He turned then and resumed cleaning the smoking grill with a wire brush.

Amy left the kitchen confused about whether Bob was referring to himself or if he was just making a general statement. She took a coffee mug from under the waitress's counter to pour herself a fountain drink and then sat down at the booth nearest the kitchen, which Frank designated for staff use. Amy had the table to herself but could see that some of the waitresses were sitting down with various friends in the diner. It gave Amy a little time to think about all that she just learned.

Since Gabe Petersen had been friends with her uncle John, she thought she might check with the Petersens to see if Gabe knew where her uncle was now. Amy decided to talk to Beatrice before her shift at the grocery store tomorrow. *If Uncle John hung out with her son, I'm sure she'd be happy to tell me some good stories about him from when he was my age, too—Oh, didn't Denise say that stranger in town might have been named John?* Amy briefly wondered if it could have been her uncle they'd seen, but then shook the thought away, confident at least one of them would have recognized him if it was. She sighed, thinking it would be wonderful to hear some pleasant stories about her uncle instead of the hate-filled stories of resentment she usually heard from her aunt.

Maybe she could even figure out when and where his life had gone wrong.

Amy's shift at the diner was repetitive: clearing tables, washing dishes, stacking clean dishes, and starting all over again. At about ten p.m., Frank entered the kitchen, where she was stacking clean plates.

"Thanks for coming in today," he smiled at her like Amy imagined a father would. "You were a great help. We were busy with all the extra people in town for the big ball game. Come up to the till, and I'll pay you out for your time."

She wiped her hands on the apron to dry them and followed Frank from the kitchen. The main part of the diner was reasonably quiet, with mostly just older couples drinking coffee. Only a few guests were eating. Jeannie stood near a table, talking to some teenagers in a booth near the front windows. Amy turned back to watch Frank use a calculator to figure out her wages, pressing the buttons with his fat fingers. She looked at her watch, trying to figure out how many hours she had worked. *Probably about eight*, she decided. Frank rang open the till, counted out four crisp ten-dollar bills, and handed them to her.

"Thanks for the work," Amy said as she slipped the apron off from around her neck so that she could stuff the bills into her pants pocket. "Let me know if I can help again." Amy turned then, scanning the room for her aunt and spotting her over at the staff table now, settling in with a cup of coffee. She made a beeline towards her.

"What time are you off?" she asked her. "I'm done now and want to get home."

"I'm here until three a.m. closing." Jeannie sighed as she reached for her mug of coffee, taking a sip of the hot liquid. "You'll have to find your own way home tonight, kid."

Amy stared at her incredulously. "I didn't know that when you asked me to come in. It's late. Can't you drive me?"

"Nope," was her curt reply. "Guess you're walking."

Amy threw the apron down on the table in front of her and briskly turned to stalk towards the front doors. Brushing past people waiting at the till, she angrily pulled on the door handle to exit.

"Have a good night, Amy!" Frank called out to her as the door closed.

The air was cold and damp. Amy rubbed her hands up and down her arms, trying to ward off the chills. If she had known she was going to have to walk home, she would have brought a jacket, not to mention her bike. She anticipated the dozen or more blocks would seem long and cold in the dark without a sweater or jacket. Turning to her right with a sigh, Amy started to trudge towards home.

"Hey!" a male voice called out behind her. "Do you need a ride?"

Amy stopped dead in her tracks and turned slowly around to see Shane, the tall stock boy from the Family Grocers, standing on the sidewalk in front of the diner with two of his friends. *Well,* Amy thought, *I'm probably safer catching a ride with these guys than walking home alone in the dark.* Beatrice Petersen's words of warning were still echoing in her mind.

"Okay, I guess," Amy replied, eyeing Shane's companions as she walked towards them. Amy recognized one boy from her math class, but she couldn't quite place the other. Looking around to mask her awkwardness, she asked, "Where's your car?"

"Right here," Shane gestured towards a two-tone brown, 1977 Chevrolet Chevette parked a few cars down from Frankie's Diner.

As his friends argued about who would sit in the back seat with Amy, to "put the moves" on her, Amy started to have second thoughts. Maybe she was safer walking home alone than risking being trapped in the back seat with one of them. "Um ..." she hesitated, looking up at Shane. "On second thought... maybe I should walk. I don't think I trust your friends."

Shane looked over at them. "You guys are both going to sit in the back! Amy sits up front." He turned back to her, grinning as he pushed his glasses back up on the bridge of his nose. "Problem solved! Everyone, get in!"

"Thanks," Amy said as she tucked a loose strand of hair behind her right ear before twirling the end of it nervously. She stepped off the sidewalk around to the front passenger-side door. As she climbed in, the two boys in the back were already pushing each other, vying for leg and elbow room. Amy was happy to be in the front seat.

Shane shifted into neutral and started the engine, revving it several times but not driving away from the Diner. After a few moments, Amy turned to see him looking at her expectantly.

He shrugged. "Uh ... where do you live?"

Blushing at her assumption that everyone in this little town knew everything about everyone, Amy answered, "At my aunt's place on 8th Street West, near the Circle K gas bar." He nodded and started driving, his fingers tapping with the music playing quietly on his stereo.

As he finally turned onto her street, Amy pointed. "It's the little blue house right there. The only one without any lights on."

He pulled his car into the empty gravel driveway. "There doesn't seem to be anyone home."

"There never is," Amy replied as she pulled the string from around her neck, the house and farmhouse keys jingling together. She reached for the handle and opened the car door.

"See you at work tomorrow," Shane said, ducking low and looking over at the Petersen house.

"Thanks for the ride. See you later." Amy got out quickly and shut the door, not wanting to linger longer than necessary. When she looked up, Amy saw the living-room curtains at the Petersen house swish closed just before her lights went out.

What the heck? Is she spying on me?

Chapter 11

The dim room in the back of Ace's Pawnshop & Used Goods was thick with smoke. The only light in the room was from a naked bulb dangling from the ceiling over the round, green-felt poker table. The dealer was unexpectedly fast at handling the cards; indeed, more skilled than Bobby expected to find in Glenmere tonight. He wondered where Fred had even found this dealer. He seemed far too skilled to be a part of the small-town backroom poker scene. Four of the seated men seemed just average players for the most part, except this one smug guy. He wore flashy clothes, gold rings, tinted glasses, and called himself Chuck.

Bobby was sure Chuck wasn't from anywhere near Glenmere. Recognizing some of the man's prison tattoos, Bobby assumed he was related to gang organizations out east but doubted he was anyone of significant standing. Why would Chuck be spending time in Glenmere, of all places, if he were? He felt like he might have met Chuck once before but tried to ignore the sense of familiarity that kept nagging at him.

Did I play poker against him in Ontario? Or was he in the same prison as me? Is that where I recognize him from? He sighed mentally and tried to shake it off. *Maybe, I just recognize the type.*

Bobby looked at the gold watch he was wearing and wondered what Darren did for a living to afford a watch like that but still had to move to a small town. It was getting late, and Bobby's chips were still ·piled high after an incredible night of winning. He smiled to himself as he looked at the three cards in his hand, confident that he might have the start of a flush. With a bit more luck, Bobby hoped to make a few thousand dollars tonight, which wouldn't be a bad takeaway from this little amateur poker game.

He studied his opponents around the green felt, confident in his experience playing many different back-room poker games over the years. After all, playing in the back of a pawnshop wasn't much different from playing in the backroom of a bar. Usually, it took Bobby only a few quick hands to feel out his competitors' skills and decipher each of their tells.

Suddenly, Bobby noticed that the players were no longer particularly talkative and that the mood around the table seemed to have changed. *Shit! What's happened? I should have been paying more attention instead of letting my mind wander.* The other players sat stiffly in their chairs, silently giving each other sideways glances. And everyone was eyeing the pile of chips in front of Bobby.

Chuck squinted, shifting his eyes towards the dealer, which sent chills running up Bobby's back, souring the whiskey in his stomach. Bobby kept his eyes locked on the dealer as he slowly reached over, picking up his last two cards. They had been playing five-card draw all night, and the stakes for this hand were unusually high. He knew that he would lose this round and most of his winnings unless he could pull off a convincing bluff. "Two cards," Bobby said, coolly laying two of his cards face down on the table for the dealer to exchange. Because he hadn't gotten the flush he was hoping for, he would have to bluff this hand or try to build on his pair of threes.

He picked up his new cards, but he still had nothing. Bobby's heart sank, but he tried to keep his face neutral as he thought about his strategy. He couldn't decide if this lousy deal was just the luck of the cards after his winning streak or if the dealer was cheating. Maybe he was being paranoid. Perhaps it was just one bad hand. He looked around the table for clues as to what everyone else could be holding. Chuck glared at him. Bobby glared back, thinking, *Screw it. I might as well have a bit of fun with this hand.* He tossed back the rest of the whiskey in his glass, allowing the burning sensation to run down his throat and feeling cocky. Grinning broadly at Chuck, he made his move.

"All in!"

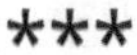

August 18, 1985 Sunday

The birds were making a racket that echoed in Bobby's pounding head. The sun seemed extraordinarily bright this morning. He struggled to sit upright on the park bench to survey his surroundings through squinted eyelids. "Ugh," he groaned as memories of the late-night poker game came flooding back to him. Dizziness and nausea made him realize that he'd moved too quickly. He couldn't remember how he'd ended up sleeping in the park, but Bobby did remember losing all his chips and the gold watch he'd been wearing.

With a few fingers, he gingerly touched the swollen tissue around his left eye, a vague memory coming back to him of the fight that had broken out after he'd accused the dealer of cheating him out of all his money. Chuck and the dealer were in cahoots. He was sure of it. Maybe they all were. He would confront Fred, the pawnshop owner, about the crooked game he'd invited him to attend, but not until tomorrow when he was less hungover.

Bobby bent over, put his elbows on his knees and his head in his hands, taking deep breaths and trying to stop the world from spinning. He needed some strong coffee before he could crawl his way back to the house where he was hiding out. It was difficult to know how long he sat in that hunched-over position as he quickly dozed off again.

He was woken by a man's hand gently patting his shoulder.

"Son?"

Bobby opened one eye, looking up at the bald man leaning over him.

"I'm Pastor Bill. I think we may have met last week. Why don't you come with me to the church and enjoy some hot coffee? You look like you could use some company this morning."

"Thank you. I think the coffee would help, but I'm unsure about the company part." Bobby looked back down at his hands. "I'm not feeling so great. I don't think I'm up to much talking today."

"That's alright," Pastor Bill said gently. "We can sit together in silence, and when you're ready to talk, I'll be right beside you, waiting to listen." He reached his arm under Bobby's elbow and helped him into a standing position. Bobby swayed a little with the movement, but Pastor Bill steadied and then guided him over to the little community church.

Once there, Pastor Bill led Bobby into the basement, where he'd accidentally attended the Alcoholics Anonymous meeting the previous week. A robust woman wearing a white apron over a pink floral dress was busy in the kitchen, baking something that smelled delicious. Bobby's stomach gurgled in response to the aroma.

"Missy, I brought someone for coffee!" the pastor called over to her with a smile.

The woman nodded in response and brought out two mugs of hot black coffee. She smiled and was about to say something, but Pastor Bill shook his head silently, so she dutifully returned to the kitchen. "My wife, Missy, is baking cookies for after the Sunday Service today. Please don't feel like you have to rush out when I go upstairs to conduct it. You can join the service or hang out down here as long as you want and have a few cups of coffee. After the service, the church members will come down for coffee and Missy's cookies."

"Thanks," Bobby mumbled, sipping his coffee and thinking he'd never felt this low about his life. The knot in his stomach felt rock hard. He'd lost everything he had and more. True to his word, the pastor didn't press him for small talk or any kind of conversation. He drank another cup of coffee after the pastor had gone upstairs. Swirling the last bit around in the mug, he decided he couldn't wait around any longer. He had to get his big score, to leave this miserable life behind. Friendly noises of people coming in the main front doors of the church reached his ears. As the music started playing for the service, Bobby put his mug in the kitchen sink and slinked up the stairs to exit from the main doors.

He dragged his tired feet down the road, heading to the house owned by Darren and Tanya. He made one wrong turn, forcing him to circle the block, but eventually found his way back to it. Unlocking the door, he entered the living room, collapsing onto the cozy striped couch. With his weary body hitting the plush fabric and one foot propped up on a cardboard box next to the couch, Bobby pulled the brown and orange Afghan over himself. As he closed his eyes, he hoped his dreams would show him how to get the money he needed to change his life.

Chapter 12

August 19, 1985

Monday

The law office of Donald Tracker was a block past Main Street in a largely residential area. It was a small white house with green trim and shutters that someone had converted into a law office. The fresh hand-painted sign read "Donald Tracker, attorney, Wills & Estate Planning, Real Estate, Matrimonial Agreements."

Bobby looked up and down the street, ensuring no one was around. He was at least twenty minutes early for his appointment with this Tracker guy to read the Last Will and Testament of Dorothy Young. Bobby hoped that, by being early, he could avoid being seen by anyone who might recognize him. Straightening the tie he'd put on that morning, compliments of homeowner Darren, and patting down his black hair, he walked up the sidewalk to the front door to put his big plan into motion.

The wooden door of the office was sun faded and had three narrow little windows in it. Bobby turned the brass knob and pushed the door open. Directly inside was the front office, which would have, at one time, served as the home's living room. A young blonde lady in a light-blue frilly top sat at a desk, typing something on her typewriter. Manila folders were stacked on an inbox tray on one side of the desk.

She stopped typing and greeted him with a smile, "Do you have an appointment today?"

Bobby shook his head to clear it. "Yes, I'm John Young. I have an appointment to see Mr. Tracker about my ... um, mother's will." He coughed into his fist to clear his throat, looking around the room nervously.

The receptionist looked at her watch. "Your appointment isn't for another twenty-five minutes. He's just finishing with another client, but you can sit over there to wait until he's available." She pointed to a leather sofa behind him, in front of the big picture window.

Bobby leaned slightly over the pile of papers and folders on the receptionist's desk, placing one hand on the desk and the other on his back hip. "Is there somewhere else I can wait?" he asked quietly. "My ex-wife is expected here soon. I don't think it's a very good idea if we catch even a glimpse of each other unless you're planning on having security keep her off me." He winked at the young receptionist with a flirtatious smile.

The receptionist raised her eyebrows, picking up the telephone receiver in front of her. "Just one minute, please... Donald, John Young is here to see you. He requests to be put into a private room to wait for his appointment ... Yes ... He doesn't want to be in the same room as his ex-wife ... No ... No

... Yes ... Okay." She hung up the phone, smiling at Bobby. "Right this way, John," she said, standing up and nodding to the hallway. "Follow me, please."

Bobby followed the young blonde down the hallway to the second door on the left, which was closed. She knocked before opening the door and then waved Bobby inside. A man in a three-piece brown suit and matching brown-striped tie stood up, shaking Bobby's hand, "Good afternoon, John. I'm Donald Tracker. Sorry to be meeting you for something like this, but I moved to town a few months ago to take over Stanley Buchanan's clients when he retired and moved to Vancouver. Have a seat."

He gestured to a wooden chair across from his desk. Bobby sat down without speaking, unsure of what he should do now that he'd gotten this far.

"So, you're John. Finally! I have been anxious to meet you since your phone call three weeks ago. I'm sorry that I didn't have everything ready sooner. I'm still trying to catch up with the paperwork around here. Can I get you a cup of coffee?"

"Uh, no, I'm fine." Bobby cleared his throat and crossed his right leg over his knee. He had never been to this sort of reading before and wasn't sure what was supposed to happen next. Of course, he was sure that was the case for most people. But deep down, a storm of anxiety was brewing, threatening to disrupt his calm façade, knowing his plan rested on this meeting.

Donald shuffled several stacks of paper file folders around on his desk and reached for the telephone. "Doris, could you bring me the Dorothy Young file, please? Thank you." He hung up the receiver. "Sorry. I thought we would all be meeting in the conference room. It's a little less cluttered."

Bobby looked Donald directly in the eyes and shrugged. "Yes, I'm sorry about that. I tried to explain to your receptionist ... Doris, is it? My ex-wife and I cannot be in the same room without starting a nuclear war." He grinned sheepishly, but the tension in the room was palpable, as if a single wrong move could set off an explosion.

Donald frowned a bit. "When I talked to Jeannie, your ex-wife, she didn't say anything about being divorced. She just said that she had not seen you in several years since you left for Ontario. If you are divorced, the paperwork must be on file. I'll need to get a copy from the records office. A divorce would definitely change things for Jeannie, regarding how your mother has worded her will. She didn't name Jeannie specifically in the will, as you'll soon hear when I read it. It only mentions you inheriting a share with your 'current wife.'" Donald put the phrase in air quotes with his fingers. After a short pause, he asked, "Are you currently married to anyone else?"

Bobby sat up a little straighter, wishing he was more certain of what John had said about his wife at their last poker game in Toronto. He was fairly certain they'd been celebrating the actual divorce, but could it have just been a separation? His mind raced with the implications. It had been too many years to be completely certain, not to mention the fact that they'd both been quite drunk by the end of the night. He decided this was definitely not the time for uncertainty, not when his entire future could be at stake.

"Nope. After my disastrous marriage to Jeannie, I'm staying single. I don't think I ever want to walk that road again." Bobby stared back at the man sitting across the desk from him, unblinkingly presenting him with his best poker face. The man was hard to read, and Bobby smiled slightly, thinking about how good a poker player he would be. He couldn't yet tell whether Donald believed him or not.

There was a knock at the door then, and Doris walked in quietly, laid a manila folder with several pages of documents on the corner of the desk, and then left again. Once the door was closed, Donald opened the envelope and shuffled some pages around before looking up at Bobby. "Alright," he said, smiling. "I'll begin by reading the will in its entirety, and then you can ask your questions before we talk about the follow-up paperwork involved."

Bobby tried to concentrate while he listened to what the lawyer was telling him and what he could get by impersonating John Young, but his mind kept wandering. He would steal John's inheritance to get his revenge and pay back the loan sharks at the same time. Or maybe he would grab the money and run away, creating another identity elsewhere. Bobby's heartbeat was increasing as his mind started racing through all the possibilities, his breathing becoming irregular just thinking about John Young, his high school "friend," who'd lost him all his winnings at the big poker game, making him mad enough to beat some random guy half to death in an alley. He clenched and unclenched his fists as he thought about how all his misery could be traced directly back to John Young. Well, it was payback time, and he was cashing in one way or another!

After the lawyer finished reading the will and answering questions, he instructed Bobby to wait in his office until the rest of the expected parties arrived. Donald's secretary, Doris, would then let him know when the front office area was clear so he could leave without meeting anyone else. Bobby was a little more relaxed when he heard that he wouldn't have to face anyone who would recognize him and know that he was only impersonating John. Jeannie would know right away, of course. He would have to keep his distance from her. Even though John and Bobby had very similar builds and even hairstyles now, anyone who'd known him well would be able to see right through his act. Luckily, other than his niece, John had no family left. Bobby was reasonably confident that he could fool most people in town since no one had seen John, or him, in years.

Bobby sat in the wooden office chair for at least another half hour, listening to the voices of people going in and out of the room across the hall. He wondered how many people would be inheriting from Dorothy's estate. *How wealthy could the old lady have been?* He strained to listen to the muffled voices, hoping to figure out how many there were.

After what seemed like at least thirty minutes, Doris softly knocked on the door before poking her blonde head in. "The coast is clear. You can leave the office now."

Bobby nodded, not wanting to speak out loud in case someone should hear him, although he suspected that no one would recognize his voice. He moved quickly towards the front door and out onto the sidewalk. There was a 1983 Black Buick Riviera and an old, faded green Ford truck parked at an angle to the sidewalk out front of the building. An older man sat in the driver's seat of the black Buick, reading a newspaper.

Bobby quickly turned his face away from it, walking swiftly down the sidewalk with a bit of a bounce in his step. His life was finally headed in a good direction. The lawyer hadn't revealed what the estate was worth, but Bobby figured the farmhouse and the land alone had to be worth enough for him to live much more comfortably than he ever had before. Turning onto Main Street, he decided that a real estate agent would know its value. Still, He had to figure out how to avoid John's ex-wife until his plan was fully executed.

He grinned. "Tonight, I'll celebrate and drink to the start of my new life!"

Chapter 13

The sound of a lawnmower somewhere on the street woke Amy up on Monday morning. Her back and arms hurt from all the heavy bins of dishes she'd carried around after another shift at Frankie's Diner last night. *There has to be more to life than working at the Family Grocers and busing tables at the diner. At least it's just for the summer. I wonder how Jeannie manages to juggle her life when she's always working two jobs,* she thought, sighing and rubbing her face.

Crawling out of bed, she pushed the curtain aside to see what was happening on the street. It wasn't unusual to see George Petersen happily working around the yard. The sun was shining brightly for him while he mowed. He would most likely mow Jeannie's lawn, too, because she didn't own a mower and relied on George to mow it whenever it needed cutting. Luckily, because she didn't want to pay for all the water the lawn required, it didn't tend to grow very fast unless there was a lot of rainfall.

Amy wasn't sure when George Petersen started cutting the grass, but her aunt had told her that he had always done it since she'd moved into the house all those years ago with Uncle John. Amy couldn't be sure if it was an agreement her uncle had made between them and the Petersens or if it was just something George Petersen had taken on himself out of disgust for the weeds growing wild in her front yard.

She noticed that her aunt's truck was sitting in the driveway, which meant Jeannie was probably still sleeping. Deciding that she should take this opportunity to take over the bathroom before her aunt got up, she quickly left her room, heading across the hall to shower and get dressed. Since she still had an hour before her shift at the Family Grocers, she knew she had time to eat while browsing the library books again for clues to opening the puzzle box.

Amy arrived at work five minutes late and ran into the staff room to hang up her sweater before starting the shift. Then she ran up the stairs to the manager's office to get her till-drawer float from her boss, Dan. Gasping and breathing heavily, Amy burst into his office without knocking, took a deep breath and blurted out, "Sorry! So sorry I'm late! I lost track of time!"

Dan spun around in his chair to face Amy. He held the receiver of the phone with one hand and gestured to the chair against the wall with the other. "Yes, she's here now. What time?"

Amy sat down on the edge of the chair, trying to slow down her hammering heart and gulping to catch her breath. She figured that Dan had phoned the house looking for his late employee, but it seemed an overreaction. It was only five minutes, after all. Instead of slowing down, Amy's heart started to beat faster. *Am I in trouble with my boss?*

"Alright, I'll discuss it with her ... Goodbye, Doris. Thanks for calling." He hung up the receiver, raising his eyebrows to look at Amy.

Before he had a chance to say anything, Amy started nervously talking. "I'm sorry, but I didn't sleep well last night, and I slept in. I tried to—"

"It's fine," he said, raising his hand to interrupt. "You're usually pretty good at getting here on time. I just got off the phone with Donald Tracker's receptionist, Doris. She said that you have an appointment today at one o'clock. You can use that time as your lunch break, but take whatever time you need; the other girls will cover for you until you return. You'll have to ensure the other cashiers are back from lunch before you leave, though."

Amy blinked, brushing her hair out of her face. "I knew I had a meeting sometime this week, but I didn't know it would be today! Thanks for your understanding. I'll keep an eye on the time. And I promise I won't be at the lawyer's office too long."

The phone on his desk started ringing, so Dan gestured for her to leave the office before picking up the receiver. "Good morning, Family Grocers, Dan speaking."

Amy nodded, sliding the float off his desk, taking it with her as she headed down the stairs and wondering why her aunt Jeannie hadn't mentioned the time or date of the appointment.

Her shift wasn't anything out of the ordinary. The store started getting busy just before noon when some customers bought ready-made salads and sandwiches from the deli section for their lunch breaks. Amy's stomach started gurgling to let her know she was getting hungry too, but she didn't know if she would have time to eat today, thanks to the appointment at the lawyer's office. She regretted only eating a granola bar this morning while reading her library book, mentally kicking herself for forgetting to pack a lunch the day before.

Anna, the cashier on register one, was already taking an early lunch break and was due back at 12:30, giving Amy enough time to ride her bike to the appointment. Unfortunately, at 12:50 p.m., Anna still had not returned.

Amy kept looking up at the clock, biting on her bottom lip as the lines of customers at all the open cash lanes started to grow, many of them with full cartloads. One tall man with slicked-back hair, a leather jacket, and gold chains around his neck sauntered over to sweet-talk his way to the front of the line since he just had to buy a pack of cigarettes. He winked at the woman he'd cut in front of as he left the store, leaving her blushing crimson red.

At one o'clock, Amy slid the "Please use another register" sign behind her current customer's items and rushed to finish the order. She was almost done when a young woman with two screaming kids pulled her cart up to her lane, ignored the sign, and unloaded her cart.

Amy shouted over the noise her children were making, "Excuse me! Could you please use another register? I am taking my break now."

The lady ignored Amy, turning to her youngest child. "I said no more candy! You'll have to go sit in the car if you keep touching everything!" She looked up at Amy with a sour expression on her face. "I only have half of a cart. I can be quick!"

Looking around to see if her co-worker had returned, Amy wondered where she was. Then she pulled the microphone down towards her mouth, switching it on. "Packer to register three, please." Amy pressed the lever on the side of the counter with her left hip to start the belt moving and leaned out to snatch each item and ring it in as soon as it was within reach. Her mind was whirling, and Amy felt sick, knowing that she would be late to the lawyer's office even if she pedaled as fast as she could. Sweat glistened on Amy's neck as she tried to rush the woman's cartload of groceries through. It didn't help that the woman kept stopping to wrangle one of her children to stay by her side or stop putting candy in their pockets. At this point, Amy was willing to let the kids shoplift if it meant getting the rest of the order through.

"Aren't you supposed to be somewhere right now?" asked Shane from behind her.

Amy turned to answer him but was startled to see Beatrice Petersen standing anxiously beside him.

"It's already past one o'clock," she scolded. "Why are you still working? Didn't your aunt tell you to be at Donald Tracker's office at one this afternoon? Hurry up and finish what you're doing!"

Amy blinked back tears, sputtering, "I'm trying! I tried to close my cash lane, but this person forced her way in ... and ... well—" She tilted her head towards the misbehaving children arguing with their mother.

Beatrice quickly assessed the situation, pushing her way over to the woman, and said in an exaggerated, sing-song voice, "Let me help you empty your cart onto the belt so you can get going!" Without waiting for an answer, Beatrice Petersen finished unloading the cart so that Amy could continue to ring the items through.

"That will be $173.54," Amy said after hitting the total button.

The woman started fumbling with her purse, pulling out her wallet, and slowly handing over various bills as she rummaged around her purse for more. It appeared that the woman hadn't brought enough money with her.

"I'm afraid I'm going to put some items back," she said as she squinted and rubbed her temples.

Amy picked up the money and counted it. "You have one hundred forty-two dollars," Amy said, punching the numbers into the till to get a quick look at the amount still owed. "You're short $34.54. What do you want to return?" Amy turned to Shane, who had just finished bagging the last items. He looked up at Amy with raised eyebrows.

"What's the hold-up?" Beatrice Petersen asked.

"I'm short on cash, so I'm deciding what not to take," the woman said as she began rummaging through the packed bags.

Beatrice leaned towards the cash register, reading the subtotal amount. "Oh, for heaven's sake, Wendy!" She rolled her eyes and pulled her wallet from her purse. "I'll pay the rest!" She handed Amy forty dollars and turned back to the woman. "Don't worry about it. Just get your children home!"

The woman, apparently named Wendy, thanked Beatrice and walked away, leading Shane with her load of groceries and the children following.

Amy handed Beatrice the change and put the closed sign back up. It was almost one-thirty. "Thanks, Mrs. Petersen," Amy said, frowning. "I don't think I will make it to the lawyer's office after all." She felt so bad, knowing her aunt Jeannie would have to just tell her what would happen to her beloved farmhouse.

"Nonsense!" she exclaimed. "There is no meeting without you! My husband, George, is waiting in the parking lot with the car. Let's go, honey! There is no time to waste!"

Amy followed Beatrice Petersen into the parking lot to her car and saw George Petersen jumping out to open the doors for his passengers. Amy slid into the soft leather backseat and rested her head backwards, feeling exhausted and emotionally drained. En route, she closed her eyes while Beatrice told her husband about Wendy, the lady with the two children holding Amy up at work. As Beatrice recounted the story, silent tears ran down Amy's face, but she didn't have the energy to wipe them away. She just wanted to crawl into bed and sleep away the rest of the day.

Amy felt the car's tires bump the curb as George Petersen put it in park. "There we are, dear," he said quietly.

Amy slowly opened her eyes and wiped her cheeks with the back of her hands. Her nose was running, and she sniffed. George Petersen reached over the seat to hand her a neatly folded handkerchief. She used the soft cloth to wipe away the tears and the drip from her nose. Amy wasn't sure what to do with it now that the hankie was soiled. Looking up, she saw Mr. Petersen watching her in the rearview mirror. He nodded and exited the car, walking around to the passenger side to open their doors. The sense of urgency seemed to have disappeared, replaced with calm.

George Petersen leaned over to his wife, whispering something in her ear. Then Beatrice nodded, dabbing at a little tear glistening at the corner of her eye with a daintily embroidered blue handkerchief. She put her arm around Amy to guide her up the sidewalk to the front door of the lawyer's office. Amy held tightly onto the damp handkerchief balled up in her fist, telling herself that she would wash it and return it later.

Beatrice Petersen took a big breath and let it out. "Let's get this over and done with, shall we?" She opened the front door and then marched into the office with a sense of purpose.

Amy copied her, taking a deep breath, exhaling, and then marching through the open door with her head held high. The room smelled like dusty papers, stale coffee, and cigarette smoke, though neither the secretary at the desk nor the man sitting on the corner of the desk talking on the phone was smoking. To Amy's surprise, Mrs. Petersen used her full name to announce their arrival to the secretary. Amy hadn't realized that her neighbour even knew her full name. Since Beatrice seemed to have more information than she let on, Amy decided that she needed to ask her some questions about her relationship with her family.

"Oh, good! You're back," Doris, the receptionist, said. "Just follow me to the conference room." The secretary led Amy down the hallway to a closed door on the right, then opened it and stood to the side. "Please have a seat, ladies. Donald will be with you shortly."

Amy looked over her shoulder, surprised and confused, to see that Mrs. Petersen had followed Doris down the hallway, too. *I thought Aunt Jeannie said the meeting was just for the estate's heirs. Is*

Beatrice Petersen one, too? Is that why they came to get me for the appointment?

Entering the room and looking around, Amy admired the big wooden desk with its high-backed, green upholstered chair. Four heavy wooden chairs were arranged in a semicircle facing the desk. Jeannie sat on the edge of the chairs to the far right, chewing on her fingernails.

"What took you so long to get here?" Jeannie huffed at Beatrice, tapping her watch. "I'm missing work right now." She crossed her arms over her blue and orange apron, frowning at Amy.

"Well," Mrs. Petersen said as she took her seat, leaving an open seat on either side of her, "I'm back with Amy as I said I would be. It's not the girl's fault that the store is busy. You could have just picked her up on your way here and saved us all some time and trouble." The tension hung heavy between the two of them as Jeannie glared at them and slid back into her chair.

Amy took a chair on the far side of Mrs. Petersen, leaving an empty chair between her neighbour and her aunt. She didn't know what conversation had occurred between Beatrice and Jeannie earlier, but she knew it was her fault everyone had been kept waiting. The door opened then, and the man who had been talking on the phone when Amy arrived entered the room.

"Alright, this is all of us. I am Donald Tracker, the lawyer who took over this office from Dorothy's long-time lawyer, Stanley Buchanan, a few months ago. I'm sorry it took so long to get to the reading of the will, but let's get started. This is the Last Will and Testament of Dorothy Mary Young and—"

"Wait!" Jeannie interrupted. "You told me on the phone last week that all the heirs to Dorothy's estate would be here. Where's John?" Jeannie sat forward, looking behind her at the closed door. "This is ridiculous," she continued. "First, we were waiting for a new lawyer to take over this office and then for you to locate everyone listed in the Last Will and Testament, but everyone sitting here today has been right here in Glenmere this whole damn time! What's going on?"

Donald Tracker sighed, taking a minute to formulate his answer before speaking. "We have tracked down all of the heirs. John met with me earlier today, and since there are no other grandchildren but Amy," he nodded at her, "we are ready to proceed."

Jeannie raised her eyebrows and shifted in her seat. "Do you mean to tell me that John was here? Today?" Her voice started to get louder and higher pitched. "The son of a bitch was here in town and never bothered to see me?!" She straightened her diner uniform. The awkward tension in the room was palpable as Amy looked back and forth between her aunt and the lawyer following their exchange.

Jeannie leaned forward to make eye contact with Amy past Beatrice, but Amy looked away, suddenly interested in the bookcase to her right.

Donald Tracker swallowed hard, pulling at his necktie like it was trying to choke him. "Yes, he was here today. He requested a private appointment ... um, separate from the rest. He has already heard me read the documents and particulars of his inheritance."

Jeannie crossed her arms over her chest and leaned back, looking at Donald. "I'll find the prick later. I know where he liked to hang out. And anyway, it's easy. I will find him playing in the closest backroom poker game." She fluffed her frizzy hair, then with an air of smugness. "You can proceed, Donald."

Donald Tracker shuffled the pages on his desk before him and began reading. "This is the Last Will and Testament of Dorothy Mary Young: The farmhouse and all of its land and contents, owned in full rights, are to be given to John William Young, Junior and his current spouse, or his children if he should predecease me at the reading of this will. If he should have no children and be deceased, then his claims shall be inherited equally by other grandchildren of Dorothy Mary Young. The house in Glenmere, at 102-8th Street West, plus 25 percent of all monetary assets, will be given to Sandra Mary Young, also known as Sandy, and her current spouse, or her children, if she should be deceased. Of the remaining monetary assets, 10 percent will be donated to the town's public library, with 25 percent given to Amanda Michelle Young, the only grandchild at the time of the document, to be held in trust by Beatrice Eleanor Petersen until said grandchild reaches the age of eighteen. The remaining 40 percent of monetary assets will be divided equally among all other grandchildren. If no other grandchild exists at the time of my death, then that 40 percent will be held in trust, with an appointed trustee, until Amanda Michelle Young should legally marry. This statement is my last will. Signed Dorothy Young, June 2, 1973."

Donald looked up from the documents then. "Because Sandra is deceased and never married, her portion of the inheritance is transferred to her daughter."

Amy sat in silent shock for a long moment before speaking, trying to sort through all the information Mr. Tracker had presented. "So ... Grandma left the farmhouse to Uncle John and Aunt Jeannie, but she left the house I am currently living in to my mom ... And since she never married and is deceased, it goes to me. The house in town where Aunt Jeannie and I live is ... *mine*?"

She found this both confusing and exciting. She'd always thought the little house belonged to her aunt and uncle, but it had been her grandmother's. Deep down, she'd always hoped to move back to the farmhouse, though she didn't know who would be her appointed guardian if she did. She certainly hadn't expected it to be Beatrice Petersen. She looked over at her neighbour and saw that her blue eyes were shining with unshed tears as she looked back at her.

Before Amy could ask her if she'd known about the guardianship all along, Aunt Jeannie jumped out of her chair, unable to contain her excitement any longer. "I get the farmhouse and all of its land! Finally! Something useful I can sell to get out of this miserable little town!"

"Now, just a moment," Donald said, clearing his throat before he continued. "That's not quite true. John Junior inherits both the farmhouse and its property. I understand you are no longer his spouse, and both of you signed divorce papers, which have been filed with the courts. As such, you do not inherit anything. The document clearly states that John inherits with his 'current wife.' Unless you deny that divorce, you are not his current wife and have no claims to inherit in any other capacity in the terms of the will."

"Well, where's John then to prove there was a divorce? Is it his word against mine? What if I say we're still married? He abandoned me several years ago, leaving me with a mountain of debt! Is he scared to look me in the face and deny what he's put me through?"

"He was here this morning. He stated that the two of you are no longer married and that he didn't want to... um, be in the same room as you. If you say that you are still married, then we will need to verify your claim with the record's office before proceeding with the other necessary paperwork."

Donald shuffled some papers around as Jeannie slowly lowered herself back into her seat, her earlier excitement dissipating now. When he found what he'd been searching for, he looked back at his clients. "As it stands now, Amanda inherits the house on Eighth Street, and the 25 percent of monetary assets that would have gone to her mother had she lived, as well as the 25 percent of monetary assets that were left to her by name, both of which will be held in trust by Beatrice until she is eighteen. In that same trust, though held until she chooses to marry, will be the 40 percent that had been earmarked for other potential grandchildren, who do not exist. In terms of the farmhouse and its property, if you are, in fact, still married to John Young, we will go to the court's records to verify this and—"

"Stop," Jeannie interrupted, with clenched fists and her eyes squeezed shut. "Just stop."

Donald did as she asked and fell silent, watching as she let out a long, slow breath, seeming almost to deflate entirely, her shoulders slumping more with each passing moment. Years of playing the victim of a cruel abandonment to cash in on the guilt of John's mother wouldn't stand up in the face of her signature on the actual divorce papers, which, apparently, the lawyers could easily retrieve if needed. She'd lost, and she knew it. "Don't bother. We're divorced."

"I see," Donald said with surprising understanding. "Well, in that case, I have—"

"Who is this Amanda anyway?" Jeannie said then, interrupting once more. "If she's inheriting the house I live in, and John gets the farmhouse, where am I supposed to live?" She stood up then and stepped towards the desk.

The lawyer frowned. "I'm sure I don't know. But perhaps if—"

"Can I at least get reimbursed for taking Amy in? Had I known it would take almost five months for things to get divvied up and that I'd be left out in the cold, I would have let social services take her! But I didn't! I took her in, even though I had nothing to spare! I should get something for that! Right? What's the law say about that?"

The lawyer nodded in Amy's direction. "I suppose that's up to Amanda and her trustee to decide."

Wide-eyed, Jeannie looked from Amy to Beatrice and back again. "You?" She shook her head. "And You?"

Feeling almost numb by everything the lawyer had unearthed at the meeting, Amy looked at her aunt. "Amy's just a nickname," she said, the sadness in her voice almost completely hidden beneath a veil of misleading calm. "My given name's Amanda. How do you not even know that? Do you know me at all?"

Jeannie suddenly turned back to Donald. "Can I still go after John for support even though the divorce is already final?" Not waiting for an answer, she spun back to face Amy, then, pulling at her hair almost hysterically now, her eyes as wide as saucers as she looked back at her niece. "Are you going to make me move out and live on the streets?! I let you live with me for free!"

Neither Amy nor Donald seemed capable of responding to this stunning behaviour. Thankfully, Beatrice Petersen stood up then, taking control of the situation.

"As Amy's legal guardian and trustee, her inheritance and well-being are my responsibility until she is of legal age. I'll consider what is best for her in terms of the house in Glenmere and everything else after I've had some time to think about the situation. Maybe you should wait until John settles his portion of the inheritance and then see what he will provide for you in terms of a divorce settlement. But in the meantime, I am sure that Amy won't just kick you out onto the street."

Jeannie snorted derisively. "Right. Like, I'm going to wait for John to sort things out! I'm sure he hasn't changed since he left town. He cut himself off from his whole family years ago to hide the sort of man he was, and it was just as well! It was much easier dealing with Dorothy, who always felt so bad for my situation, than with him abandoning me like that. But I will find him. And mark my words, this time, I'll be the one who comes out on top!" With that, she nodded with determination and stormed out of the office.

Donald leaned back in his chair and clicked the end of the pen he was holding, unsure whether or not even to acknowledge the ugly scene that had just played out in his office. Finally, he cleared his throat, shook his head slightly, and then returned his attention to the matter at hand.

"Alright, so ... in terms of the actual financial figures, the monetary assets, there are still a few more hoops for me to jump through before we can finalize those numbers, but hopefully, it won't be too much longer." He looked down at the papers on his desk. "The rest of the paperwork I have pertains to Beatrice's guardianship of Amanda ... Amy ... and her role as trustee. I need your identification, Beatrice, and your signature on various papers, and we can settle that part of things immediately." He pushed the papers and a pen closer to the edge of the desk. Beatrice Petersen pulled her wallet out of her purse and showed him her driver's licence.

With a nod, he said, "Please sign next to the arrows on these three pages." He pointed them out to her. "You'll also need a copy of Amanda's—Amy's birth certificate to fill out this form," he handed another piece of paper to her, "which you'll need to return to me as soon as you can."

Once Mrs. Petersen had signed the documents, he leaned back in his chair and crossed his hands on his desk. "Thank you. And I'd advise you not to worry too much about Jeannie's claims. She can try to sue John for his portion of the inheritance to cover any financial debts they incurred while they were still married. Of course, I can't represent her due to a conflict of interest." He looked at Amy with a sympathetic expression. "But none of that is your problem. Or your responsibility. Alright?"

Amy nodded but was still too numb to speak.

Finally, he pushed a few documents towards Beatrice, who thanked him and stood up, reaching out to shake his hand, "Thank you very much, Donald. Now, if you're finished with us, Amy and I will be going."

With that, Beatrice, Amy's new guardian and trustee, neatly tucked the page requiring Amy's identification into her purse, nodded to him, and turned to go. Amy stood slowly and mindlessly followed her outside. It all seemed so strange. It had never occurred to her that her guardian could be someone who wasn't even related to her.

A few moments later, Amy stood stunned on the sidewalk, facing the Petersens' shiny black car. George Petersen had already gotten out and was getting ready to open the doors, but lost in thought, she didn't notice. When Amy finally looked up, they were both looking at her.

"What happens to me now?" she asked quietly, too astonished to express any real thought or emotions.

"Well," Mrs. Petersen answered, "First, I think we will tell your boss, Dan, that you won't be coming to finish your shift today. You need a meal and a nap after this stressful day." She put an arm around Amy and then led her around the car's open door to the back seat. Amy's mind spun with new information and countless questions as she slid into the leather seat. Her head throbbed, her eyes felt itchy, and her mouth felt like cotton. She was tired, hungry, and thirsty, and her brain struggled to process everything.

Mr. Petersen drove to the Family Grocers and parked the car. "I'll go talk to Dan. You two can stay here. I'll be right back." After twenty minutes or so, he returned. "You have the rest of today and all day tomorrow off, but he wants you here first thing on Thursday."

Chapter 14

They drove in silence until Mr. Petersen pulled into his driveway. "Go change out of your uniform, Amy, and then come over," he said. "We'll all have something good to eat with our afternoon tea."

Amy climbed out of the back seat, heaving the heavy car door shut behind her. Seeing that Jeannie's old Ford truck wasn't in the driveway, Amy felt relieved, not ready to face her aunt after she'd made it pretty clear that she'd only been letting Amy live with her in the hopes of cashing in on Grandma Dorothy's estate. It made her uneasy, knowing that she had been an unwanted guest for the past few months while Jeannie was waiting for her big payout. She wasn't the person Amy thought she was.

Amy unlocked the front door and pushed it open. Where was her Uncle John anyway? She'd only ever seen dusty photos of him at the farmhouse. Her aunt Jeannie certainly hadn't kept any pictures of him, too angry at him for "abandoning" her. She doubted he would want Amy to move in with him at the farmhouse, considering that he'd shown no interest whatsoever in her while she was growing up. And he'd never even visited the farmhouse the whole time she'd lived there. He'd probably sell it and leave town again. The meeting she had hoped would finally give her some answers had left Amy with even more unanswered questions and a sick feeling in her stomach.

She went inside, changing out of her work clothes and into a pair of well-worn blue jeans and a faded shirt. After a quick check in the mirror, she walked back to the neighbours' house, hoping to eat something that might settle her stomach.

Mr. and Mrs. Petersen lived in a grey stucco home with white trim and a white picket fence. The yard was neatly kept with colourful flower beds edging the luscious green lawn—in great contrast to the neglected house Amy had been living in with her aunt. Now that she knew she was inheriting the little house, Amy wondered if she was expected to keep up the yard and house as part of her responsibilities.

There was a soft-pink rose bush close to the front door of the Petersens' home, and she reached out to gently stroke its petals, inhaling the fantastic aroma. Nodding to herself, she decided she would like roses in her yard, too and tried not to think about how much that would cost.

Amy knocked quietly on the door, waiting until Beatrice Petersen opened it to invite her inside.

"Come on in! I just about have the table set. Don't be shy. You don't have to knock."

"Thank you, Mrs. Petersen," Amy mumbled, looking around. She couldn't recall whether or not she had ever been in this house before. The kitchen and dining room reminded her of the farmhouse. The space was wide open, running from the front of the house to the back. The kitchen cupboards ran along the right side of the room, with a large island in front of them. There were couches and chairs near the front living room window. Mr. Petersen sat at the round wooden kitchen table, waiting for his wife to finish setting food on it.

"You look hungry. Come sit with me," Mr. Petersen said, gesturing to the empty chair beside him.

As she settled in, she mumbled, "Thank you, Mr. Petersen."

He shook his head. "Enough of that now. Since we're your guardians, we should be on more familiar terms. Please, call me George and my wife, Beatrice."

She just nodded, looking at all the items on the table: fresh homemade buns, homemade raspberry jam, cold cuts, pickles, and cheese slices. Finally, Beatrice placed a jar of canned peaches and a jar of zucchini relish on the table. Then sat down across the table from Amy, who couldn't take her eyes off of the peaches and the relish, which brought Amy right back to sitting around the table with her grandma.

Beatrice must have noticed Amy staring at the jars. "Yes, the peaches were made by your grandmother, Dorothy. We always traded. My zucchini relish for her canned peaches." She pushed the jars a bit closer to Amy.

"I knew she traded for the relish, but I didn't know with whom."

"Your grandma and I used to have tea sometimes while you were at school. I have known her for a very long time. Our boys used to hang out together in high school." She smiled as she poured herself a cup of tea, swirling in a bit of honey.

Amy nodded, smiling shyly. "Actually, I meant to come over to talk to you about my uncle, John. I wanted to see if you could tell me anything. Grandma was searching for him. She was using a private investigator. The lawyer today said he was there this morning, but neither of us have seen him. Jeannie and me, I mean."

Beatrice reached over and gently patted Amy's hand, a gesture of kindness and understanding. "A lot of information was presented today at the lawyer's office, but you need to know that I already knew about my role as your guardian and trustee. It wasn't a surprise to me. Not like John's sudden return, a man well known in Glenmere. He would have made a dramatic entrance to show off to his family."

"Bea and I have talked about your guardianship," George added. "I know I wasn't named as one, but I feel like I'm your guardian, too. We both feel the best thing for you would be to move all of your stuff over here as soon as possible so we can take proper care of you." He watched her reaction to this before proceeding with a cautious tone. "After our little lunch, I suggest that we go next door and clear out your belongings. To be honest, we wanted to have you move over here months ago, but your aunt insisted that she was your only family and that she would take care of you. But I have to say that we've been worrying about you. She seems to leave you at home by yourself a lot."

Amy swallowed hard. Everything was out of control. She had so many emotions running through her right now that she was confused about everything. "What about my aunt?" she asked before shrugging and shaking her head. "Though I don't know why I'm concerned about her. She was only concerned about Grandma's estate."

George shrugged. "There's no reason she'd have to leave the house. You own it, of course, but it's up to you if you'll allow her to continue living there. With or without paying rent."

"I always thought it was hers. That Aunt Jeannie owned it."

He shook his head. "Your aunt and uncle used to own it, but it got repossessed by the bank: gambling debts and whatnot. In any case, Dorothy repurchased it from the bank to help your uncle John. In any case, when you're older, you can decide whether you want to keep it, rent it or sell it for the money."

Amy nodded, silently sipping her tea. It was a lot to think about.

They ate in companionable silence, and when they finished, Beatrice stood up. "I think we have a few empty boxes in the basement, George. I'll grab my two laundry baskets, too, and we can start moving Amy over here." Beatrice scooped up the empty plates and then set them in the sink.

Together, they carried the empty boxes and two laundry baskets to the little house. Amy unlocked the door and pushed the door open. The house felt different somehow, and a sad, hollow emptiness consumed her. Despite everything, it felt like she was betraying her aunt. The Petersens followed Amy to her bedroom, then set the laundry basket on her unmade bed. Amy turned to look at them, unsure if she should tell them what to do or let them take the lead. "The furniture isn't mine, but just about everything else is. I have a few things in the little closet and some under the bed."

Beatrice surveyed the room, making a quick assessment. "This won't take very long. I was expecting you to have more stuff."

"Actually, I do have more stuff, but it's all at the farmhouse. I guess I'll have to go there before Uncle John takes it over or sells the place." Amy was trying to calculate how much stuff she had at the farmhouse. She frowned, realizing there probably wasn't much there either since even her bedroom furniture belonged to the farmhouse.

"Let's just focus on this for today," George said. "We can go out to the farmhouse after we get the approval from John if we see him, since it's his property now, or else from Donald, the lawyer.

It didn't take long to fill the boxes and baskets, and then they carried them over to the Petersen house and dumped the contents on the bed in the spare room before repeating the process. It seemed they would get the last of it on the third trip. Amy reached under her bed, pulling out the folder with the documents, the messenger bag, the cloth bag with her grandma's valuables, the puzzle box, and a few other random things shoved under there. Putting everything in the basket, Amy turned to leave the room. "I think that's everything," she said, smiling at how quick and easy it had been to move her stuff out.

George looked at the objects Amy had put in the basket and stepped closer. He ran his right hand across the smooth surface of the wooden puzzle box, following the patterns across the top. "Where did you get this treasure box?"

"It was my grandmother's. She called it a puzzle box. She wanted me to have it. It was important to her." Amy shrugged, acting like it was no big deal. She didn't want to talk about it with him.

"Have you opened it?"

"No," Amy replied. "I haven't figured it out yet."

He cleared his throat. "I could help you break it open if you want."

In her somewhat frazzled state, she was horrified that he would suggest breaking it open. "No! Thank you. But I think I can get it. I just haven't had much time to figure out the solution."

After they finished bringing the last load over, the three collapsed on the soft living room furniture of the Petersens' home—now Amy's home, too. George suggested that he would order take-out pizza from the diner. He said he would pick it up and talk to Jeannie while he was there. Beatrice and Amy agreed. Amy was relieved yet again that she didn't have to confront her aunt directly to tell her about the new living arrangements. She realized that having guardians who could make the hard things easier might not be so bad.

As the door closed behind George, Beatrice began to reminisce. "As I told you before, your uncle used to hang out with my Gabe and a few others. The group of boys used to come over a few times a month to play cards. I think I have a photo of them, actually." Beatrice got up and walked over to the bookshelf to run her fingers along the spines of several albums before pulling one out. "Maybe this one, from 1967, will have the shot I'm thinking about. They didn't play cards as often once the girls started showing up with John. He was a really handsome boy, with bright eyes and black hair. I'm surprised more girls didn't follow him around." She flipped quickly through the photo album until she found the book she wanted to share with Amy.

"So... Who's who?" Amy asked, her eyes fixed on the black and white photo taken from the Petersens' kitchen. She noticed the same cookie jar on their counter now, sitting in the middle of the table in the picture, and it sparked a deep curiosity about the people in the photo.

"Well, the dark-haired boy is your Uncle John." She pointed to him and then to the others as she named them individually. "That's my son, Gabe. His hair is much lighter than John's, though it's hard to tell in black and white—brown instead of black. Okay, so this bigger boy is Steve. A redhead, though again, it's hard to tell. And the two blonds here are Eddie and Leon, though with their backs to the camera, I couldn't tell you which was which."

Amy squinted closer at the photo. Gabe and John seemed to be laughing at some inside joke. She suddenly jolted upright, a wave of panic washing over her. "Oh no! Is it okay if I use your phone? I just realized that I haven't told my friend Sarah what happened today! She doesn't know where I am!" Her heart raced until Mrs. Petersen gave her reply.

"Of course. It's in the kitchen on the counter behind the cookie jar," Beatrice replied. "Help yourself to some cookies if you like. You can take as many as you want. I can make more tomorrow."

Amy walked into the kitchen, scanning the counters until she spotted the large, white ceramic cookie jar with yellow daisies on it. The telephone wasn't a wall mount. Instead, it sat on its base on the counter. Amy lifted the receiver to place it in the crook of her neck, holding it in place with her chin while she spun the dial with one hand and held the base steady with the other. As the call connected, Amy lifted the lid of the cookie jar. The sugar-coated molasses gingersnaps, their aroma wafting through the air, were a temptation impossible to resist.

Amy had a mouth full of cookies when Sarah answered, so she chewed quickly and swallowed. "Hi, Sarah? It's me, Amy."

"I tried to call you earlier, but you weren't home yet. How did it go today?"

"Oh my god, it was horrible!" Amy rattled off the events of the day, starting with being late for work and proceeding through the experience at the lawyer's office. "My uncle John came back to town to claim the farmhouse, and Aunt Jeannie got really mad because he told the lawyer they were divorced, which she's been lying about all along, and then she said she wished she would have let Social Services take me! Can you imagine? She was using me this whole time! Can you believe it?" Amy paused to reach into the cookie jar, fishing out her third or fourth cookie. They were so chewy and good.

Sarah gasped. "Is she home? Is she listening to you talk to me? Maybe you should be careful what you say around her."

"She's not here. I mean, I don't know where she is right now. I'm not at her house. I'm at George and Beatrice Petersen's house. That's why I'm calling you. I moved next door. Beatrice is my appointed guardian and the trustee of my inheritance."

"Wow!" Sarah exclaimed. "That's … Wow! I don't know what to ask you first! What did you inherit? Did Jeannie get into a fight with your uncle? Is it weird over there? Wait, don't answer that last one. You can tell me that later!"

"Actually, I didn't see Uncle John. He met with the lawyer before us. I own my aunt's house now. I guess Grandma bought it so they would have a place to live rent-free. They must have been in debt because the bank took it from them. Grandma repurchased it!" Amy turned then, looking towards the living room. "And no, it's fine here. Everything is fine. My brain hurts, but I'm fine."

"Wow ... So, I guess you haven't had time to go to the police about your list of missing items from the farmhouse."

"No, not yet. I guess I should give it to them soon and let them know that Uncle John owns it now. Then he can deal with it."

They talked for a few more minutes; then, she gave Sarah the phone number at the Petersens', telling her they would talk soon. After saying their goodbyes, Amy hung up the phone and replaced the lid on the cookie jar, realizing she'd lost track of how many she'd eaten.

Chapter 15

The new real estate agent in town, Edward Greene, was a tall, heavy-set man with perfectly combed and styled hair. He wore a long-sleeved dress shirt with a black tie and black pants. He slung his checkered sports jacket over the chair behind him. The paperwork he had just finished filling out lay scattered across his large desk in front of him. He seemed to think properties like the Young family farmhouse were extremely desirable and would sell quickly for a handsome price.

Bobby stood and reached across the desk to shake the hand of the man listing it for sale. Grinning, he popped an unlit cigarette into the left corner of his mouth. "Thanks for your time, Ed. You go ahead and put up the sign and start advertising right away. You can get the key from Donald Tracker, the new lawyer, to get things started. I'll drive out to meet you after I take care of a few things in town."

"Thank you, John. It was nice meeting you. My realtor friend from Saskatoon is looking for just this kind of property for a client of his with five children. I'll call her today and see if they're still interested." Ed smiled broadly, pulling a lighter out of his breast pocket and handing it to Bobby to light his cigarette.

Handing it back, Bobby blew the smoke up into the air before turning with a nod and leaving the office. While he walked back to his hideout, he thought about whether or not he should move out to the farmhouse while he waited for someone to buy the place. He would need a vehicle if he did, though. Bobby looked up and down the streets as he walked, stopping to look into any parked cars he passed, hoping that someone might have left their keys in the ignition. It was a small town, after all, and people were laid back about such things here.

His search for an accessible vehicle to steal turned out to be fruitless, and he arrived back at the house where he was squatting, feeling defeated. As he pulled out the keys for the door, fumbling for the right one, a woman's voice called out to him.

"Hello there!"

Startled, Bobby jumped slightly, turning around to find the next-door neighbour sitting on her front step. "Hello to you as well." He let out a slow smile as he lifted his hand with the key ring to wave at her. "Just, uh, checking up on the place while they're out of town."

"Ah! Friend or family?"

"Family. I'm Darren's nephew. He and Aunt Tanya are gone until the twenty-fifth, so I said I'd check on the place for them."

"Yes, that's what she told me, too," she answered with a slight smile. "I met them when they moved in earlier this month. Imagine my surprise when they said they were going away again when they weren't finished unpacking yet. I gave them my number in case they needed me to check in on things, but they didn't give me a key, so I'm just watching from the outside."

Well, that makes the decision of whether or not to leave a lot easier, Bobby thought. He'd better get in to pack up his few possessions quickly before anyone else comes to check in on the place. Bobby jangled the keys again. "Well, I appreciate you looking out for them." He turned, inserting the key into the lock to open the door. He could feel the prying eyes of the neighbour on his back. As soon as the door opened, he slipped inside and hurriedly shut the door behind him.

Moving quickly from room to room, he gathered his few belongings around the house and placed them all on the kitchen table. Then he scanned the kitchen, wondering if there was anything else of value that he could take with him.

No, he decided. *That'll look too suspicious if the neighbour's still watching.* He shoved everything from the table into his pockets and then walked over to the side of the kitchen window to peek through its curtains. The neighbour wasn't on her doorstep any longer. Just to be sure, he looked out the window facing the backyard. All he could see was a view of the single-car garage and the alleyway.

"Hmmm. I wonder—" Bobby mused aloud to the empty kitchen, bouncing the set of keys in his hand. There was a set of keys for a Chrysler on the key ring. Going out the back door, he followed the pathway to the garage's small side door. Someone locked it, but the same key that unlocked the house's front door unlocked the garage, too. Bobby smiled as he opened the door and stepped into the dark space. He fumbled around a bit before finding the light switch near the door and flicking it on.

He smiled brightly. There was a car inside, hidden beneath a cover. Eagerly, Bobby pulled on the light parachute fabric to reveal his prize: a yellow 1973 Chrysler Imperial LeBaron. Bobby skimmed the lines of the car with his fingertips as he admired its streamlined frame, completely devoid of tacky chrome or flashy trim. He chuckled. "Well, Darren, you have great taste in cars!"

The main garage door opened directly into the back alley. With a strong push, Bobby lifted it open. Thankfully, it didn't make too much noise. Bobby looked up and down the alley, deciding that he was in the clear, then opened the heavy door of the car and slid into the driver's seat. "Hopefully, it starts on the first try," Bobby mumbled. He pumped the gas pedal twice before turning the key to the first click. The dash lights and the radio lit up. Bobby turned down the radio, waiting a few seconds before engaging the ignition. The car sputtered to life! After revving it gently a few times, he shifted it into first gear and slowly exited the garage. Looking in the rear-view mirror, he left the garage door open, not wanting to linger and risk the neighbour checking on him in the back alley.

Bobby didn't want people to see him driving around town in this beautiful car, but he still needed to make one stop before heading out to the farmhouse. He needed to visit the little house John had lived in when they were still playing poker regularly. He had to sneak in and find the divorce papers so that John's ex-wife wouldn't get a cut of his inheritance. Just thinking about his old poker buddy brought a sneer to his face as he gripped the steering wheel tighter and made his way a few blocks over to John's old house.

His revenge couldn't come quickly enough!

Chapter 16

August 20, 1985

Tuesday

Amy refolded her fuzzy sweater, placing it on top of the others in the open drawer of the dresser. "How well did you know my grandmother?"

"Well enough that we traded canning recipes and canned goods," Beatrice called out behind her as she rummaged around in the small closet. She was busy clearing out items from the bedroom where Amy would now be staying and moving them to other rooms in the house. "We talked about books when I was at the library. And sometimes, we reminisced about the old days when our children were young. They were good boys, but sometimes they got into some mischief. The poker games they played got a little heated sometimes, but it was all fun and games." She chuckled, shaking her head as she carried an armful of jackets and coats out of the room.

While she was busy in the other room, Amy continued to move her clothing items from the laundry basket into the six-drawer dresser. When Beatrice returned, Amy asked, "Did my uncle John hang out with your son before high school?"

"Yes, actually. Both my sons, Thomas and Gabe, hung around with your Uncle John for a couple of years before that, and then Edward, Leon, and Steven joined their group in high school. Thomas eventually pursued different interests when the other boys started playing poker for fun. I guess it wasn't his thing. After graduation, both my boys went to the city to attend college. Once in a while, Gabe would mention that he still picked up the odd poker game with his friends, but it eventually stopped as they matured. As you already know, John married Jeannie right out of high school. They lived next door until one day, John suddenly left town. I guess divorcing Jeannie as well."

"It's so odd," Amy said. "My aunt has been telling everyone for years that Uncle John abandoned and left her with all of his debt. Never said anything at all about a divorce."

Beatrice turned, raising her eyebrow knowingly. "Did you see how Jeannie's face dropped when the lawyer said that John didn't want to be in the room with his ex-wife? Oh, they were divorced, but Jeannie never mentioned it since John cut off all ties with his family. All births, marriages, deaths, and divorces are recorded and documented, but I'm sure she never thought someone would look up the paperwork." She nodded to emphasize her point. "I'm sure she wanted everyone to believe in her abandonment story so that Dorothy would feel bad and still help her financially, even though John had left town." She grabbed the last few hanging items in the closet and carried the armload out of the room to make more room for Amy's clothes.

Amy tried cramming another sweater into the drawer, struggling to close it when Beatrice returned to the bedroom. "It doesn't want to close!" Amy grumbled.

"Are all the drawers full already?" Beatrice asked as she looked around at the piles of clothes still on the floor.

"No, I just want all the sweaters in the same drawer," Amy answered.

"Maybe you want to hang something up in the closet. There's lots of space." She gestured at the empty closet, laughing. "The frown on your face makes you look a lot like your mother! Once you finish putting away your clothing, we can have lunch and run some errands." She turned to leave.

"Wait!" Amy held up her hand. "Did you know my mom, too?"

"Yes, of course," she explained. "Sandy sometimes tagged along with him and the rest of the group. Eventually, Jeannie and a few other girls joined the group, while each boy started dating. I think one of Jeannie's friends dated Thomas for a while. Because your mom was the youngest of the group, she had an early curfew, so John or one of my boys always had to drop her off at home partway through the evening."

After that enlightening piece of information, Beatrice left the room as Amy continued to organize clothes and random items on the nightstand. She tossed a few things into the bottom of the closet. After placing the puzzle box on top of the doily on the dresser, she left the room to join the Petersens for lunch.

"You can bring your bicycle to our house today and put it in my workshop," George said as she sat down to eat.

"Thanks. It's okay for now, though. Maybe I'll do it later." She was too tired from organizing and moving. Dreading the idea of having to get all of her things from the farmhouse and leave it forever gave her a sick feeling in the pit of her stomach. She was going to miss it. Somehow, knowing that she could always return to it had been comforting, but now, with her uncle John taking possession of it, she knew it wouldn't be the same. "Oh, I just remembered; I have a list of things stolen from the farmhouse that I'm supposed to drop off at the police station. I also need to check the mail at the post office."

"It's not a problem," George said. "We can take you. We need to check our mail, too."

Beatrice smiled. "I want to stop at the fabric store to get material for new curtains for Amy's new room. Something bright and cheery. And more feminine."

George and Amy exchanged a look. "There's no point in arguing with her. She always gets her way." He smiled, patting the back of his wife's hand.

After lunch, George drove everyone to the fabric store first. Beatrice told Amy to walk around the spools of fabric to see what attracted her the most. There were so many designs and colours, but Amy eventually picked out a blue fabric with little pink flowers for the curtains. Beatrice seemed pleased that it would go well with the light blue walls.

Next, they hurried to the post office, where Amy anxiously retrieved a letter from Grandma's mailbox with her own name on it. It was the same manila envelope as the other letters that had come from the private investigator. Unable to contain her curiosity, Amy tore the envelope seal open with her fingers as she slowly walked down the post office steps.

The stationary was from Alister Morgan, the private investigator. She read the contents of the letter with a growing sense of unease. In it, Morgan gave her the name of a man she'd never heard of and explained that it was very important that she go to the local law enforcement and tell them about him having been recently released from prison. He had reason to believe he was headed their way. He also warned her not to approach the man because he was a repeat violent offender. She turned the page over to see if there was any other information. The back side of the page was blank. No description of the dangerous man, just his name. Amy's confusion deepened. *Well, that's not very helpful.* Amy knew they were going to the police station next anyway, so she decided to just hand over the letter to the police along with her list of stolen items for the farmhouse. Was this the very important information the P.I. had wanted to talk to her grandmother about? Did she know this guy? Amy frowned. *What does he have to do with me?*

Amy returned the letter to the envelope and walked closer to George's car. He was leaning against it, and when he spotted her, he moved to open the passenger door for her. "That's quite a frown. Is something wrong?"

"No," Amy shook her head. "It's nothing. I guess it's just something else for me to give the police: a letter from a private investigator that my grandma hired, saying to watch out for some guy that just got out of prison. See?" She shrugged as she flashed him the letter before refolding it and sliding herself into the backseat. George closed the door and waited for his wife to emerge from the post office.

Beatrice politely greeted and smiled at people as she approached the car, stopping just in front of George. He had his back to Amy, but he must have been saying something to her about the letter because Beatrice leaned around him to look at Amy before looking back at George again. After a short conversation, George opened the door for her. Once she was seated, he shut the door and walked around the front of the car, pausing on the sidewalk to take a long look in both directions, up and down the street. Beatrice said nothing but waited patiently for her husband to get into the driver's seat.

"I think we'll make our stop at the police station and then call it an afternoon," George quietly stated, starting the engine and backing out of the parking space.

Amy noticed that Beatrice seemed oddly quiet and wondered what their little conversation had been about. She wiped her sweaty palms on the sides of her jeans, her anxiety growing. As the Buick turned down Railway Avenue, Amy chewed on the corner of her lower lip, watching a train reverse tracks over in the train yard. The police station was just ahead. Amy just wanted to get this over with so she could go crawl into bed and hide under the covers for a little while. It has been such a long day.

"I'll go in with you," George said as he parked the car.

Amy lifted the handle latch and pushed open the heavy door with her foot. After she climbed out, she pushed the door shut again, using her whole body for leverage.

George had gotten out as well and smiled as he approached her. "If you would be patient and wait, I would open and close the door for you. There's nothing wrong with accepting help from people who want to help you, Amy." He looked like he was about to mess up her hair with his hand but quickly changed his mind.

Amy stared blankly at him without making any kind of acknowledgement, then pulled her crumpled list of missing items from the farmhouse out of her pocket. She walked past George to the police station's entrance doors, went inside and approached the front desk.

"What can I help you with?" asked the woman behind the counter, who was wearing civilian clothes.

"I'm here to talk to Officer Gerard about the list of missing items from my grandmother's farmhouse."

The woman looked over her shoulders at the uniformed officers sitting at their desks behind her. "What's your name? Is he expecting you?"

"Amy Young. He stopped by my place to ask for a list of missing things. I went there to check, and now I'm here to give it to him." She slid the list across the counter.

The woman scanned the list before addressing George, who stood behind Amy. "Is this all, George?"

"No, she also has a letter from a private investigator to give him." He nudged Amy's arm.

"Oh, yeah, this too." She presented the envelope to the woman.

The woman wrote "George Petersen & Amy Young, for Officer Gerard" on a scrap of paper and fastened everything with a paper clip. "I'll see that he gets these. Have a great day!"

"Thanks, Gladys," George said. "Have Gerard call me if he needs me." With that, he turned to head back outside.

Amy stood awkwardly for a moment before realizing that she should follow Mr. Petersen. "Um, thanks," she mumbled to the woman just before leaving.

Chapter 17

George pulled into the driveway and parked the Buick. Amy noticed he was staring out the side window towards the little house next door and followed his gaze to the broken glass in the front door. The hair on the back of Amy's neck seemed to instantly stand on end, sending a prickly feeling up and down her spine as she realized that someone had broken the little window to gain access to the house!

In a soothing, calm voice, George quietly said, "Bea, take Amy inside and call the police. Ask for Gerard or Randy. I'll listen outside the door to ensure no one is still inside while we wait for them." He never took his eyes off the house next door. "Stay inside our house."

Slowly, Amy exited the car, followed Beatrice into her house, and watched as she called the police. Then, the two of them sat silently at the kitchen table until Beatrice suddenly announced, "I should put on the coffee and take out something to eat. The police could take a while to figure things out."

She busied herself with preparing enough food to feed an army while periodically checking out the kitchen window. Once she had as much food on the table as she could reasonably fit, she nudged a stack of plates onto one corner and handed Amy the top one. "You go ahead and eat. It'll settle your nerves and stop you from chewing your lip off."

Amy licked her lips, tasting the metallic flavour of her blood. Yes, she had been chewing them a bit too much today. Amy's bottom lip, in particular, was raw and tender. She thought she would need some salve if this day got any worse than it already had been. Thank goodness she didn't have to work today or tomorrow. She wasn't sure she could handle any more stressful situations.

When Amy finished eating, she put her dishes in the kitchen sink. Beatrice was still looking out the window, watching what was happening next door. Amy looked out, too. Two police cars with flashing lights but no sirens were now parked in front of her aunt Jeannie's place—well, technically, Amy's place. George was talking to one of the officers.

Amy could hear a police siren off in the distance, getting closer. The siren shut off abruptly once the patrol car arrived, stopping at an odd angle across both driveways. Amy recognized Officer Gerard when he got out and walked over to George. He seemed to quickly take over the situation, sending two other officers into the house while talking to George. Both men looked in the direction of the Petersens' kitchen window a few times.

Eventually, the police officers and George came into the kitchen. Beatrice greeted everyone by their first name, handing them each a cup of coffee as they walked into the kitchen. "I didn't know you would send the whole force out over a break-in, Gerard," she teased.

"There seems to be a little more going on than you think." Officer Gerard sat down at the table.

"I just read the information that George left at the station. I still need to call Alister Morgan for more clarification. I have a few questions for you, though, Beatrice, and you, Amy. First of all, where is Jeannie Young?"

"We haven't seen her since yesterday at the lawyer's office," Beatrice said. "And I haven't seen her truck at home since the day before. Did you check her workplace?"

"I'll check with Frank at the diner. Where else does she work?" Officer Gerard asked.

"That's it, actually. I heard that Jeannie was let go at the doctor's office for missing too many shifts," Beatrice supplied. Amy was shocked to hear this, but when she thought about it, she realized that Jeannie was working late at the diner most days, picking up double shifts. Amy didn't think Jeannie could work in two places simultaneously with those sorts of hours.

"She was really upset that she might not be inheriting anything from my grandmother," Amy supplied sheepishly. "I don't know what kind of information you're looking for in connection to the break-in next door and at the farmhouse, but my aunt did show up unexpectedly while I was there with Sarah." The officer nodded and made a note in his little pocket notebook.

"Have you talked with Alister Morgan or had any other reports from him?" Officer Gerard asked, looking around the room.

"I have some letters that he sent to my grandmother. Mostly, it's about my uncle John. And then there's the one we got today about the guy we must watch out for."

"If you don't mind, I think I'll need to read those letters before I call him."

Amy went to her room to dig the folder out of the bottom of the closet and then brought the whole folder into the kitchen. The officers were all seated around the table, filling up their plates. Beatrice was topping up coffee mugs. Amy started to wonder if so many of the officers had come because they'd known Beatrice would feed them a delicious meal. Reaching into the folder and grabbing hold of the stack of letters from the private investigator, Amy handed all of them to Officer Gerard.

He reached for the pages with only a couple of fingers because he held a rather large sandwich in both hands. With his mouth full, he managed to offer a mumbled thanks. He scanned each page and passed it around the table to his fellow officers. George looked at each of them over the shoulder of one of them.

"Where did you find these letters, Amy?" Officer Gerard asked after passing the last one to the officer on his left, eyeing the folder she was still holding under her arm.

"I still check Grandma's mail. The few that came recently came to her mailbox. The rest I found with a bunch of other documents in her room at the farmhouse when I was trying to figure out what all was missing."

"The letter you left at the police station was addressed to you. Why is that?"

"I phoned and left the investigator a message after opening the one that said he needed Grandma to call him immediately. I called but got cut off before I could give him Aunt Jeannie's phone number, so he would have only been able to contact me by the mailing address."

"I'll need to know if any additional letters come to you. In the meantime, I'll have Officer Doyle call him to find out anything we don't already know." He nodded in the direction of the youngest officer at the table. Officer Randy Doyle was chewing a large mouthful and responded with a thumbs up.

"I'll let you know if we hear or see any sign of Jeannie," George said. "Do you want us to ask her to call you?"

"Yes," one of the officers replied. "Tell her we need to discuss a few things with her. We'll file a missing person report if we don't see her by tomorrow. Maybe she's just skipped town, but that might be the fastest way to find her if she didn't."

Amy figured that everyone finished asking her questions, so she went to her room to return the folder to the bottom of the closet. She was confident she'd given everyone all the information she had from the private investigator. Although Amy wanted to call Sarah to give her another update, she also wanted to wait until all the people were out of the kitchen.

Chapter 18

It was a while before the noise from the kitchen seemed to die down. Amy stayed in her room, looking through the library books she had about woodworking. She knew she could let George break the puzzle box open, but Amy wasn't ready to do that just yet—not if she didn't have to. Besides, what if there wasn't anything important inside of it, and they destroyed it for nothing?

A little knock on the door sounded just before Beatrice entered the room. "Are you doing okay?"

"Yes." Amy stretched, yawning. "I'm just reading. Did all of those police officers know you were going to feed them? Is that why so many police officers came to see about the break-in?"

Beatrice glanced around the room at the few items Amy still had lying around and picked up the puzzle box on the dresser, turning it over in her hands. "Yes." She smiled. "That's part of it anyway. Officer Gerard and my husband, George, are very good friends. His first name is Michael, but he's gone by his last name, Gerard, as long as I've known him. And Randy is married to my youngest daughter, Samantha. The officers all work under Gerard and know us quite well, so when George called the police station, they all came to help. It's a bit over the top, but I appreciate it. I put out food for them because they often don't take the time to eat whenever they are on shift."

"Do they all know that you're my guardian?"

"Yes. The officers haven't known as long as I have, though. It wasn't until just recently that we told our family and friends about the new arrangements. I imagine Randy told his fellow officers because no one was surprised to hear about your new living arrangements, or at least they wouldn't have made a big deal over it if they had. I'm sure they want to respect your privacy."

Amy shrugged. "I wasn't sure what to think or say."

"Randy was the first to know about you," Beatrice explained. "I told him the night I sent him to the farmhouse to get you when Dorothy was in the hospital."

Amy swallowed and sat up straighter. "That was in April! Where were you?"

"I'm not surprised you don't remember, as it was an extremely difficult night for you, but I was at the hospital. Dorothy asked me to fetch you, but I called Randy to pick you up in his cruiser because I thought it would get you there faster. I was so upset when Jeannie told me you had to go to her place or Social Services would have to take you. I knew about the guardianship, of course, but I believed Jeannie when she told me it would have to wait until the lawyer made it all legal. George and I thought we could wait, assuming that it would only take a few days. We had no idea it would take this long! But Jeannie refused to let us assume guardianship until the lawyer processed the will. But then things got sidetracked when Donald Tracker was taking over the practice. I'm sorry this didn't happen sooner, and maybe we should have tried harder. We didn't want to upset you by barging in next door." She wiped a tear from the corner of her eye with the edge of her sleeve. "Some days, it was all George could do to keep me from running next door to scoop you up and move you over here."

Amy's mind was spinning, but one question seemed more important than anything else. "How did you know Grandma was in the hospital? My aunt was surprised to see me the night I was dumped on her doorstep. She didn't know what was going on."

Beatrice cleared her throat and took a deep breath. "I'll tell you what I know from that night. Dorothy came to my house, very upset after a fight with Jeannie."

Amy felt like she had been waiting to find out more about that night ever since Denise Schneider had hinted that Dorothy's death was mysterious. Her only regret was not asking someone about it sooner.

"When she told me she'd just had fought with Jeannie," Beatrice continued, "She was red in the face and not making much sense. I still don't know what the fight was about, but Dorothy began having difficulty breathing. I tried to get her to sit down, but she kept pushing me away, and then suddenly, she collapsed right on the kitchen floor! I called the ambulance, which came right away, and I went with her to the hospital. The doctors told me that she'd had a heart attack, and her condition was critical. I was so worried you wouldn't get to her in time, which is why I called Randy to go get you in his police cruiser." She wiped the tears that started rolling down her face with the back of her hand.

"Then, after she died," Amy finished for her, "The police dropped me off to stay with my aunt because she was the only relative that I could name to the police. That's why they brought me to her house that night. I didn't know you were my guardian."

Beatrice sighed, took a deep breath, and nodded. "Yes. I'm sorry the legal work took so long, but I'm so glad you're finally here where Dorothy wanted you to be. We'll take good care of you. I promise." She turned to leave then but suddenly turned back to Amy. "Oh! I almost forgot! I have Dorothy's purse! She dropped it on the kitchen floor that night. I found it after I returned home. Just a minute. I'll go get it for you." She left the room, returning a few minutes later with Dorothy's black handbag, which she handed to Amy. "This is as good as yours now. Keep it."

Amy turned the handbag over in her hands as Beatrice left the bedroom. She could smell the leather and even a hint of her grandma's flowery perfume. Slowly, she opened the handbag's gold clasp, and looking inside, she slowly pulled out one item at a time, laying them on the bed in front of her and inspecting them. The wallet had a few pieces of identification, a credit card, and photos of Amy, Sandy, and John. There was also a red bankbook, a few pens, a cheque book, a small sewing kit, and a folded piece of paper, which Amy realized was the same colour and texture as the letters from the private investigator.

As Amy unfolded it, it quickly became clear to her that it was indeed another letter from Alister Morgan, which she read out loud to herself. "John Young, Junior. filed divorce papers, signed by himself and Jeannie Young, in 1979, after being released from the Rehabilitation Centre in Toronto, Ontario. I have enclosed a copy of the certificate filed with the Toronto Records Office. Call me if you need the details of the divorce." Amy reread the short letter a few times before checking all of the compartments in the handbag. There didn't seem to be a divorce certificate anywhere inside the purse. She returned the items into the purse except the letter, which she decided she needed to tell Officer Gerard and Donald Tracker about. As John's ex-wife, Jeannie knew she wouldn't inherit anything, and since no one knew where she was, it was probably safe to assume that Jeannie was out looking for John, hoping to get some money from him.

Amy brought the letter out into the kitchen, showing it to Beatrice. They didn't know if it mattered that the divorce certificate was missing or not, but just to be sure, Beatrice called Officer Gerard and read the letter to him over the phone, adding her suspicions that the police would find Jeannie where they found John. She also phoned Donald Tracker's secretary, Doris, letting her know that John and Jeannie filed for divorce, but the document was missing. When Beatrice returned the letter to Amy, she folded it and put it in the back pocket of her jeans.

Chapter 19

Bobby turned down the dusty gravel road, slowing down as he passed a farmyard, looking for anything that seemed familiar to him. It had been a decade or two since he'd been out at John's parents' place. His memory of his high school days was a little fuzzy. Back then, he'd been more interested in having a good time and attending parties. Luckily, he recognized the white stucco with the green roof and trim as he drove towards it along the main road and turned the yellow Imperial LeBaron down the driveway.

Bobby tensed after seeing a small car parked near the front steps, which made Bobby feel a little uneasy until he recognized the person coming out of the house as his new real estate agent, Edward Greene. Relieved, he gave the man a little wave and parked the stolen yellow LeBaron beside Ed's red Ford Escort.

Getting out and closing the car door, he smiled broadly at him. "Hello, Ed! It's nice to see you're here to get your photos of the place. Did you bring the sign?"

"Yes, it's in the trunk. I'll put it up near the end of the driveway. I was about to lock up when I saw your car drive up. I guess I won't have to now."

"Yes, of course!" Bobby rocked on his heels, unsure what to say next, waiting impatiently for the guy to leave. He wanted to get into the farmhouse to scope the place out. Bobby needed to check for valuables to hock or even have an auction of all the furniture so he wouldn't be seen selling it on his own. There was no sense in waiting to start cashing in on the place and getting as much money as he could.

"Nice ride," Ed said, pointing to the car Bobby arrived in.

"Thanks," Bobby turned to admire it. "It was irresistible. This beauty stole my heart as soon as I saw it."

"Are you staying at the farmhouse while you're in town?" Ed asked him.

"I am, yes. Did I mention that when we met? Sorry. I never thought of it. If I move in, I could keep up the place until it sells, so it's always ready for showings."

"It's not a problem," Ed assured him. "It's not very often that we sell a house without someone still living there. Do you need me to call you before I come out to show people the place?"

Bobby felt a sense of panic. It would be strange if he couldn't tell the man the phone number, and even if he could, he didn't know if the phone was still connected. "Uh ... no. I think you can just pop on over whenever you want since it will just be me. I'll try to keep the place ready at all times. When people are here, I'll go for a walk or something."

Ed nodded, reaching out to shake Bobby's hand. "Sounds good, John. I'll see you around. I've got to get going! I want to make flyers with the photos to generate interest for the place and put an ad in the papers."

Bobby smiled, waving at the man as he drove away. The first thing he would do was park the flashy yellow LeBaron in the garage. It was too noticeable to leave out front. He walked over to the attached garage and pulled on the lever to lift the door open. The door groaned as Bobby heaved it open. It was a single-car garage but filled with various-sized boxes, old furniture, and worn-out tires. There was no room for the LeBaron.

"Damn it." He walked around the house to see what other outbuildings were on the property and found a barn, a large shop, an empty chicken coop, and a few granaries. "I guess the shop is my best bet," Bobby muttered. He walked over to it, but someone locked its large, vertical-swinging doors. He discovered a side entrance, though hidden behind a copse of trees, and soon realized that someone had locked it, too.

Finally, Bobby's eyes fell on the unlocked attached garage he'd already searched. "There was just junk in there. So, what's in here worth locking up, John? Something expensive, I bet." His gaze shifted, trying to figure out how he would gain entry into the shop, and that's when he spotted it. A slightly worn path in the grass led Bobby away from the door and into the surrounding trees. Bobby followed the path, his heart pounding with anticipation, until it abruptly ended. He looked around, his eyes scanning the area, and there it was. "Bingo!" A single key, hanging on a nail on one of the trees, glinting in the sunlight.

Bobby unlocked the door to the shop and stepped inside. The three-bay shop was large and didn't disappoint him. The Young family filled the space with tools, welding equipment, and lumber, but there was enough room to store the LeBaron.

He would park it in the middle bay beside a car that was already nestled there under a protective cover.

Bobby hit each electric door opener on the wall until he managed to open the middle one. He parked the stolen car in the shop and then closed and locked the shop doors once again. Even without a careful inspection, Bobby was pleased with the items he'd already seen there, knowing that they would bring him a lot of money in an auction sale. He strolled over to the farmhouse then to investigate his new hideout for revenue potential and to try to find John's divorce papers so he wouldn't have to wait for a record search at the courts or share his windfall with John's wife.

He walked around the farmhouse, looking for expensive items that could fetch a reasonable price at auction. He found mostly furnishings and some china. He wasn't sure what anyone would do with personal items, like clothing and footwear, so he supposed he could just leave them in the house for whoever bought it. Dealing with that stuff would be the new owner's problem.

It dawned on Bobby then that the land and farmhouse could be auctioned just as easily as the items found in it. He hurried to the kitchen, his mind racing with possibilities, to search for a telephone book to look up auctioneers in the area. The Yellow Pages had ads for two companies that handled estate-sale auctions. Bobby tore the page out of the book and set it on the kitchen counter so it would be easier to find later. He knew he should continue searching the outbuildings to get a better idea of what to tell the auctioneers. It wouldn't look good if he couldn't talk about the farmhouse and its holdings like it was his family home. The anticipation of the potential windfall and the life it could bring him filled Bobby with a mix of excitement and nervousness.

Bobby sighed then and lifted the telephone receiver, pleased to hear a dial tone. He had a different call he needed to make. He dialed the long-distance number to connect him to the man he was indebted to for more money than Bobby had ever thought he could pay back in his lifetime. But that had all changed. Hopefully, the man would give him enough time to execute his plan if it meant he could finally pay him off in full, with interest. Only then would Bobby feel like a free man, able to restart his life once more.

After several rings, a gruff voice with a thick Eastern accent picked up on the other end. "Yeah?" it said.

"I need to talk to him again," Bobby said, pleading as he heard a few clicks over the line. "I've got the property and assets to repay all of my loans. He just needs to take the hit off of me so I can get the money from the sale. I-I'm going to set up an auction of this farmhouse I scammed from a guy I know so that it will be quick!" Bobby's heart was hammering in his chest, and sweat gathered on his brow.

"One moment."

It seemed like an eternity before the man came back on the phone with the answer Bobby was waiting for. "One month." With that, the call was ended abruptly with a click, followed by the disconnected line loudly buzzing in Bobby's ear.

Well, a month isn't much time, but hopefully, it will be enough. Bobby had to work fast, though, or he'd never be able to pull this off. Emptying his pockets on the kitchen counter, Bobby removed the jacket and tie he'd been still wearing, hoping to avoid getting them dirty while he explored the barn and outbuildings. He looked around, not particularly optimistic about finding any men's clothing in the farmhouse, which looked very feminine, and mentally kicked himself for not taking some clothes from Darren or Darryl or whatever his name was before he'd bolted out of there.

A quick look in the closets confirmed Bobby's assumption about the men's clothing. He found nothing except an old pair of coveralls and a plaid jacket that would fit him. *These will work, I guess.* He stripped out of his dress shirt and dress pants and climbed into the coveralls with just his underwear on underneath. At least he could keep the dress clothes clean for when he needed them later.

Chapter 20

B obby had already looked around the property and in the smaller outbuildings before walking into the large barn, which was dark and smelled damp. A few barn swallows flitted about in the rafters when he entered. Deciding he could use more light, Bobby opened the two big sliding doors on the front before looking around.

Someone parked a red Case tractor with a lawn-mowing attachment in the middle of the barn. It appeared to be dusty but well-maintained. He discovered the keys still in the ignition. Bobby decided he should mow the yard after he had snooped around to make the place look better for the sale. It's not like he had much else to do while waiting for his big payout. He was sure that he could remember how to work the tractor from the old days when he'd helped John with his chores.

There wasn't much of anything else of value in the barn that Bobby could see. He surveyed the abundant gardening tools, ropes, and some old saddles and bridles that didn't look like anyone had used them in years. There was also a wooden ladder that led up to the hayloft. Deciding that the ladder looked sturdy enough for him to climb, Bobby moved over to it, wanting to take a quick look around up there to ensure that he wasn't missing anything of value.

The second rung from the top broke in half as Bobby reached the top, giving him a jolt. Then, the floor in the loft creaked as he started walking across it. He stopped and listened to the creaking of the wood. *Maybe it wasn't a good idea to come up here after all. There wasn't anything up there except a few cardboard boxes in the far corner.* Bobby decided it wasn't worth the risk to walk across the loft floor to check them out and started climbing back down.

"What do you think you're doing, avoiding me, John?!"

The angry voice from behind startled him, and he looked over his shoulder and down to see the woman standing at the foot of the ladder. He shook his head, smiling at the confused look on her face.

"Well, look what we have here!" he said. "The ex-wife of John Young, junior. You're trespassing on his property, you know." He continued climbing down the ladder until he reached the bottom and turned to face Jeannie.

"I ... I can't believe it!" Looking him up and down, she was amazed at how much this man looked like her ex-husband, John. He was an excellent likeness of the man she hated.

"That you're trespassing?" he said with a laugh. "Well, believe it."

Jeannie crossed her arms in front of her, stomping, and raising her voice. "No! I mean, I can't believe that you, of all people, would be *here*! Are you behind this scheme? Are you trying to get my inheritance from John? Where is that idiot anyway? He owes me a big payout for handling all his gambling debt for him." She glanced around the barn, calling out, "John? Are you here?"

Slowly, the realization that his scheme was about to fizzle out dawned on Bobby. "I'm trying to settle all of my gambling debts before I get killed! I'm the one John owes! Not you! John screwed me out of a lot more money than you ever had. And you are not going to ruin everything!" He grabbed her arms, squeezing them tightly.

Leaning in closer and gritting his teeth with anger and desperation, he growled, "You cannot be here! This place is John's inheritance! Not yours!"

Jeannie fought against his hold, kicking him in the shin, "Get your hands off me!" She spat in distaste. "I'm the one who's going to inherit this place! All I have to do is go to the police and tell them you're pretending to be my estranged husband to steal his inheritance!"

Bobby stepped closer to her, snarling now. "You didn't marry John because you loved him. You just wanted his family's money!" Releasing her with a push that sent her sprawling to the dirt floor, he continued in a taunting tone. "I knew your scheme even back then, and I'm sure you haven't changed any over the years. I bet you've been sucking the old lady dry ever since he took off."

Jeannie scowled up at him. "It was going extremely well, too, until Dorothy said she would stop her monthly support payments to me. She came by on the night she died to tell me that she was evicting me from my house! My house! That bitch! It's not my fault that John borrowed against it and lost it in a poker game!" Her lip quivered in anger and resentment as she wiped drool from the corner of her mouth. "He didn't even tell me!

The bank took it, and his mother repurchased it, so we'd still have a roof over our heads. But I guess you already know all that. And knew more back then since you were still hanging out sometimes, playing that god-damn poker." She pushed herself up, brushing the dirt off of her jeans.

"I know he divorced you," Bobby said, hoping to get confirmation since he still couldn't remember if it was true. "He told me at a poker game."

Sighing, crossing her arms, and slowly pacing back and forth across the barn, she said, "Yes … We were divorced. I didn't think anyone knew, though. I told everyone that John had just abandoned me. Everyone felt sorry for me, so I used it. I still needed the monthly support payments from his mother. It's not like I've been debt-free either, you know. I like nice things."

Suddenly, she stopped directly in front of Bobby, softening her tone. "I can help you think of a new plan. We could be great together! I'm sure no one will find John in whatever little hole he's dug for himself, and you've already stolen John's identity. I know I can come up with a plan that will benefit us both. We could share the money!"

Bobby couldn't believe what he was hearing. "No! I need it! Are your debts going to get you killed? Because mine will! You can't have any of it! Whatever you need is not my problem! Hell, you could get yourself killed for all I care!" Bobby's voice intensified with his increasing anger.

"My plan is perfect! Since John hasn't already shown up, and no one has seen him in years, it's a safe bet that he won't be showing up anytime soon!" Bobby eyed the rope that was hanging on the wall behind Jeannie, wishing he could tie her up in the barn, but with people coming in to view the property, there should be better ideas than that. He looked up at the loft, wondering if a perilous solution might exist.

"You're going to have to make a deal with me," Jeannie stated matter-of-factly. "I need to move out and find a new place, and I need money for that, so you're going to pay me off. If you don't, I'll expose you as a fraud."

"Well," Bobby said, slowly shaking his head. "That deal will create a big problem for me. I just told the Big Boss I would have all his money by the end of the month. I can't cut you in on the deal." His mind was racing, and he was clenching and unclenching his fists. She was going to mess up everything!

She smirked at him. "I guess I can always let the police work out their deal with you. I know your true identity." She shrugged. "If you want me to keep quiet, you'll have to hand over a lot of John's money."

Her blackmailing attempts to extort money from him suddenly pushed Bobby too far, and he leapt towards her in a burst of blind rage, knocking her down and striking her with his fists as she scratched and fought against him. Gasping, she was about to unleash a torrent of screaming, but as she looked past him, she suddenly stopped, her eyes going as wide as saucers. Suddenly, Bobby's body came crashing down on top of her, sinking Jeannie into darkness.

Chapter 21

August 21, 1985

Wednesday

Beatrice stopped by Amy's open doorway and leaned in. "Do you have any dark clothes to wash? I can take them."

Looking around the floor of her room, Amy spotted a few things. "Just a second." She scrambled to grab a pair of jeans and a few T-shirts and added them to Beatrice's dirty laundry basket.

Beatrice started to turn away and then stopped. "Oh, there seems to be something in the pocket of those jeans. Better take it out if you don't want it going through the wash."

Amy reached into the laundry basket, pulled out the jeans, and checked the pockets. "Oops. It's the letter from the private investigator." She pulled the crinkled letter out.

"You better put it in your folder for safekeeping. You should to give it to Donald, the lawyer, as confirmation that Jeannie is not eligible for any inheritance. Though I suppose he'll still need to find the divorce papers they filed."

Shrugging slightly, Beatrice turned away again and headed back down the hall, calling back over her shoulder, "When you finish putting that away, if you could pick up the rest of the dirty clothes and put them in the hamper in the corner, I'd appreciate it."

"No problem." Amy looked around, nodding. She opened the closet door to dig out the folder on the floor and then took it over to the bed. Amy unfolded the letter and tried to rub some of the creases out, as it wouldn't sit neatly in the folder. She finally had to pull out all the papers and flatten the letter in between them, restacking everything twice before she could get them back inside. In the process, her birth certificate and the two copies of her grandfather's death certificate slid off the top of the pile and onto the floor.

Amy rolled her eyes as she slid off the bed and onto her knees to pick them up. As she stood back up, she looked at one of the death certificates again and noticed that a doctor listed her grandfather's cause of death as "kidney failure." When she looked at the other one, though, she saw that another doctor listed the cause of death as a "drug overdose." She frowned, not understanding why or how the copies wouldn't be identical. Putting the two side by side, she compared them carefully. It took a few moments, but then the connection clicked. What she held in her hands weren't duplicates of the same document!

Amy replaced the first document in the pile of papers on the bed and reread the one she was still holding. It was a death certificate for John William

Young, Junior. Her grandfather was John William, Senior. Junior was his son. Her uncle John. According to this document, her uncle John had died of a drug overdose on March 21, 1983.

The divorce papers suddenly seemed utterly irrelevant. "Uncle John is dead? Wait! So, who was at the lawyer's office?" Whoever it was, it hadn't been her uncle. Amy took off running out of the bedroom and down the hallway, turning into the kitchen and bolting down the stairs to the basement.

Beatrice was sorting laundry on the cement floor but quickly straightened, looking at Amy with alarm. "What's the matter? You're as white as a sheet!"

"Uncle John is dead!" Amy was gasping for air. "He died!" Her throat felt tight, making her voice much higher than usual. "They were divorced, and then he died! He's dead!"

Beatrice put her arms around Amy, trying to reassure her. "What happened? Did someone phone?"

Amy tried to calm herself with a few deep breaths, swallowing hard as she held up the document and pointed to the date. "He died in 1983 of a drug overdose in Toronto! Someone must be impersonating him to take over Grandma's farmhouse!"

Beatrice took the certificate from Amy's shaking hands, reading what it said. "We better call Gerard!"

Beatrice ran up the stairs into the kitchen, with Amy close behind her, and dialed the number to the police department. While she waited for her call to connect, she moved to the kitchen window to frantically wave to George outside.

"Yes, this is Beatrice Petersen! I have an emergency! I need Officer Gerard right away!"

George came bursting into the kitchen. "What's all the fuss about?"

Amy snatched the certificate from her hands and pushed it into George's. "Someone's impersonating my uncle John! My uncle died a long time ago!"

George and Amy waited, listening as Beatrice left a message with one of the officers at the station before hanging up the phone. "He's out of the station, investigating a crime scene. We'll have to wait for him to return to the station to call us."

George calmly sat at the kitchen table, with Amy sitting across from him.

"What do we do now?" she asked him.

He looked thoughtfully at the clock on the wall before answering, "I think we'll have some coffee and cookies. Maybe play a game of cards or something while we wait. Who knows how long it will be?" He looked over at his wife, still standing by the kitchen window. "Did you try asking for Randy?"

She nodded. "It seems that just about everyone is out of the office today. They have been working on another emergency. We'll have to wait."

It turns out that they had to wait almost four hours, drinking coffee, eating snacks, and playing a seemingly endless game of Monopoly before the phone finally rang. George jumped up to answer it.

"Hello?" he said breathlessly. "Yes, of course! Amy found a death certificate for John Young ... No, not the old man. The son, John, Junior." After briefly exchanging details, he hung up the phone. "He'll be right over. I think he'll need to see that document." They all took turns anxiously watching out the window for Officer Gerard.

"He's here!" exclaimed Beatrice from her shift at the window.

At the door, George hurriedly greeted him and the two other officers who had accompanied him the day before to investigate the break-in at the house next door. They refused to come inside this time because they said the police unit was in a hurry to finish the day's paperwork from the other crime they were currently working on.

"Amy found the death certificate for her uncle, John," George said.

Amy took the paper off the kitchen counter, carrying it over to the door to hand it to the officer. "Someone was at the lawyer's office on Monday claiming to be my uncle John so he could inherit the farmhouse from my grandma. Then, Aunt Jeannie claimed she was still married to Uncle John and entitled to half of his inheritance, but it was a bit confusing whether they still were or not, but then the lawyer said he could check the court documents..." Amy rambled on for a bit longer, not knowing how much information the police needed.

The officers exchanged glances, and Officer Gerard nodded. "Alright. We definitely need to look into this. It's essential information, and we will use it to connect it to another crime we are investigating. Perhaps even the break-in next door. If you don't mind, I'll borrow this and photocopy it at the office before returning it."

He handed George a business card. "I have a new direct line. Call me anytime if you find out who might be impersonating John Young, Junior. Meanwhile, we'll check with the neighbours around the farmhouse." Nodding again, he turned to leave but stopped as one of the other officers whispered something to him.

Officer Gerard listened and continued down the front steps, waving to them. "It looks like we're headed out of town again, and I won't be reachable until tomorrow."

After a short exchange of reactions with Beatrice and George, Amy went to her room for a bit of quiet reflection. It had been a strange day. She felt antsy and couldn't figure out what to do with herself. She tried reading but found that images and memories of the farmhouse kept interrupting her concentration. Frustrated, she threw her book down on the bed and walked over to the dresser, running her hands along the smooth surface of the puzzle box. *What was its secret? And why hadn't her grandma just told her whatever it was hiding?*

She picked up the wooden box, flipping it over in her hands. The checkered pattern on the sides made it look like a woodworker designed it using many smaller pieces of wood. As Amy turned it around, she felt her fingers slip slightly on one side. Upon closer inspection, Amy realized that her fingers had moved a little square panel on one end. She pushed it back into place and then moved it again. It would only move a fraction of an inch and no more. Amy tried pushing different patterned areas on the puzzle box but couldn't make much else happen. *What am I missing?*

She turned it over to look at the bottom again, sliding her fingers along all the different colour patterns in the wood until another piece moved just ever so slightly. Thinking that this might be like a Rubik's cube, she kept trying to move things in a particular order until she could make a few more almost invisible panels move slightly. Remembering that some of the Rubik's cube squares didn't move individually, like the corner pieces and the center square, she figured that this box might have some similar trick involving moving one piece at a time in a specific order to open it. Amy thought that if she kept working on it, she might eventually be able to open it enough to see what was inside without breaking it open.

Chapter 22

It was late in the evening when Officer Gerard and Doyle knocked on the door of the Petersen house. George talked with them briefly in hushed whispers before calling Amy to join them. She put her book down on the couch and walked into the kitchen. The officers held their hats in their hands. There was an awkward silence in the room, very different from their previous visits' casual laughter and banter.

"Amy," Officer Gerard sighed, "I am very sorry to inform you that we discovered your aunt Jeannie deceased this afternoon. We will know more after we finish our investigation. In these circumstances, we order an autopsy to confirm the cause of death because there was suspicion of foul play involved."

Amy was stunned, overwhelmed by countless questions and feelings that hit her all at once. Beatrice put her arm around Amy to steady her. "

Swallowing the lump in her throat, Amy asked, "Where was she found? I haven't seen her since she left the lawyer's office. What happened to her?"

Officer Gerard looked Amy straight in the eye as he answered. "A real-estate agent from Saskatoon was showing the farmhouse property. She found an unknown male lying on the floor of the shop.

After an initial search, we also found your aunt in another building on the property. Is there any chance you know who she might have been with at the farmhouse? Did she go there with someone to confront the man pretending to be John? Is it possible that the imposter attacked Jeannie and her boyfriend?"

She shook her head, frowning. "No, if you had asked me earlier today, I would have said that only my uncle John would be at the farmhouse," Amy offered. "But we know Uncle John is also dead. Maybe she also figured that out and went to the farmhouse to confront the imposter. Or maybe she didn't and thought she would find Uncle John there. I ... I just don't know."

"Do you know if she was dating anyone?" Randy asked.

"Not really. However, Auntie Jeannie went out on a date last week. I don't know who she was dating but was gone all night." Amy shrugged, looking around the room at everyone, realizing she had never really known her aunt at all like she thought. She didn't even feel very sad that her aunt was gone, though that in itself made her miserable. And she was worried. Did that make her a horrible person? Jeannie had lived in town all her life, but until she'd been dropped on her doorstep by the police, she'd never really visited her or even talked about her much with her grandma.

"Anyone you know who might have shown an interest in her?" Officer Gerard asked, continuing his questioning.

Amy thought carefully. "Bob Crookedneck, one of the cooks at Frankie's Diner, seemed to like her. He used to send leftovers home with her so we would have something to eat. He once told me my aunt Jeannie wouldn't know happiness if it was right in front of her."

Officer Gerard wrote this down in his notebook. "And what was her financial situation?"

Beatrice fielded this one. "She was deep in debt. Dorothy had bailed John and Jeannie out by buying their little house back from the bank for them a long time ago. They'd lost it to gambling debts. At the reading of the will, she got agitated when she found out she wouldn't be entitled to inherit anything from Dorothy because she divorced John. Perhaps you should talk to Donald Tracker. He told us he'd met with John Young, Junior, just before the Monday meeting with us about the will. But now we know it must have been someone impersonating him, as Amy found John's death certificate."

"Did you see the man at the office? Or hear him? Anyone you recognize at all?" asked Officer Randy.

"No," Beatrice and Amy answered in unison.

George cleared his throat. "I didn't go in with the ladies, but I didn't see anyone entering or leaving the building. I was reading my newspaper in the car."

Officer Gerard snapped his notebook closed. "Alright. We need to identify the man we found at the farmhouse. We'll search the database for a photo ID, but that'll take some time—longer than normal even since we'll probably have to use a police artist to estimate what he actually looks like. He was pretty badly beaten, so we may have to wait until his face heals or his fingerprints come back as a match for someone."

"The man's alive?" Amy asked, suddenly realizing that she'd been assuming he was dead as well.

"That's correct. Unfortunately, the man had no ID on him. We're waiting for him to regain consciousness so we can question him. He's receiving treatment at the hospital." He tucked his notebook into his breast pocket. "Well, I am finished questioning you. Call me anytime. I hooked up an answering machine, so I won't miss anything, though there could still be a delay."

The officers left the Petersen house once again. Amy rubbed her forehead, blinking her eyes a few times. She could feel pain starting behind her eyes and hoped she wasn't getting a migraine. Beatrice suggested that she take a hot shower and go to bed. There was no point in arguing. It had been a crazy week, and Amy thought her guardian's suggestion sounded like what she needed now.

Chapter 23

Unable to move, Bobby woke up feeling sore and stiff. He couldn't see anything with his right eye and barely anything with his left. There was also an annoying ringing in his ears that Bobby found disorientating. He felt a wave of nausea when he tried to move his head to try to locate the source of a rhythmic beeping noise somewhere nearby. It made his head throb just listening to it. He tried to lay still and take some shallow breaths. He couldn't breathe in too heavily without causing severe pain in his right side.

Finally, he tried to open his left eye again to take a look around. Through a tiny slit of an opening, he was surprised to find that he was in a hospital room. Looking down at himself on the bed, he realized why he couldn't move too much. He had leather restraints on his wrists and ankles, securing him to the bed. Not a particularly good sign, but Bobby had been in worse situations than this. He tugged on the restraints to test their strength and confirmed that he wasn't going anywhere anytime soon.

His memory was cloudy. *What happened?* He tried to piece things together. He could remember walking around the farmhouse property, trying to estimate his upcoming payout. Then, memories of

Jeannie arguing with him in the barn came flooding back to him. Knowing who he was, she demanded he cut her in his scheme, hoping to get a big payout of her own. He closed his eyes, trying to remember the heated argument. He remembered rushing at her in a fit of rage, swinging his fists and yelling, and telling her that she wouldn't get any money from him and that it was all his!

But then what happened? He urged his subconscious to think. Just barely, he could remember seeing Jeannie's eyes widen as she looked past him over his shoulder—then someone hit him over the head from behind. He hadn't heard anyone else enter the barn, but someone must have. *Was it one of Big Boss's heavyweights? It had to be. Right? But why?* He'd said he would give him a month to repay his debt. Bobby suddenly realized that the increasingly rapid beeping noise was his heart monitor. He forcibly took a few calming breaths to slow his heartbeat rhythm and prevent the nurses from barging in.

His efforts to calm himself hit a setback when he realized he was likely being punished by the Big Boss for asking for another payment extension. It had to have been the Big Boss's men. No one else would know where to find him. If he ever got out of this mess, he promised himself that he would never gamble again!

Male voices outside his door seeped into Bobby's thoughts, getting his attention. He strained to hear the conversation, but the door muffled it, and he could only pick out the occasional word or phrase. He hoped that none of the nurses or doctors were about to burst into the room to prevent him from eavesdropping.

"—woken up yet?" one voice said.

"No, ... will question... morning," said another.

The next voice to speak up was deep and male, sending a chill through his whole body. "Has ... What ... his name ...?"

He lay as still as he could, trying to listen over the drumming of his heart. If they knew he wasn't John, he'd be sent back to prison for fraud. And the Big Boss could get his guys on the inside to kill him.

"—not right!" Random words kept floating into the room, and despite his efforts, he couldn't figure out how many people were standing out in the hall.

"She said ... went ... Are you sure? I—"

Bobby assumed the voices were talking about Jeannie. Bobby knew just what kind of girl Jeannie was from the very first time he'd met her back in high school. Initially, she faked some interest in Bobby until she found out that John's family had a lot of money. Bobby sneered, just thinking about her. It was obvious that Jeannie couldn't be trusted, but John had been oblivious to her manipulation, blinded by her charms. He'd tried to warn his friend, but John wouldn't listen, which had strained their friendship.

At the big poker game in Ontario, on the night that would eventually land him in prison, he hadn't been surprised to hear that they'd divorced or that he wanted to celebrate finally ending a relationship with her. Of course, as soon as John realized the host had rigged the game, the dealer ruined the celebratory demeanour, and he'd flipped the table, ending Bobby's chance of taking the pot with his winning hand and kicking off the downward spiral that had ruined Bobby's life.

The noises in the hallway finally quieted. Bobby wished he knew what the police had on him, figuring it had to be incrimination, though, since they'd had him restrained to his hospital bed. Luckily, it seemed like he would have until morning to figure out a story to sweet-talk his way out of this mess.

He would be a dead man if he ended up back in prison, but Bobby would also be a dead man if he stayed out but couldn't pay his debts. Bobby had escaped many sticky situations before, but this one was bad even by his standards. He'd have to carefully weigh all his options and come up with a decision and a plan before morning.

Chapter 24

August 22, 1985

Thursday

Bobby felt like he'd barely slept at all that night in his hospital bed, the restraints being the only things keeping him from tossing and turning despite his injuries. By morning, he'd realized he had only three options to get him out of this mess—and the restraints. No matter what, Bobby knew he would have to avoid revealing his true identity or getting sent back to prison, directly into the hands of some mindless goon. Beyond that, he had a number of possible hands to play, once he figured out who the police thought he was, and if he played them right, he figured he just might be able to walk away from this crappy little town and start his life over again as someone else. It was risky, but Bobby knew his life was worth the gamble.

When a young nurse came in to check Bobby's intravenous and his vitals, she noticed that he was watching her with the one eye he could open. "Did you need painkillers? I could check your chart and see if the doctor has prescribed some." She inserted a thermometer into his mouth.

"No, I think that will make me drowsy," he mumbled around the thermometer, trying to smile at her. "I need to speak to the police officer in charge. For some reason, I find myself tied to a hospital bed."

"The police have been stationed outside your door since you arrived here yesterday," she whispered. "I think they're waiting to talk to you, too." After a few more seconds, she removed the thermometer, studied it for a moment and made a quick note on a pad she kept in a side pocket of her uniform.

As she wrapped a blood-pressure cuff around his arm, Bobby stole a chance to learn a little information from her. "I must have been unconscious when an ambulance brought me in. I don't remember how I got here. I vaguely remember getting hit from behind, but that's it. Geez, they must not even know who I am—" He let the sentence trail off, hoping the nurse would fill it in for him.

"They don't. Your chart just reads John Doe. You didn't have any identification with you. The police are very interested to know who you are and what you were doing at Dorothy Young's farmhouse."

"It's John Young's farmhouse," he said without thinking.

The nurse paused, looking at him momentarily before turning to study the gauge on the blood pressure monitor. "That's not what I heard," she said, then pulled back the Velcro and removed the cuff.

Thank goodness for small-town gossip. Bobby smiled at her, trying to look harmless and intrigued. "Really? What did you hear?"

The young blonde nurse smiled mischievously, glancing at the door before leaning in and sharing her news. "Well, everyone thought he had just skipped town on Jeannie and never came back. But apparently, John died years ago. So, I guess he'll never return now. John can't if he's dead. Can he?"

Bobby had a sinking feeling in the pit of his stomach, realizing that option one had just been struck off the list. It had been his favourite option, giving him the best outcome. "No, I guess he can't."

The nurse smiled at him and left without another word, leaving Bobby to decide between his remaining options. Both of them carried the risk of being arrested, but option two seemed to have a better chance of walking away from it all.

Suddenly, four police officers entered the room, interrupting Bobby's thoughts. The senior officer was an older man who moved around the bed to get closer to him. "Good morning. I'm Officer Michael Gerard." He pulled a notepad and a pencil from his shirt pocket. "And who are you?"

"What happened?" Bobby asked, trying to play up confusion from his injuries. "How did I get here?"

"Just tell me your name, please," Officer Gerard responded gruffly.

Bobby looked around at the police officers, deciding that they weren't falling for his act. "Bobby Wilham. I'm from a small town just outside of Toronto."

The officer blinked a few times before writing the name down, obviously having expected a different answer from him. "Do you have any identification?"

Bobby knew he had to stick with his plan and dive in head first. "I was mugged in town just before I went to visit an old friend of mine. John Young." Bobby said this as calmly and innocently as he could, looking around the room at the officers—each showing apparent impatience in their posture and body language. "So, I don't have any money or identification. I think the only person in town who could verify my identity is Pastor Bill at the Community Church. I've met him a few times since I came to town about a week ago at a meeting."

Officer Gerard nodded at another officer, who promptly left the room. "And what is your business here in town, *Bobby*?"

Bobby ignored the officer's doubtful emphasis on the name he provided and sighed as he answered the question. "To be honest, I've been down on my luck for the last few years. I met John as a young adult and ran into him a few times in Toronto at various poker games. These games were a few years back. We even had a night out on the town once to celebrate his divorce. To be honest, I came to town hoping that he could help me out or at least give me a couch to sleep on for a few days while I looked for work."

Inspiration struck him then. "It's my own fault, really," Bobby said, hoping to garner a little sympathy and make his story more believable. "The hardships, I mean. Almost all of them I brought on myself with my drinking and gambling. Shortly after I got to town, I met Pastor Bill at an Alcoholics Anonymous meeting. He also fed me after I spent the night sleeping in the park. I'm sure he'd remember me if you asked him." Bobby knew the pastor could confirm all those details, which would go a long way to support the rest of his made-up story.

One of the younger officers spoke up then. "Did you know John's wife?"

Bobby suppressed a smile. The officer was competent, already trying to test his story. "Yeah, though Jeannie is his ex-wife. They divorced a long time ago. As I said, I celebrated with John in Toronto the night he told me." Bobby felt his jaw tightening a bit, worried that he was saying too much. Forcing himself to relax, he looked Officer Gerard in the eye and waited for more questions.

"That's a shame," the officer replied. "About the divorce, I mean. It's always sad when things don't work out. In any case, we'll have Pastor Bill come down here to confirm your identity. We're just waiting to uncover some additional facts with of our investigation before removing your restraints. For now, I have posted an officer outside of the door, and you should consider yourself in police custody. I'll return with more questions later. Until then, get some rest and try to heal up." The officers all filed out of the room after Officer Gerard. When the door clicked closed behind them, Bobby closed his eyes to think about how he was going to avoid arrest. At least it would help if he knew why the police were holding him and what exactly they were investigating. Since someone had severely beaten him, it seemed odd that they were obviously looking at him as a suspect and not a victim. He was mentally kicking himself for not asking for details about what had happened when it occurred to him that maybe the police weren't sure what charges they should be filing against him. If they didn't find any incriminating evidence, maybe—just perhaps—Bobby would walk away from this with the pastor's help, who had already demonstrated his willingness to aid a man as destitute as himself.

Chapter 25

The day began like any other day. Amy woke up very early, wondering where she was before remembering that she now lived at the Petersen place. How she'd managed to forget that fact while sleeping was a wonder to her. When Amy remembered that she was due back at work again today, she groaned, sinking her head back under the warm covers and trying to figure out an excuse not to go in, but she couldn't come up with anything.

Sometime later, Beatrice came in to gently shake her awake. "Amy? Randy is here. He needs us to go with him to the farmhouse so he can search the property. You need to get out of bed and get dressed."

Amy yawned and stretched. "I have to work today—I think."

"Don't worry about work. I'll call in your excuse while you get dressed. The police have more important things to discuss, and they can't wait until you finish working your shift. I'll make you a sandwich, and you will eat it in the car on our way out of town."

As she left the room, Amy sighed and looked around for her alarm clock. It was almost eleven. Apparently, she'd fallen back to sleep after it had gone off the first time. She pushed the covers off, got dressed, and then looked in the mirror in the bathroom. Judging by the state of her hair, which was standing up all over the place, she decided that she would have to wet her head down if she wanted to get a comb through it.

Twenty minutes later, with her wet hair pulled into a ponytail with a scrunchie, she walked into the kitchen. The adults, who had been talking, all stopped and turned to look at her. "Hi," she said, standing awkwardly in the doorway. "So, what is it you need me to do today?"

"This is Officer Tate Barnes," Randy said, pointing to the uniformed police officer sitting to his right at the table. "We want your permission to search the farmhouse for any evidence in regards to your aunt Jeannie's death and the man we found on the property."

"Why do you need my permission?" she asked, but then it dawned on her that by presenting proof that Uncle John was dead, she had become the sole heir, with his part of the inheritance now falling to her.

Randy and Tate exchanged glances. "Well," Randy hedged, "We could get a warrant, but that will take more time than we have. We want to investigate this as soon as possible."

"No, no. That's okay. You can go ahead." Amy was still confused about what else they needed her to do. "I just don't know why you need me there. I've never been to a crime scene before, and I'm not sure how I would handle it, especially because—well, you know." Not only had it been her aunt who had died, but it had happened at her childhood home.

Randy nodded, understanding. "We just need you to point out anything that stands out to you as being different around the property and anything else that might be missing. It would help our investigation tremendously. I don't think you'll have to see anything particularly upsetting or gruesome."

Beatrice handed Amy an egg salad sandwich wrapped in wax paper as they headed out the door. George was standing beside his vehicle, talking to two men in suits with police badges hanging around their necks from thin chains. Amy noticed a police cruiser and an unmarked police car parked in front of the house. George opened the doors of his vehicle for Beatrice and Amy as they waited for the men to get in their cars so they could follow them out of town. While they waited, Amy unwrapped her sandwich, practically inhaling it before they backed out of the driveway. Then Beatrice handed Amy three chocolate chip cookies wrapped in a napkin. Amy appreciated that she was always trying to feed her something.

"Thank you," she said to Beatrice around a mouthful of warm, chewy cookies, realizing that she must have just baked them fresh this morning.

Amy wasn't sure what she would see at the farmhouse, but nothing seemed out of the ordinary when she got out of the vehicle. The officers and detectives stood just outside the farmhouse door, and she realized that everyone was waiting for her to unlock it. Out of habit, Amy reached for the blue string she always wore around her neck with her key, but she wasn't wearing it. She hadn't needed it since moving into the Petersen home.

"Oh, I'm sorry. Here you go," Beatrice said, realizing what Amy was looking for. She pulled the blue string out of her purse, and Amy's keys dangled from the end of it. The keys rattled together as she handed them to Randy so that he could unlock the door.

Randy let the detectives and Officer Tate into the farmhouse but stepped in front of the door to block Amy and the Petersens from entering. "Just give the officers a moment to clear the house before you go inside. Then, I want you to have a look around and point out anything that's out of place or doesn't belong. Whatever you do, though, don't touch anything. We might be able to get more fingerprints."

"I was just here last week, so I don't think it'll take long to see what's different." Amy tried to look around Randy into the kitchen, but he was much taller than her and blocked most of the doorway.

After several minutes, Randy got the go-ahead to allow Amy to look around the farmhouse. She started pointing to everything in the kitchen that hadn't been there before. "Those are all wrong: the wallet on the counter, the suit jacket and tie on the table and the torn-out yellow page over by the telephone. They weren't here before." Frowning, she cautiously approached the kitchen table and picked up a single rusty key. "This is the spare key for the shop. It's supposed to be somewhere else. Like, hung on a tree beside the building."

"Please, don't touch things," Randy reminded her. "But we will need that. The shop doors were open when police officers arrived on the property, but someone else had locked them back up before we left. We'll look around over there after we finish in the house."

Amy wasn't sure what to do with the shop key now that she'd already touched it, but she put it into her pocket since Randy had said they'd need it to open the shop. Over the next little while, they slowly went from room to room. Amy found men's clothing and some partially eaten food from the pantry. The only thing that interested the detectives was the wallet's contents, scraps of newspaper articles, and her grandma's telephone, which was already being smudged with black powder to check for prints.

Once everything of interest in the house had been bagged and tagged, they all went over to the shop. Amy pulled the key out of her pocket and unlocked the door, then stepped back, letting Officer Tate and one of the detectives go in ahead of her.

"Where is the key usually kept?" Randy asked, blocking her from entering the shop.

"It hangs on a nail on a tree just over there," Amy pointed towards where the tree stood. "You can follow the little path to it. My grandma said that my grandfather had liked it that way, so she never changed it."

Randy frowned a bit. "Not very secure." Glancing over his shoulder, he indicated that it was safe for her to enter the shop.

Amy shrugged, not knowing what to say about the security. There were times they didn't even bother locking the shop. "I don't remember the last time I was in this building, so I don't know if I can be much help to you." She stepped into the three-bay shop and started looking around. Nothing of importance stood out to her. All she saw were her grandpa's tools and various building supplies stacked against the walls. Then she looked over to the far end of the shop and saw that the car cover on her grandma's vehicle had been rolled up from the back end, exposing the light, metallic blue colour of the rear panel.

Before Amy could say anything, George spoke up. "Someone has lifted the cover on Dorothy's car. I put it away and covered it over properly after she died in the spring. She'd just bought it the year before. A 1984 Oldsmobile Ninety-eight—a real beauty."

Amy walked towards it. There was a streak of brown across the back bumper. "What's this?" she asked.

Randy cleared his throat a bit awkwardly. "Dried blood. That's what it looks like. A man was found here in the shop. He'd been badly beaten and was unconscious." He squatted down to look closer at the bumper and the floor in the surrounding area. "What other vehicle was parked in here?"

Amy followed his gaze and saw tread marks made from some other vehicle that someone would have parked beside her grandma's car. "There wasn't one. Or, shouldn't have been. My grandma only ever had one car. Maybe it belonged to whoever beat that guy up and killed my aunt?" Frowning, she noticed a small round object on the floor and nudged it with her toe. "What's this?"

Randy Doyle crouched down by the back tire and used his pen to drag the object closer so he could look at it. "I don't suppose your grandma played poker?"

"No," Amy said, shaking her head and laughing a little. "I'd say that probably came from either the beat-up guy or the guy that beat him."

"You're probably right. What does it say on it?" Officer Barnes asked.

Randy slid the poker chip into a clear evidence bag and held it up so he could read it. "Niagara Falls Casino and Bar. We'll have to check into that."

"Uncle John went to Ontario after he left my aunt Jeannie. Or after he divorced her, I guess. And the private investigator, Alister Morgan, said that Uncle John had gone to rehab there for drug addiction." She sighed a bit sadly. "Of course, we now know that he died of a drug overdose, so it must not have worked. Anyway, I guess that means it must have belonged to either the guy who the police found or his attacker."

"Yes, I would agree." The detective took the evidence bag from Randy, holding it up so he could get a good look at it, too. Then he looked at Amy. "You'll make a good detective one day. You have a good eye for details."

Regardless, Amy didn't see much else in the shop, although she did point out that the garden shovel in the corner should have been in the barn with the other garden tools. The officers told them that they didn't need to go into any other buildings on the property since they'd already processed the area surrounding the barn, where someone had found her aunt Jeannie dead.

Officer Barnes told her that the police hadn't discovered Jeannie's body until later in the day. Instead, they had come out to the farmhouse property in response to a real estate agent's call for an ambulance after finding an unconscious man in the shop. The police searched the property for an assailant but only found a dead body.

Amy could feel a sinking feeling in her stomach. She didn't want to think about Jeannie possibly dying slowly and alone while the unknown man was being examined and taken to the hospital. She was relieved that she didn't have to go into the barn.

She looked back at the shop. "I don't understand. How was the unconscious man discovered but not my aunt?"

The detective answered. "The overhead door on the last bay was left open. A family who had come to view the property found him as they were looking around. When the ambulance arrived and medical personnel took him to the hospital, the driver radioed the police about the possibility of foul play, based on the nature of the injuries. It wasn't until officers rushed out to search the outbuildings on the property that they found Jeannie's body in the barn. Someone left the barn door open."

Amy looked over her shoulder at the farmhouse. The feeling of nostalgia was still there, but now it held a lot of sadness for her, too. It was at this moment that she realized that she could never return to her childhood home. It had only been a few months, but everything had changed so much that it would never be the same. Wiping a tear away from the corner of her eye, she expelled a deep breath.

She must have known what Amy was thinking because she stepped closer and said, "You can't change the past. You have to keep moving toward your future by making good decisions today that will change tomorrow. You don't have to have your whole life planned out." Beatrice put her arms around her then, wrapping her in warmth.

"I can't live here again! If the farmhouse does belong to me, I'll have to sell it."

Beatrice released Amy from her hug so that she could look her in the eyes. "Alright. Well. George and I can help you pack things up when you're ready, but I would recommend renting it out for a while first rather than rushing into that decision while everything is still so fresh. The rental income would cover any upkeep expenses on the place and things like property taxes and still leave you with some pocket money. Actually, we could do the same thing with the little blue house you lived in with your aunt. But none of that needs to be decided today." She gave Amy another small, reassuring squeeze.

Amy nodded. It was something she would think about, but not today. *Maybe I'll just focus on trying to open the puzzle box.* With everything happening around her lately, she was starting to feel increasingly anxious to find out whatever secret her grandmother had hidden inside it.

Chapter 26

Bobby pried his heavy eyes open when a voice nearby started talking. "Is this the man you know as Bobby Wilham?"

"Yes." Pastor Bill nodded, pulling up a chair beside the bed. "He's beaten up, but I still recognize him as the man I know as Bobby."

The officer raised his eyebrows in surprise as the pastor sat down. "Are you staying for a visit? I don't think he's the kind of guy who'd want to hear a sermon."

"This man needs a friend," he said, staring the officer down. "I'm here to listen and keep him company."

The officer shrugged. "It's your time you'll be wasting. I'll be right outside." With that, he took his leave.

Bobby looked at the pastor. "Thanks for coming."

"I know you don't like to talk much, so if you want to sit in silence, I'm fine with that, but I'm a good listener. It takes a lot of practice, but I try my best." He patted Bobby's hand, easing back in his chair to get comfortable. It looked like he would be there for the long haul.

Bobby had so many questions, but he wasn't even sure where to begin. While he struggled with what he wanted to say, Pastor Bill patiently sat in the chair beside his hospital bed. Finally, Bobby blurted out, "Why did you come?"

"The police told me they wanted me to confirm that you'd told me your name was Bobby," he said matter-of-factly.

"But ... But you're still here." He was shocked that anyone would stand beside him, especially someone who'd seen him sleeping in the park with one heck of a hangover. That should have made it evident to anyone that Bobby was of little worth or value. "Why would you stay here for me?" He was shocked to feel his eyes starting to water, feeling completely unworthy.

"To be your friend."

Bobby's throat constricted, and his vocal cords tensed, his voice periodically breaking as he spoke. "Look, Pastor, I'm not a very good person, okay? I gamble and drink. I steal to survive. The people to whom I owe a huge amount of money are threatening my life. It's dangerous for me to stay in one place for too long." Tears started running from the corner of his eyes and onto his pillow.

Pastor Bill sighed. "I'm not offended by who you are or what you may have done. And I'm not scared to call you, my friend. It doesn't take a rocket scientist to see that you're not in a good place." He leaned forward, resting his elbows on his knees. "We've all hit low points in our lives, Bobby. Consider this your rock bottom. But you can climb out of this dark place if you stop lying to yourself and others. You can't change your past, but you can change your future if you are willing to make better choices. Start your new life today."

"What makes you think I'm lying?" Bobby countered defensively, almost out of habit.

"I think we both know you're lying. The question is whether or not you want to change your life and start over because the only way to do that is to accept both the truth of your actions and their consequences. I think you're ready to do that." He paused and looked closely at him then, with an oddly gentle, almost forgiving expression. "But the only one who can decide if I'm right ... is you."

He didn't have an answer for Pastor Bill and was already lost in his thoughts before he realized the man had stood up. "I'll come by to see you again. Please, just think about what I said." He turned then and quietly left the room.

The pastor's words kept echoing in Bobby's head. It would be great to feel free to start his life over again. He had always planned to get whatever he could for himself out of life, with the fewest possible consequences—especially now, but he was starting to wonder if maybe that was the wrong way to look at his options.

As he started drifting off to sleep, listening to the heart monitor's rhythmic beeping, he realized that he didn't even know what his options were at this point. Maybe he needed a good lawyer, but where would he find one in Glenmere? Right before sleep took him, he decided that he would ask for a lawyer the next time someone came into his room.

Bobby opened his eyes. The swelling on his face felt like it was getting slightly better. He could see a lot better out of his left eye now and open his right eye slightly. He was surprised that he wasn't feeling any actual discomfort. Then again, maybe he was being fed painkillers through his intravenous.

He didn't know, but either way, he felt good. The only thing that didn't feel good was his conscience. Pastor Bill's words about him needing to accept the consequences of his actions before he could start his life over again scared Bobby more than anything he had ever faced.

The hospital room door opened, and Officer Gerard and a young officer entered the room. Officer Gerard nodded, looking at him. "Well, Bobby, you're under arrest for attempted fraud, theft under a thousand dollars, and the first-degree murder of Jeannie Young. Officer Randy will read you your rights." He turned to his young partner then and motioned for him to begin.

Bobby wasn't listening to the words spewing out of the kid's mouth. Instead, he tried to wrap his head around the accusation that he was responsible for Jeannie's murder. Bobby hadn't killed her! Or at least, he was pretty sure he hadn't. He started to replay the scene from the barn in his head. He remembered she had wanted to cut a deal to get in on the action, but he'd told her he wouldn't share it with her. He couldn't. *And then she wouldn't shut up!* She was mocking him and making threats. He remembered jumping at her ... punching her in the face ... three times for sure with his right hand, as she'd kicked and scratched back at him, raking his face and chest with her nails. Then he'd—

"Hello? Do you understand these rights as I have read them?" Officer Doyle said for the second time, interrupting Bobby's train of thought, but he didn't answer, too busy trying to work things out in his mind.

He remembered a glancing blow with his left hitting Jeannie in the shoulder before sliding into the barn's dirt floor. He remembered seeing her eyes widen in surprise at something she saw over his right shoulder, and something had struck him from behind. Then what happened? Think! Bobby screamed at himself inside his head.

"Sir?"

"Wait … Jeannie's dead? And you think I killed her?" Bobby was genuinely confused, and it showed. He kept playing the scene over and over in his mind again until he finally remembered waking up in the shop with two ambulance attendants standing over him. "Oh, my God! I-I didn't kill anyone! There were other guys! B-Big guys sent by the Big Boss! They beat me up!" Bobby pleaded desperately. He had done a lot of terrible things in his life, but he'd never killed anyone, and he would never have killed Jeannie. The officers exchanged questioning glances, but no one spoke.

After a moment's thought, Officer Gerard leaned in closer. His brows furrowed as he pulled out his notepad and pencil. "Which guys? Do you have names? Descriptions?" He flipped the notepad open, holding the pencil poised over the page.

Bobby shook his head, laughing humourlessly. "Look, enough is enough. I'll tell you everything I know. All of it! Because there's no way in hell you're pinning a murder on me. I didn't do it." Taking as deep a breath as he could manage, he let it out slow, trying to gather his thoughts before continuing. "I just need to talk to a lawyer first. I'd really appreciate it if you'd please send me one. I'm kind of tied up at the moment." Bobby splayed out his fingers as he tugged on his wrist restraints.

Officer Gerard closed his notebook gently, putting it back into his shirt pocket and tucking the pencil beside it. Then he looked Bobby in the eyes. "I'll work on getting you a lawyer, and then we'll talk again. Meanwhile, you are in our custody, in this room, until the doctor releases you to one of our holding cells."

The officers left the room without another word.

Chapter 27

"Goodbye! See you Saturday," Amy's boss called behind her as she left the Family Grocers after finishing her shift.

She stopped midway through the open front doors. "Oh, I almost forgot! I left the till deposit on your desk!"

"I got it! Thanks!"

Amy waved over her shoulder as the doors closed behind her. She walked over to the bike rack, unlocked the chain to free her bike, and headed out. It had felt good to ride it into work again. She never realized that she would miss the feel of the wind through her hair as she whipped down the streets. George had said he could drive Amy to work, but while the weather was nice, she'd decided to use her bike to stay healthy and maintain her independence, only asking for rides when the weather was terrible.

As she rolled up into the Petersens' driveway, she noticed quite a few black garbage bags stacked beside the front steps of the house next door. That seemed weird. She dropped her bike on the Petersens' front lawn without putting it in the garage and rushed over to the little house where she used to live with her aunt Jeannie. As she approached the first step, Beatrice emerged with two more black garbage bags.

"W-what's going on?" Amy asked, holding her hands out towards the bags.

Beatrice brushed off the front of her white apron and then used the bottom corner of it to wipe her hands. "While you were at work, I called a few friends over to clean up your little house and get it ready for renting. Don't worry. We're just discarding the trash. We will donate Jeannie's clothes and clean everything to prepare for the renters. Edward Greene, the realtor, will come over tonight to help us list it." She turned and went back inside, then called out instructions about rearranging the furniture to someone inside.

Amy lingered outside for about a minute before her curiosity got the better of her, and then she walked through the open door to look around. Denise Schneider had her back to her in the kitchen, washing dishes at the sink. She was wearing a brightly multi-coloured flowered apron with lots of ruffles over a yellow and brown bumblebee pattern. Amy smiled at her confidence in wearing such bold patterns.

Lena Merasty, the librarian, was quietly putting canned food items into boxes while Denise talked non-stop about someone she knew who rented houses. Amy wondered if Lena had many opportunities to add to the one-sided conversation. Lena raised her eyebrows at Amy, giving her a bit of a wave when she noticed her standing there. She pointed in the direction where Beatrice was, so Amy turned and walked down the hallway.

No one was in her old room. Amy and the Petersens had already moved her things to the house next door. By the looks of things, someone had freshly vacuumed its green shag carpet. Across the hall, a grey-haired lady Amy had seen a few times at the grocery store was scrubbing the bathroom sink. Amy could hear Beatrice talking to someone at the end of the hallway, so she followed her voice to her aunt Jeannie's old bedroom to find out what was happening in there.

The bedroom looked a lot different than what Amy remembered. The closet doors were open, and someone had removed all the clothes. The mattress was bare, and there didn't seem to be any blankets strewn anywhere. Beatrice and a lady Amy didn't know were standing near the dresser, discussing the items inside one of the open drawers.

"I can get a box for the papers, jewelry, and money. I'm sure Jeannie's family will want to claim them," Beatrice said to the woman.

"Has anyone contacted Aunt Jeannie's family?" Amy asked, interrupting before wondering if she should.

The ladies turned towards her, and Beatrice nodded. "Yes, but they won't be coming to town until the day of her funeral. Did you want to change out of your uniform and come give us a hand?"

"Sure. I can help," Amy said as she wandered over to peek in the drawer. "I didn't think my aunt had any jewelry worth saving except her gold locket." When she looked down into it, her eyes widened at the sparkling collection of jewelry at the bottom, scattered among assorted papers.

She gasped, "Oh! I don't believe it!" She reached into the drawer, pulling out her grandmother's anniversary ring. "This is my grandma's! She would never give Jeannie her anniversary ring! That doesn't even make sense!" The ladies leaned in while Amy pointed to each coloured stone on its band. "The two in the middle are my grandparent's birthstones; this is my uncle John's, and this one is my mom's!" She rubbed her finger over each stone, remembering the last time Amy had seen her grandma with it. It was at the farmhouse on the same day she died. Before she'd started making cookies, she'd taken it off with her wedding ring, placing them in the dish on the window ledge above the kitchen sink so she could wash dishes.

"Okay," Beatrice said, interrupting Amy's thoughts. "Perhaps we need to check with the police about the jewelry. We'll need to ensure these items actually belonged to Jeannie before we deliver them to her family. Also, Amy, since that ring belonged to your grandma Dorothy, I think it would be appropriate for you to reclaim it as part of your inheritance. It's yours."

Amy held her breath and nodded as she slipped it onto her finger, horribly missing her grandmother. Once she'd gathered herself a bit, she moved a few things around in the drawer, just to make sure that she didn't recognize anything else.

Finally, Beatrice asked, "Anything else look familiar?"

"Nope! I'm good. I just had to be sure." Amy withdrew her hands from the drawer and looked fondly at her grandma's ring on her finger. "I'll just go change and then give you a hand with whatever you want to do next."

When Amy returned a few minutes later to the little house, in her regular clothes, she saw that the women were still looking at more jewelry from her aunt Jeannie's dresser drawers. Denise extended her right arm, holding up a long gold necklace for everyone to see its sparkling, red-jeweled, star-shaped pendant.

"The one my daughter bought at Sherri Martin's jewelry party last month is just like this one except in blue," she said, then picked up another piece. "And this lovely brooch is the same one that I bought. It was a fun girls' night out. And it's so nice to go to a different kind of home party for a change. I already have enough food-storage containers to last me a lifetime."

Beatrice held out the box and allowed everyone to place the costume jewelry back into it. "Once it all checks out, I'll give the jewelry to her family when they come. I'm glad we could sort that out."

Amy looked down at her grandma's family ring on her finger. Looking up again, she noticed Beatrice watching her momentarily before approaching. "I'm sorry, Amy," she whispered, "but I'm sure she took it when she brought you back from the farmhouse last week." With that said, she moved past her and left the room with the box.

Amy only shrugged. She couldn't remember if she had put the ring on the list of missing items she'd given to the police or not, which was frustrating, as knowing if it was would give her a better idea if the ring had already been missing before Jeannie had appeared there. Amy shook her head and then gasped silently, remembering that she had put all her grandma's jewelry in a bag before her aunt Jeannie arrived at the farmhouse that day. She wondered then how many other trips Jeannie had made to the farmhouse pantry in the last few months and what else her aunt had taken.

Deciding to focus on something else, she plugged in the vacuum cleaner to start on the carpets that still needed doing. She figured it was best just to leave Beatrice and her friends to finish clearing out unnecessary items since she had no interest in any of her aunt's things or the furniture.

Actually, Beatrice had suggested that the better-shaped furniture could stay in the house for the renters to use, and Amy thought she'd just follow her lead since she seemed to know what was best.

Chapter 28

August 23, 1985

Friday

After Bobby had pulled on the grey sweatshirt and matching pants, he pushed his feet into the shoes, noting they had no laces. Then he stood up to place both hands on his head, his feet slightly apart as instructed, facing the wall with the officers behind him. One of the officers bent down to shackle his feet while another secured a chain around his waist and locked it with a padlock behind his back. Then, a young officer took Bobby's hands one at a time and retrained his wrists in the handcuffs attached to the waist chain. The officer, bending near his ankles, reached for the chain hanging from the waist and secured it between the ankle restraints with another padlock.

Then, Officer Gerard waltzed into the room, straightening himself to his full height. "We're ready for transport," he informed the other three officers in the room. "Is there anything you would like to confess before we bring you over to lock up?"

Bobby took as deep a breath as he could without wincing in pain from his fractured ribs and then let it out slowly. It worked to calm his heart rate down a little. "Not without my lawyer present. You haven't contacted a lawyer for me yet, have you?"

Officer Gerard adjusted his utility belt. "I did. Your lawyer will arrive at the station to consult with you once we get you processed. He's probably reviewing your charges as we speak. Bert Illingsworth is a defence lawyer from Saskatoon, where you'll have your court hearing. Sound familiar?" After waiting a short time for a response but receiving none, Gerard looked at the other officers, indicating it was time to complete the transfer. "Just so you know, before the day is over, we will be adding obstruction of justice to your list of charges and probably a few more things as well." He turned then, leading them out of the room.

It had been a while since armed officers had transported Bobby in shackles and chains. Still, he quickly remembered to take small, shuffling steps to avoid tripping over the chains and keep the shackles from digging into his ankles. As he turned into the hall, the chains jingled and dragged across the polished linoleum floor, loudly announcing the movement of their entourage to anyone in the area. The officer standing guard outside the hospital room took a position in the rear as the group passed him.

All eyes turned towards Bobby as the group of six rounded the nurses' station. Bobby shrugged off some of the cold stares. As far as he knew, they didn't know his story, let alone what he'd had to do to survive daily. Indeed, this would keep the town gossip wheel churning for a while as they speculated about all his dastardly deeds. Bobby smiled mockingly and winked at one of the nurses. *These people in this stupid little town are clueless! They have no idea what it's like to have to fight to survive.*

Chapter 29

Amy walked into the kitchen to take a cookie or two out of the seemingly bottomless cookie jar, but Randy stood in front of the sweet treats, leaning against the counter. Amy almost didn't recognize him without his uniform. He was wearing blue jeans and a T-shirt. She wasn't sure if she should address him as Officer Doyle or just Randy, so she decided to say nothing. He had a partially eaten cookie in one hand and a cup of coffee in the other. Amy reached behind him to drag the cookie jar out and get herself one of the delicious treats.

He raised an eyebrow, taking another sip of his hot coffee. "They're just downstairs, looking for some boxes in the storage room."

Admittedly, Amy wasn't sure who "they" were, but she could hear two female voices coming up the stairs from the basement. One voice belonged to Beatrice, but she didn't recognize the other. She slid into a chair at the table to nibble her cookie.

A moment later, Beatrice emerged from the basement with a large cardboard box, which she set on the floor in the middle of the kitchen. "You can carry this out once you finish your coffee, Randy." She dusted off her hands on her apron, walking over to the coffee pot to pour herself a cup, just as a younger woman emerged from the basement. "What do you want to drink?"

"Nothing," the other woman said, sitting at the table. "Hi. We haven't met yet. I'm Samantha—the youngest of the Petersen clan. Randy's my husband." She had the same blue eyes and brown hair as her mother.

"Nice to meet you," Amy said once she managed to swallow her mouthful of cookie. "I've met your husband a few times this week, but never when he wasn't in uniform—" Her voice trailed off, leaving the reasons she'd met him in his professional capacity to hang unspoken between them.

"Is my mom feeding you enough?" Samantha asked, laughing knowingly.

Amy smiled and nodded, trying to be polite. "I have been very well-fed since I got here. And the cookies are amazing!"

Beatrice brought up the story of finding Amy's grandmother's ring in her aunt's drawer, and the mother and daughter talked about it while Amy just listened. After several minutes, she excused herself from the kitchen to return to her room to work on the puzzle box. The pieces were starting to move, but it was painfully slow, with each piece only moving a tiny fraction, and only if she worked it in a particular order. It sometimes took her a while to remember which piece needed to move next in the sequence. At this rate, she felt like it would take forever to open it. George's suggestion to break the box open started sounding more tempting.

Frustrated, she blew her bangs out of her eyes with a huff, setting the puzzle box back onto the dresser.

Beatrice called from the kitchen, "Amy, can you come here for a minute, please?"

When she entered the kitchen, Officer Gerard stood there in uniform and addressed her immediately. "I would like you to carefully look at these photos and tell me if anyone looks vaguely familiar." He opened a portfolio to show Amy six photos of six different men, each standing before a height chart. There were no names or other identifying information.

Amy looked closely at each photo, recognizing two of them before she started to speak. "This guy with the moustache has been in the Family Grocers. Talking to Dan." She pointed to the last photo. "And this guy with slicked-back hair was hanging out across the street from the grocery store, near the pawnshop—That was a different day. I don't remember seeing any of the others, though. My friend Sarah said she thought some creep was following us one day when we met up at the post office. Maybe you should ask her to look at these photos?"

Officer Gerard nodded and then flipped to another page. "What about these men? Was one of them the creep that was following you and Sarah?"

Amy leaned in to take a good look at each photo. The men in this grouping seemed to fit the thick-neck, square-jaw stereotype of a hardened criminal. She shook her head, "No. I don't recognize anyone. Though Sarah might." The hair on the back of her neck stood up a bit as shivers started to crawl down her spine, and her stomach seemed to do a belly flop. "Those photos creep me out. Were those men involved in the break-ins? Was one of them after me?" Her eyes widened a bit further as each question exploded from her lips. "Did he kill my aunt Jeannie? Was one of them the imposter? Am I in danger?"

Officer Gerard quickly shut the portfolio, tucking it under his arm. Then he looked at her directly before answering slowly and clearly. "We do not believe that you are in any danger. We have already apprehended the man believed to have killed your aunt. We are just trying to piece together the puzzle of the recent crimes in town. It's possible; we are still looking for the one piece to bring it all together. We're simply gathering and sorting through what we do know right now." He looked over Amy's head at Randy then. "Did you say George was next door fixing a sink?"

"Yes," Randy answered.

"Alright. I'll see you tonight at shift change," Officer Gerard said, letting himself out and heading next door to search for George.

Amy stood rooted in place, trying to figure out if she had seen the guy with the moustache anywhere else or any of the men from the second grouping of photos until she became aware that Beatrice was speaking to her.

"—get some fresh air and ride your bike to clear your head."

"What?" She concentrated momentarily, trying to piece together what she'd been saying. "Oh. A bike ride? That sounds great. Yes, I think I'll do that." With a nod, she reached for her windbreaker on the hook by the door, pulling it over her head as she left the house. She got her bike out of the garage and walked it out to the street, looking at Officer Gerard's police vehicle, which she found still parked in front. Finally, wondering what it would be like to be a police officer, she hopped on her bike and started pedaling.

Not having any real destination, Amy rode aimlessly around town. She caught a whiff of the food at Frankie's as she crossed Main Street near the post office. Eventually, she rode past the library and the lawyer's office before switching directions to zigzag her way home. It felt good to have the wind on her face and the sun on her back. She even smiled, waving at a few people out tending to their flowers and mowing their lawns as she passed near their houses.

As she rounded the corner on Fifth Street and started pedaling down it, she noticed a little elderly woman with curlers in her hair and wearing a housecoat over a pink nightgown, trying to peek into the windows of someone's house. As she rode past, she couldn't help but keep looking back at her. It was just odd. Finally, it occurred to her that the woman might have locked herself out of the house and needed to get back inside. Rounding the corner to turn up the back alley running behind the houses on that street, she passed an open garage door and slowed down, spotting the same woman again. The woman had gone around to the backyard to try her luck with the back door. That door must be locked as well, though, because she started peeking into the windows again.

"Are you locked out?" Amy called out to her.

The older woman jumped a little at the sudden sound of Amy's voice before answering. "No, I live next door. My neighbours are away until Sunday. They just called me to check on the place, but I don't have a key."

"The garage door is open to the alley back here," Amy said, pointing to the building.

The small woman made her way to the back alley. "That's strange. I didn't notice this being open before." She peered into the empty garage but had no way to know if anything might be missing.

"There have been a lot of break-ins lately," Amy offered. "My aunt's house and my grandma's farmhouse both got broken into. I had to report a few missing things to the police."

"Darren, my new neighbour, phoned me to check in on the place. I mentioned seeing his nephew several times, but he didn't know who I was talking about. He said he'd never made arrangements with anyone and asked if I could check on things."

Amy gasped, thinking about the police photos. "It wouldn't have been a small guy with a moustache, was it? Black hair?"

The woman's eyes widened. "Yes! He had a black moustache. He also wore a hat!"

"You need to call the police. Ask for Officer Gerard. He's already gathering evidence on that man. He can show you a photo of him too! I think he's dangerous. If you report it, maybe you can help the police lock him up for a long time!" Amy rambled on a bit longer about how he'd been seen around town and might have even followed her and her friend Sarah.

As the elderly lady touched the curlers on her head and adjusted the buttons of her flowered house coat, she finally got a word in. "I better make myself presentable if I'm going to talk to the police officer in person! Thanks for stopping by!" She waved, then disappeared back around the garage and headed home.

Amy turned her bike around to rush straight back to the Petersen house. If she was lucky, Officer Gerard or Doyle would still be there so Amy could direct them to the right street.

Chapter 30

Sighing, Bobby rubbed his eyes. The chain that attached him to the interrogation table jingled with his movements. Over the last few hours, he had repeated his story several times to his appointed lawyer, laying out the whole thing, complete with the troubles and scams that had led him to his current situation. Bert Illingsworth just kept scribbling down notes and repeatedly asking questions to try and get more details.

Bobby flicked the empty Styrofoam cup across the table and onto the floor. "Yes. That's right," he said, staring across the table at the man.

He'd been expecting to find a snot-nosed kid representing him. That was usually all you could get for free representation. So, he'd been shocked to meet the brown-suit-wearing, middle-aged lawyer with his loud tie. This guy seemed at least somewhat experienced, or so Bobby had fathomed from the man's smug grin and matter-of-fact attitude, which he almost appreciated.

For the first time in his life, Bobby amazingly told a court-appointed lawyer everything he knew and everything he had done to land him in police custody, as well as why he'd done it. He hoped that by exchanging information on the Big Boss and his men, he could make some ironclad deal to help himself. His lawyer looked like he had enough experience to handle the particulars.

Still, the repetition was tedious and tiring him out. He sighed. "Yes, I stole a car and a few items from that house. I also used John's name to try and steal his inheritance. It was when I was at the farmhouse that Jeannie Young showed up, threatening to expose me if I didn't give her a cut in the estate, crying about not getting anything in their divorce."

"And to be clear," the lawyer said. "You were arguing with Jeannie when someone who you cannot identify struck you from behind with something hard?"

"Yes, we were arguing. Like I said, Jeannie suddenly looked over my shoulder at something, and then I was knocked out cold. I didn't become aware of anything else until I woke up in the hospital in bad shape." Bobby tried to shift on his chair to a more comfortable position, wishing he could pace back and forth around the room if only to stretch his legs.

"And did you at any time strike Jeannie during this argument?"

Bobby scratched the stubble on his chin, taking a deep pull from his cigarette. "Yes. Like I've already told you, I did. I lost my temper and punched her a few times because she kept threatening me and wouldn't shut up!" He blew smoke upwards to the ceiling.

Bert stared back at him, holding the end of his pencil in the corner of his mouth as though he were smoking, too. After briefly pausing, he said, "I can get you out on bail at your hearing. So, you won't have to wait for trial in a holding cell." He took the pencil out of his mouth again, pointing it at Bobby. "But it could be a few months before they get to your case. Would you rather spend that time on the outside or in a cell?"

Bobby clasped his hands together and leaned on the edge of the table, "I don't have bail money, and no one else is going to bail me out. More importantly, I don't have anywhere to live!" He shook his head and sighed again. "At least inside, I'll get a private room and three meals a day—at least until I get taken out by one of the Big Boss's thugs."

"Well then, I'll see what I can do. In terms of the hearing in a few days, it doesn't matter if you're there or not. I can do what needs to be done in court either way. You'll continue to be held in custody only if the Crown can convince the judge to deny bail and keep you there. If I get released on bail pending trial, assuming someone will pay it, then I can make arrangements for you to stay in some dumpy little apartment in the city—unless you'd prefer the homeless shelter."

The lawyer grinned then and shrugged. "I think I can make arrangements with a businessman I know who'd be willing to help provide you with bail money. Maybe even give you a little job while you're out so you can afford to eat." He smoothed down his slicked-back hair before gathering all his notes and what was left of his chewed-up pencil, pushing them away from the table, and walking over to the door. He knocked on it and then looked back at him. "Your bail hearing will be in a few days. I'll get everything prepared."

A guard opened the metal door and waited. Bert Illingsworth exited with a confident swagger.

Bobby shook his head in disbelief at the man's confidence in leading the case and planning to get him out on bail. He didn't feel like he would survive life in the Saskatoon prison. The Big Boss was indeed out to have his debt repaid one way or another, even if that meant sending someone inside to kill him.

With his real-estate scam foiled, Bobby had no more options left and no way to repay the Big Boss, let alone within the month. He was quite comfortable with his new living conditions in the tiny Glenmere jailhouse and relatively confident that none of the Big Boss's minions would be in there with him, and wouldn't be before his bail hearing. But would Bobby be safe out on the street? *And who is this businessman he was talking about anyway? And why would he want to help out a suspected murderer?* The scarier thought, of course, was what he would demand in return.

The metal door opened with a clang, breaking Bobby from his reverie. He pushed his thoughts to the back of his mind, clearing his head, as four guards walked into the room to escort him back to his holding cell. They unlocked the cuffs to release him from the table and put on smaller ones that fastened his hands closer together. Then, guards pulled him to his feet and led him out into the hall, passing by two more guards who followed behind, marching in close step with him until he was deposited into his cell.

Chapter 31

August 26, 1985

Monday

B obby sat in the holding cell in the basement of the Saskatoon courthouse, oddly relaxed, considering it was the day of his bail hearing. He waited patiently for his lawyer, Bert Illingsworth, to show up and wondered why the man seemed to want him here for the preliminaries. It didn't make too much sense to him, though he honestly doubted the judge would grant him bail in any case.

He allowed his thoughts to wander back to his senior year in high school and smiled slightly, remembering how much he'd enjoyed hanging out, drinking, and chasing girls. He could still remember the first time little Sandy Young had come to a party at the gravel pit with her brother, John. She'd been so cute, trying to pretend she was as mature as the seniors when she was far too young and awkward to be hanging out with her brother and his buddies. Bobby would watch her from across the bonfire and track her movements.

"It looks like they are getting close to your name on the docket for your bail hearing," Bert said, his voice breaking through Bobby's thoughts. He'd just arrived with a garment bag over his right shoulder. "I have a suit for you to put on so that you look like a decent person deserving of release on bail." As he unzipped the bag, revealing a dark brown suit, he grinned like the Cheshire Cat.

Bobby looked down at the prisoner uniform he'd been wearing since leaving the hospital room: grey sweatpants and matching sweatshirt. Although he didn't see what difference a suit would make, he had to admit that he needed a change of clothes. "I can't pay you for the suit," he said, sighing heavily.

"Don't worry about the suit. My services and this suit are both compliments of your employer." Bert paused for effect to make sure Bobby understood who he was talking about. "You look confused. You do know that your employer is paying for your defence, right? He'll also post your bail money, assuming the judge will allow you out on bail."

Bobby rubbed his hands over his face, attempting to clear his mind. *What employer?* He didn't have a job—a chill ran down his neck, and the hair on the backs of his arms stood on end. Alarmed, he stood up and walked towards the bars to get closer to his lawyer. "Who's my employer?" he asked cautiously. He had to know if he was right.

Bert cleared his throat and looked around the hallway before approaching the bars and answering in a hushed whisper. "I can't say his name, but he's the guy you'll be working for until you can repay your debts." He stared purposely at Bobby with his eyebrows raised for emphasis. "You'll be working for him whether you're behind bars or on the outside.

I'll refer to him as Mr. Stefan Bigman in court, but I think you know him better as the Big Boss." With that, he nodded, stepped back from the bars, pulled the suit off its hangers, and held it through the bars for Bobby to take. "I wouldn't recommend turning him down."

Bobby looked at the suit. He didn't have a choice. If Bobby didn't agree to work for the Big Boss, he'd undoubtedly be killed by one of his men before the day ended. He cautiously took the suit. "You can tell him that I understand, and that I'm available for a meeting, at his convenience, to discuss my ... new position."

Bert grinned. "I knew you'd make the right choice. Once you're out on bail, I'll give you the tie to go with the suit. Get changed. We'll face the judge and the crown prosecutor shortly. But listen to me very closely now. Do not even think about skipping bail, or Stefan Bigman will terminate your contract if you get my meaning."

Indeed, Bobby knew what he meant. If he skipped bail and cost the Big Boss even more money, the boss would order on of his other "employees" to kill him. He nodded to Bert. "Since you're getting paid either way, could you do me a favour?"

Bert nodded slowly. "Are you in need of some other legal work? I could see what I could do for you."

"I want you to change my name to Bobby Wilham legally. I no longer want to be associated with my given name in any way," he sighed. "It's complicated, but there's just too much history and pain associated with it."

His lawyer nodded. "No problem. I'll get the necessary paperwork together for you to sign.

Believe it or not, it's quite easy when you don't have any government-issued identification, assets or bank accounts. I'll use my office as your permanent address, just like many of your colleagues already do."

Bobby watched Bert Illingsworth turn and retreat down the corridor before turning his back to the bars to change into the brown suit. The clothing was a nicely made polyester blend. Bobby wondered if the Big Boss would add the cost to his debt or if this was to be his uniform for his new employment position. Whatever the Big Boss wanted from him, Bobby sure hoped it didn't involve killing anyone, but if it did, he knew he would not have a choice.

Chapter 32

Amy stood facing her open closet, wondering what would be appropriate to wear on a day like today. She had no ideas. She'd never attended anything like this. *Does it even matter what I wear? No one will be looking at me,* she thought as she reached into her closet and pulled out a jean skirt. After looking at it momentarily, she shook her head and threw it on the floor behind her with the other discarded outfits she had already dismissed. She thought she needed something more formal. More serious. She pushed most of her clothes to the left of the closet to get them out of the way and pulled out a navy-blue pleated skirt and a wrinkled white blouse that she'd worn to the Halloween dance as a costume last year with Sarah when they'd dressed up as old ladies. She smiled fondly, remembering they'd borrowed Grandma's knitting bag, gloves, and hats to complete their ensembles. It had been a fun night.

She held the outfit against herself and looked in the mirror, thinking back to happier days when Beatrice entered her room. She wore a black dress with large pink flowers, black stockings, and shiny black dress shoes. "That looks nice! I can quickly iron the blouse, and we'll be ready to go." She swooped the blouse out of Amy's hands and disappeared down the hall, leaving Amy in stunned silence.

Amy shook her head to bring herself out of her disbelief and called after Beatrice. "Do you honestly think that's what I should wear? I have other clothes. Maybe something more in style? Like my jean skirt?"

"This is perfectly nice!" Beatrice replied from the other room.

Amy looked down at the clothes she had discarded at her feet, wondering if she should reconsider her fashion choices. Nothing else really jumped out at her, though, except her bare feet. Realizing that she needed shoes, she dropped to her hands and knees and crawled around the bottom of the closet, looking for a pair of dress shoes. All she could find were her white jellybean plastic shoes. They weren't exactly what she had in mind, but they'd work.

Amy started to back out of her closet on her hands and knees when her foot bumped into the puzzle box. She had been working on getting each piece to open only a little more, but it seemed like it would take forever. Amy could only hope that it was worth the time she'd been spending on it. She started spinning it around in her hands again, trying each piece until she could find one to move, and then she repeated the previous steps.

She was still playing around with the puzzle box when Beatrice returned to her room. "Here's your blouse, all ready to go!" she said. "Hurry up and finish getting ready! We don't want to be late!" She handed Amy the white blouse, closing the door as she left the room.

Amy sighed, laying the blouse neatly on the bed beside the skirt so she could change out of the jeans and t-shirt she was currently wearing. After putting them on, Amy turned to look at herself in the mirror and was surprised to see that the outfit wasn't as bad as she'd remembered it. She started to pull her hair up into a ponytail with a scrunchie but then changed her mind, leaving it hanging down instead. Then, she picked up the puzzle box and put it on the dresser so she wouldn't keep tripping over it whenever she entered the bedroom.

"Time to go, Amy!" Beatrice called from the kitchen, where she and George were waiting.

When Amy entered, Beatrice was pulling on a pair of black satin gloves. Mr. Petersen, wearing a dark blue suit with a matching plaid tie, was leaning casually against the kitchen sink while he drank the last of his coffee. He placed the mug in the sink, nodded to Beatrice and Amy, and then left the house with them close behind.

As usual, George held the doors of the black Buick open for the two of them to climb in. The drive was uncharacteristically quiet. Amy's palms were sweating, and her stomach was feeling a bit jittery. Trying not to worry about what a strange and emotional experience this might be, she tried to take a few deep breaths to slow her pounding heart.

George parked the car and then came around to open the doors for them to exit easily. "This is the closest spot to the door," he said apologetically, looking up at the dark clouds rolling overhead. "We'll have to walk half a block. If we're lucky, the storm will either hold off or be over before we finish here."

Amy followed behind George and Beatrice Petersen on the sidewalk, watching them walk arm in arm. The wind seemed to distort their conversation, but Amy heard little snippets: "—I do not want ... should be with family—" When they reached the red brick building with its sombre white columns, they stopped, turning towards Amy, who was blinking back tears and trying to valiantly swallow the lump in her throat.

"It will all work out," George said to her as he reached out to put his hand on Amy's shoulder.

Amy moved, pushing past them to the big glass doors of the main entrance. Inside was quiet with just the murmuring of voices. She didn't bother looking around at anyone because she doubted that there would be anyone that she knew anyway. They entered a large room with rows of chairs on each side divided by a wide aisle. Amy slid into a chair on the left side of the room about halfway up the aisle. People sitting around her were talking in hushed voices with bowed heads. The Petersens quietly sat down on Amy's right. Somewhere behind them, she heard the words "thief" and "murder" being bandied about. George cleared his throat loudly. It looked like they were about to begin.

Chapter 33

B obby was relieved that the guards had come down to his holding cell to prepare him to enter the courtroom. His name must be next on the docket. He put his hands through the opening of the cell so that the guard could once again handcuff his wrists. At least his suit gave him a little more confidence than the prison-issued outfit he'd been wearing before. He smiled, thinking his lawyer might be exceptionally good at what he did. *The suit makes the man, after all,* Bobby mused. Whether or not he could get out on bail wasn't what he was concerned about anyway. What especially bothered him was the unknown terms of his mandatory employment with the Big Boss.

The guards escorted Bobby from a doorway near the front of the courtroom to the defendant's table, where his lawyer, Bert, was waiting. He looked over at the Crown Prosecutor's table. Three lawyers in suits were sitting there, shuffling paperwork in preparation for this bail hearing. "Impressive." Bobby smiled at Bert.

Then the bailiff yelled, "All rise for the Honourable Judge Bennington." There was a loud shuffling of feet and chairs as everyone stood for the white-haired judge to enter the courtroom and make his way over to the bench.

"You may all be seated," Judge Bennington said, picking up his reading glasses from the bench before him to read the paperwork.

A few hushed whispers reached Bobby's ears as he waited for the man to begin. Then, someone in the back of the courtroom yelled out, "Murdering thief!"

With a bang, the judge slammed the gavel down, "Order in my court!" He pointed to whoever had shouted with his gavel. "That's your only warning. Next time, I'll find you in contempt of court, and you'll spend twenty-four hours in a jail cell! And that goes for anyone else in the gallery as well."

Somehow, the sternness of the judge's voice kept the people in the courthouse quiet while the lawyers on both sides of the room did their dance. Bobby sat silent and still, as instructed, listening to them argue about whether or not he should be allowed out on bail.

The lawyer for the prosecution was a red-headed man with a big moustache who puffed up his chest while he argued against his possible release on bail. "Furthermore, he is a known dangerous offender, addicted to drugs and alcohol, which increases the risk he poses to society. Thank you, Your Honour." The man straightened his black tie with a smug smile and sat back down.

"Does the defendant still want to pursue bail?" the judge asked.

Bert stood up to address the court. "Of course we do, Your Honour. My client has indeed had a conviction that involved violence due to alcohol and drug use at the time of that offence. I should remind the court that my client has served his time for it, so the court should not consider it here in today's hearing. Since being released from prison, he has attended Alcoholics Anonymous meetings, willingly trying to better himself. He even has a sober sponsor, who unfortunately cannot be named because of the nature of the organization. My client also recently found work here in Saskatoon with Big City Dry Cleaners on 50th Street. If granted bail, he will not pose any risk to society and will continue to work on bettering himself until his trial. If it pleases the court, we will accept whatever restrictions to the bail release the court should want to impose." Bert sat down again, then added, "Thank you, Your Honour—that concludes our statement."

"Is your client prepared to enter a plea at this time?" Judge Bennington asked him.

Bert stood again. "Yes, your Honour. We will enter a plea of 'not guilty' to all charges." He sat down again as soon as he finished speaking, ignoring the murmurs in the courtroom. Bert put his elbow on the table, resting his chin on his fist.

After a moment's consideration, the judge nodded. "Very well. I am setting the bail at twenty thousand dollars, with the following conditions: He will attend weekly Alcoholics Anonymous meetings, remain employed, and will not leave the city. He will also be required to inform his employer of his pending trial. I expect him to be on his best behaviour." The judge hit his gavel on the desk, calling for the next case.

Bobby turned to his lawyer. "I assume my employer will add the bail cost to my tally?"

His lawyer put his hand on Bobby's shoulder. "You haven't a thing to worry about. It's better to be employed by the boss than to run away from him. I'll get the bail bond paid and call him to find out where the job interview will be." Bert smiled as the bailiff arrived at Bobby's side to escort him out of the courtroom and back to the holding cell.

Chapter 34

Amy struggled to concentrate on the male speaker at the front of the large room. Her eyes were swimming with unshed tears as she tried to figure out what George and Beatrice had been discussing outside on the sidewalk. Were they saying that she should be with her family instead of them? Did they not want her living with them? Although it hurt, she couldn't very well blame them. After all, she was just an orphan that her grandmother had forced the Petersens to take guardianship over.

Once she had enough money, Amy planned to leave and take care of herself. She didn't want to stay anywhere someone didn't want her ever again. Amy wished she were already making a profit from the rent of the little house she and her aunt had lived in, but for now, at least, that money would be needed to cover the taxes and maintenance of the home and the farmhouse. George had yet to rent out the farmhouse because the police had not finished their investigation, forcing him to wait until the police completed it. Amy would have thought they'd be done by now, but again, she had yet to learn how long that sort of thing could take. She'd have to stay with the Petersens until she started receiving some rental profits.

Amy shook her head to clear it, swiping her hand across her eyes. George handed her a handkerchief. She looked up at the older man speaking at the front of the room, trying to listen as his words floated towards her:

"—her untimely death leaves many questions unanswered, but let us all try to remember Jeannie as a friend, a sister, a daughter, and … an aunt. Thank you, everyone, for coming today. The church ladies have made sandwiches and treats, setting them up at the side table at the back. Please take as much time as you need to grieve." The man left the podium, stopping in front of the urn holding Jeannie's ashes and touching it gently for a brief moment before walking down the aisle.

The mourners talked in murmurs. Some people moved towards the urn, while others made a beeline for the snack table. Amy wasn't sure what to do, so she stayed in her seat, staring straight ahead.

"Take all the time you need," George's deep, gentle voice said to her before he got up to leave his seat.

Amy didn't know how long she had sat there, lost in her thoughts and considering what her aunt had meant to her. Their relationship hadn't amounted to much, but at least Jeannie had been family. She suspected that what was upsetting her more than anything was that she no longer had anyone who fit into that category. Instead of a sense of belonging, Amy felt only emptiness and loss.

Sarah suddenly flopped down into the seat right beside her. "I'm sorry about your aunt. I know you, like … didn't get along that well, but it's hard anyway.

Are you okay?" She twisted a strand of her hair behind her ear.

Amy just shrugged. "I'd had no choice but to live with her when Grandma died. There was no other family. It's okay. I'm going to be fine."

"Do you feel like eating those mushy sandwiches or do you want to just go to the diner? We could have a meal there to remember your aunt. I saw several staff members from the diner here today in their uniforms. They all left a while ago. I'm sure they had to return to open Frankie's."

Amy had to admit that this sounded like a great idea. She could swallow her self-pity along with some hot comfort food. Anything would be better than a cold, soggy egg salad sandwich.

She tracked down George, who was talking to Pastor Bill from the church on Main Street. Pastor Bill wore an old, tacky tie that didn't match his shirt or pants. She noticed that he had a habit of rubbing the top of his bald head. "Excuse me. Sarah and I want to walk over to Frankie's Diner to eat. Is that okay?" she asked, twirling a strand of her hair between her fingers as she spoke.

"Sure, go enjoy yourself. Call me from the diner if you need me to pick you up. It looks like it'll rain soon."

Amy said goodbye to both men, accepting the condolences a few people had to offer as she searched for Sarah so that they could leave the funeral home together. She found her talking to her mom near the snack table. When Amy got closer, Sarah spotted her and said, "I'm all set to go! My mom gave me some money to pay for us both. Let's get out of here."

She smiled her gratitude at Sarah's mom. "Thank you, Mrs. Tyler. That's nice of you, although I doubt we'll need it today." Amy had yet to ever pay for a meal at Frankie's Diner. With her aunt Jeannie working there, Frank had always covered the cost. He always treated his staff like family. Of course, maybe now that Jeannie didn't work there anymore, she would have to start paying for meals. Luckily, she knew she could always work a shift in exchange for a meal whenever needed

The girls left to walk the two blocks to Frankie's Diner. The weather quickly changed, and a light rain started to fall, which was more of an annoying mist than anything else. *It'll probably just flatten out my hair*, Amy thought. She looked at Sarah and asked, "When will you get a job so you don't have to keep borrowing money from your parents?"

"Well—I just haven't gotten around to applying anywhere yet," Sarah replied tartly. "What difference does it make?"

"All you have to do is talk to any store manager about hiring you or even at the diner. There's also an opening right now at the Family Grocers that you could take." Sarah didn't have a chance to reply to Amy's comment because a bright flash of lightning, followed closely by a roar of thunder, interrupted their conversation. The rain started coming down in large, heavy drops that stirred up the dust on the sidewalks.

Amy called out, "We better run for it!"

They ran the rest of the way to the diner, bursting through the front doors even as the rainfall grew heavier. By the looks of things, the town was in for quite the thunderstorm.

Once safely inside, Amy shook the water droplets from her clothes and tried to fluff up her brown hair slightly. The combination of the hairspray and rainwater felt sticky on her hands. She tucked it behind her ears, thinking it would have been better if she'd worn it in her usual ponytail as they purposely walked to a front booth to watch the storm.

Before she could join Sarah, who had already reached the booth and sat down, someone tapped her shoulder. She turned and looked up into Frank's eyes. They were puffy and red. "I'm so sorry for your loss, Amy, but I'm happy to see you here for my famous comfort food. Anything you and your friend want is on me, as usual."

He gave Amy a brief hug and then brushed past. Behind him, there was a lineup of staff. Amy stood for each one to hug her before moving on. Some seemed more upset than others. Amy felt a bit guilty that she was more upset about her circumstances than she was about her aunt Jeannie's death. It seemed like the staff had been closer to her aunt than she was.

Amy slid onto the bench across from Sarah, who was looking at the menu, and moved as close as she could get to the window. Amy didn't need to check the menu as she'd had everything on it more than once. When Tracie, one of the waitresses, came around to take their orders, she told them that Bob Crookedneck was cooking that day and that he wanted Amy to pop in to say hello.

As the teenage girls waited for their food to arrive, Amy started talking to Sarah again about her plans to leave town and go to a university in the city, but mid-sentence, Sarah looked over Amy's shoulder and waved to someone. Amy turned towards the door and saw Shane, the tall, skinny stock boy from the Family Grocers, and his friend Matt. When Amy turned back to look at Sarah, she had slid closer to the window to make room for the boys to slide into the booth. Matt slid in beside Sarah while Shane settled in beside Amy.

Frowning slightly, Amy said, "So, you two ... *know* each other?"

Sarah blushed slightly. "Yes, of course. We all go to school together." She giggled when Amy raised her eyebrows at her.

"I have news from the city to share with you," Matt explained. He removed his jean jacket, shaking the rainwater from it before continuing. "My dad called to say that the guy who the police charged with murdering your aunt is getting out on bail today!"

"What?!" Amy was shocked. Perhaps she should have paid more attention to the radio or the people's conversations at the funeral home today. "How do you know that?"

"My dad's a bailiff at the courthouse. What do you know about the case? Is the guy guilty?"

Amy had to wait to answer Matt's questions while Tracie came to ask the boys for their orders. Once she left, she shrugged at him. "The police are still looking for more evidence at the farmhouse. I know that they've taken a lot of fingerprints inside the house. There were black smudges everywhere by the time they finished gathering evidence. The police seemed to be very interested in my grandfather's shop tools, as well as the garden tools. They have collected several items into evidence, and other things have been sent to forensics. Officer Gerard informed me that they would return the items after the trial. I saw some tire tracks that were baffling them."

"What tire tracks?" Shane asked.

"There was a set of tracks in the shop, but we didn't have any other vehicles except my grandma's Oldsmobile Ninety-eight."

"Nice car! What about the people who found your aunt and that guy they charged with the murder on the property? Did one of them park in the shop?" Matt asked.

"Not from what I heard." She shook her head. The conversation continued while everyone tried to get the details of what had happened at the farmhouse. "The real-estate agent and the couple looking at the place said they parked beside the farmhouse. The wife found the injured man in the shop while she was looking around. The police didn't find my aunt until later that day. It's hard to say what would have happened had they gotten to her sooner. Maybe she would have survived and could have just told them what happened."

Eventually, the conversation moved on to other important topics, like school starting again in a few weeks, the latest music video on television, and whether or not this year's football team expected to win any games. "I'm sorry for interrupting," Amy said to Sarah, looking for an excuse not to talk about football. "I should go to the kitchen to talk to the kitchen staff. Do you want me to use the phone to call George to give us a ride home?"

"I can give you both a ride home," Shane volunteered. "I drove here anyway."

Amy left the three of them in the booth, heading towards the kitchen to talk to Bob, the cook. The kitchen was noisy with the sounds of the industrial dishwasher and the cooks banging around. Bob was working the flat-top grill. When he saw Amy, he handed his flipper over to a young kid who must have been a new hire since Amy didn't recognize him. "Hey, beautiful!" He smiled at Amy, raising his hand for a high five.

"Hi." Amy slapped his hand in greeting. "It's good to see you again." She spent a few minutes making small talk with Bob but wanted to take up only a little of his time. He seemed to want to check to see if she was doing alright. Amy assured him everything was fine and he didn't need to worry about her. He made Amy promise to continue to pop into the diner occasionally so that he could feed her for "old time's sake."

When Amy returned to the dining area, Sarah and the two teenage boys were standing by the booth, looking out the window. The skies were dark, and the rain came down hard and fast. A flashy yellow car drove slowly past through the pelting rain. "That's a sweet ride." Turning back to them, he said, "Okay, you guys stay here. I'll run out to my car and bring it as close as possible to the door." Shane pointed while he explained his plan. "I'll make sure the passenger door is unlocked. Everyone should come out one at a time so you're not standing around in the rain waiting to get in."

Amy doubted that she would be able to get into the car without getting soaked regardless, but she nodded her head in agreement with everyone else.

Matt, Sarah, and Amy waited near the front door until Shane's Chevette pulled up. Matt decided to run out first and climb into the back seat. He suggested that the next person to run out also crawl into the back so the last person could jump into the front passenger seat.

After Matt ran out into the rain, Sarah turned to Amy, "I'm going to take the back seat with Matt! I think he's kind of cute. You can take the front. Hopefully, Shane drops you off first." She rushed out the doors before Amy could comment.

Amy waited until Sarah was in the back seat before she pushed the glass doors open to run across the sidewalk. The gutters were overflowing. Still, Amy tried to jump across the fast-moving water but landed in the cold stream with a splash. Scrambling into the passenger seat, Amy pulled the door closed behind her. The windows were fogging with moisture. Shane started wiping the inside of the windshield with the sleeve of his hooded pullover sweatshirt—also known as a bunnyhug.

"Everyone stop breathing so I can see out the windows," he teased. "Just give me a minute to get ready to go." He increased the fan to blower on the windows and turned on his tape deck to start his music. Aerosmith blasted from the speakers as he backed away from his parking spot.

It was soon apparent that he intended to drop Amy off first. Eventually, he turned down her street, but instead of pulling up to the Petersen's house, he turned into the driveway of the little house next door. Amy turned towards him. "I'm sorry, but I don't live here anymore. I moved next door with the Petersens. I thought you'd heard." She pointed to the house with bountiful flowerbeds.

Shane turned the music down so he could talk. "Sorry. What did you say?" Amy smiled and repeated the news, and he nodded. "My bad—I'll get closer." He shifted into reverse, backing out of the driveway, and turned into the Petersens' instead. "How long are you going to live here?"

Amy twirled a strand of her wet, stringy hair with her fingers, a nervous habit she'd had since childhood. "I think I have to stay here until I'm eighteen. Beatrice Petersen is my appointed guardian since I don't have any family. I don't think I have much choice in the matter. It's so screwed up."

He frowned, nodding. "Mr. and Mrs. Petersen are nice people, but it's too bad you don't have any family. I'm sorry for your loss, by the way."

Amy nodded, quietly thanking him for the ride as she opened the car door to dash for the house.

Chapter 35

August 27, 1985

Tuesday

Bobby followed his lawyer, Bert, up the cement steps into the small lobby of a four-story, yellow-brick apartment building. It seemed like a decent place to live. Small metal mailboxes lined both sides of the entranceway.

Bert nodded towards the mailboxes. "I'll give you your mail key. Check it often. The Big Boss has a copy of your mail key, so instructions can be placed in the mailbox regularly depending on what he needs you to do." Pulling a key ring from his pocket, Bert used the most significant key to unlock the security doors and walked through, turning left to climb the wide staircase. "Your apartment's on the third floor."

Bobby looked around the modest one-bedroom apartment. It was sparsely furnished, clean, and had more to offer him than he'd ever managed to get himself. He still didn't know what the Big Boss would be expecting from him or what sort of instructions he would be receiving, but if it meant staying in this apartment for the rest of his life, he was agreeable to it.

"Here's a hundred bucks," Bert said, sliding a white envelope across the worn kitchen counter towards him. "Go get some groceries and some clothes for yourself from the second-hand store down the street. You'll get another hundred in two weeks, so go easy on this money. No gambling!" Bert shook his finger at Bobby. "It would be a bail violation."

"No problem," Bobby grinned. "I've survived on less."

Bert hesitated. "Don't be stealing or doing anything that would violate your bail conditions. Report to the dry cleaners tomorrow morning at eight for work. It's not far from here. The guys there will tell you what you'll be doing. The extra jobs you receive in your mailbox will earn you either credit toward your debt or cash, depending on what you think you need most. The bus stop is on the corner."

Bobby nodded. The terms of his employment were pretty straightforward: Work for the Big Boss and do what he says or be killed. "I won't disappoint you."

"It's not me you need to worry about. I'm only one of many lawyers caring for the Big Boss and his dealings. Here's my card and phone number, should you need legal advice from me. Be sure you do not need any if you can manage it." He put his white business card in the envelope with the money. "If you get sent back to jail, then the work you'll be doing to pay off your debts is—well, let's just say it would be less attractive. Your best bet is to stay out of trouble, work at the cleaners, and do the side jobs as they arise."

"I think I can manage to stay out of trouble."

"The telephone is in service," Bert said then, pointing to the green telephone mounted on the wall. "Your court-appointed liaison officer will be calling you. The police also have this number and address as per your bail conditions. Do whatever they say, and allow them access to this apartment when they stop by to check on you. Don't keep anything illegal in this place, you hear me?"

Bobby nodded. He couldn't even remember the last time he'd had a phone number. As Bobby looked at it, it suddenly rang. Bobby looked at Bert for reassurance.

"Here are your keys to the building and your mailbox. Answer your phone while I let myself out." He placed the keys on the kitchen counter and headed out.

The phone rang twice before Bobby picked up the receiver, holding it to his ear, "Hello?"

"This is Detective Branson from the City Police Department. Am I speaking to Edward Bates?"

Bobby hesitated before answering the man. "Yes, but I am legally changing my name to Bobby Wilham. Please call me Bobby instead."

There was a pause on the other end before the detective responded. "Alright, Bobby. I'm calling to let you know that my partner and I are coming to ask you a few questions. Two police officers from another jurisdiction who've also been working on your case will also join us. We'll be there in about fifteen minutes. I have the address."

"That would be fine. I'll be out on the front steps enjoying a smoke while I wait for you." Bobby returned the receiver to its cradle. He wondered what kinds of questions he would need to answer or if this was just routine procedure when someone was out on bail. His lawyer wouldn't be back at his office yet, but Bobby assumed that he was to cooperate as much as possible to stay out of trouble. He grabbed his keys and half-pack of cigarettes and headed down to the front steps of the building.

Once outside, Bobby leaned casually against the cool cement railing, inhaling the hot smoke from his cigarette. He hoped it would calm his jitters before the detectives arrived. He looked up and down the street. There were apartment buildings lining both sides of it, which would make finding a parking spot almost impossible. He noticed some buildings had little shops on the main floors that people could access from the street or the lobby.

The smell of smoked meats from the deli on the corner wafted over to him as he inhaled another drag from his cigarette. He almost choked on the hot smoke when a yellow early 1970s Chrysler Imperial LeBaron slowed down near the front of his building. Undoubtedly, this was the very same flashy car that Bobby had stolen, and he wondered who was driving it now. The driver looked pointedly at Bobby before it sped off again. Bobby slowly exhaled, watching the vehicle drive away as his heart pounded against his ribs. He thought the driver looked strangely familiar. He looked down the street after the car, trying to remember where he had seen him before. *Maybe one of the Big Boss guys is checking on me?*

"Are you Bobby?" a voice from the sidewalk asked, interrupting Bobby's thoughts.

"Uh—" Bobby hesitated, turning his eyes away from where he'd last seen the yellow LeBaron to look at the speaker. "Yes."

"I'm Detective Branson, and this is Detective Calloway." The two men flashed their detective badges hanging on their chests beneath their suit jackets. Detective Branson looked down the street. "We're just waiting for Officer Gerard and his partner to find a place to park before we ask you a few questions."

Bobby nodded, looking down the street where Detective Branson had indicated. From where he was leaning on the top rail, he could see that the police car was just a little over a block away, behind a red pickup. "I see them coming," Bobby informed the detectives from his elevated vantage point.

Suddenly, the flashy yellow LeBaron cut in front of the red pickup truck at the intersection, turning back towards the apartment building. Bobby stood up straighter; his awareness suddenly heightened as he watched the car slow down as it neared the building. Bobby's cigarette slipped from his fingers, bouncing down the cement steps. The driver of the vehicle had pulled out a gun, pointing it straight at Bobby.

He took a step back just before the force of a bullet ripped through his left shoulder, the force of it spinning him around and slamming him face-first into the glass entrance doors. Shattered glass rained down on him as his body fell through it.

Footsteps pounded up the cement steps. Someone was shouting, shaking Bobby's limp body. Bobby's ears rang. Then, there was more shouting and sirens, but they all seemed to be muffled. His vision was blurred. He closed his eyes, lying motionless, allowing the darkness to overtake him. As his mind slipped into unconsciousness, Bobby's only thought was how odd it was that he couldn't feel any pain.

This time, when Bobby woke up in the hospital bed, he wasn't handcuffed or chained in any way. The curtains were open around his bed, and a nurses' station seemed to be in the middle of the room. Bobby realized he must have just come out of surgery and that this was a recovery room. One of the nurses noticed that he'd opened his eyes and came rushing over to the side of the bed. "How are you feeling?" she asked, checking the machines surrounding him.

"What happened?"

"You just came out of surgery to remove a bullet from your left shoulder and glass from various other wounds. Those have been cleaned and stitched, but you lost a great deal of blood. You were very badly injured." He could see the concern on her face as she checked the readings on the various monitors. His vitals undoubtedly weren't good. "Police officers have been urgently waiting to talk to you and will likely be in to do so even before the doctor comes to explain the results of your surgery. I hope you're ready." She offered him an awkward smile he thought was meant to be reassuring, then turned back to the nurses' station to make a phone call.

Bert Illingsworth, Bobby's lawyer, walked into the recovery room, followed by three men in suits with their detective badges. "I'm glad to see you've woken up. The surgeon was uncertain whether you'd even get through the surgery."

Bert smiled then, which Bobby took as reassurance that he wasn't in trouble with the Big Boss over the drive-by shooting.

"I'm doing fine, considering the circumstances that brought me here. I've survived a lot worse."

One of the suited gentlemen spoke up then, saying, "I'm Detective Jameson, homicide. These are Detectives Carson and McTavish. Do you know why someone would want to shoot you and Detective Calloway?"

Bobby hesitated before answering, his eyebrows raising slightly beneath what felt like an oversized bandage. He hadn't realized the shooter had also shot the detective. "No. I'd only met Detective Calloway for the first time today, so I don't know who would want to shoot him. As for myself, I just got out on bail, so I suppose any number of people might be unhappy with me. Maybe you should check into the family of the person trying to pin a murder charge on me!"

"Pin it on you?" Detective McTavish cut in. "Didn't you kill someone?"

"Now, Detective," Bert cautioned. "My client does not need to answer that question. He maintains that he is innocent of that charge, and it's up to the courts to decide otherwise. Bobby is out on bail awaiting trial. In any case, I'm sure you don't want to waste your time asking questions about those things. Stick to the matter at hand, please."

Detective McTavish scowled. "Do you know a man named Charles Smith?"

Bobby thought about the name. It sounded mildly familiar, but he couldn't quite put his finger on why. "I'm not sure. What does he have to do with anything?"

"Charles Smith is the shooter," Detective Jameson supplied. "Officer Gerard apprehended him following the shooting today after a high-speed pursuit. We were hoping that you'd pull through to be a witness in the court case against the shooter, who also shot at the police officers, by the way. Your lawyer can help you write out your statement and have you sign it."

The doors at the end of the room opened then, and Officer Gerard walked in. "Hold on a second!" he called as he walked briskly up to the bed, looking at the detectives. "Charles Smith and his wife Edna were the couple the realtor said were viewing the farmhouse property when this man and, later, Jeannie Young's body were found. The cases are unquestionably connected!"

"If that's true," Bert said, holding up his hands to stop the questioning. "Then my client is done with your questions until I can have a moment to speak with him alone."

When the detectives and Officer Gerard reluctantly left the recovery room, Bert went to the nurse's station to use their telephone. It was brief because Bert pretty much only relayed the name of the shooter to whoever he had called. Then he returned to Bobby's bedside. "The Big Boss says you can write out a full confession of the incident as you know it at the farmhouse and everything that happened with the shooting. Do you know any poker players named Chuck?"

Bobby's eyes widened in surprise. Chuck was the card player with the prison tattoos, flashy gold rings, and tinted glasses who'd won all his money in Ace's Pawnshop back room. "Chuck? Yeah! He just recently wiped me out at a rigged poker game!"

"So, you do know Charles Smith. Chuck is short for Charles. Why does he want you dead? What did you do to him?"

As Bobby considered this new information, he fought the drugs that were pumping through his veins and tried to think about every poker player he'd ever met named Chuck or Charles. There had to be a connection somewhere. Why would a poker player who had just cheated against him in a game of cards and won want to kill him? Then, a realization came to him in a wave of confusing emotion. "I think you need to check into Craig Simmons' family. I think Chuck might be related to him."

"And who's Craig Simmons?" Bert leaned in so he could look Bobby directly in his eyes.

"He's the young guy I beat up in an alley back in seventy-eight, which got me sent to prison. If Chuck is related to him, this might have been some sort of revenge for the assault. I pleaded guilty at my hearing. I'd been caught right in the middle of the act, so denying it was no use."

Bobby shook his head slightly, causing it to throb, and pain started radiating through his chest despite the painkillers the nurses had given him. His groan sent the nurses scurrying over to his bedside to up the dose on his morphine drip. Bobby's eyes started to lose focus as he thought about how the past kept returning to haunt him. If only he could learn to follow his instincts and try to make better choices, he might not always find himself in this kind of mess.

Bert slowly stood up, patting Bobby on the leg. "You rest up. I'll talk to the detectives and Officer Gerard about Craig Simmons. I can write up your confession statements based on our previous conversations. They'll find out if there's a connection. If they need to talk to you again, I'll make sure that I'm with you because of the morphine." With that, he turned and walked away.

"Wait!" Bobby called.

Bert stopped, returning to the bedside. "What is it?"

"I just realized that Chuck was probably at the farmhouse when someone hit me over the head and beat the crap out of me! I bet he was even the one who did it!" Bobby exclaimed as the realization hit him at once. "I bet he tried to kill me then, and when he failed, he shot me! He's tried to kill me twice already! Did they check for prints on the garden tools? Someone hit me with something pretty hard while I was in the barn."

"Do you want to press charges against him for aggravated assault, attempted murder, and intent to do you bodily harm?"

"Yes," Bobby replied slowly and evenly. "I want you to tell Officer Gerard that I am pressing charges against Chuck."

"I'll take care of it for you. But I'm also going to take this one step further in your upcoming court case, suggesting that Chuck also killed Jeannie Young. I want the forensic team to check for his prints on the murder weapon, which seems to have been a shovel, by the way. Assuming that they match his prints, it will cast doubt on the prosecution's case of you as her murderer."

Bert grinned then. "I'm sure we can get your first-degree murder charge dropped. The puzzle pieces are falling into place and presenting you with a strong defence, Bobby. You are a lucky son of a gun. I'm starting to see the big picture here! I think I could even get you some leniency with the prosecutor in exchange for testifying against Charles Smith for shooting you and the other detective. The Big Boss will be extremely pleased. He has a way of getting what he wants in all situations."

Frowning, Bobby nodded. "It only makes sense that he was the guy who killed Jeannie. He was there at the same time, and I know I didn't kill her! I'm sure of it! Yes, I admit that I roughed her up a bit, hitting her to try and get her to shut up and stop threatening me, but I remember her looking over my shoulder just before something hit me, and I lost consciousness. Officer Gerard needs to check Chuck's connection with me. Seemingly, he hates me enough to want to kill me. We know he shot me, but the question is why. I thought he works for the Big Boss?"

"No, he doesn't. He's never even heard of the man, but he won't be happy when he finds out he was targeting one of his important employees. Chuck is in a lot of trouble." Bert straightened his tie and cleared his throat. "It's going to be alright, Bobby. I'll write your confession as you've explained it so you can rest easy. Then, you'll have to sign off on it. I'll be in touch with you soon. Get some rest."

Bobby watched as his lawyer turned and left the recovery room, then looked over at the nurses' station. He suddenly realized they had been listening to every word of their exchange. He didn't genuinely care though. He knew he was innocent of Jeannie's murder. The two nurses quickly looked away, busying themselves with other tasks now that the show was over. He knew that admitting to hitting Jeannie in front of still more witnesses probably wasn't brilliant, but how likely was it that they would say anything anyway? He smiled weakly over at the nurses as the morphine eased all of his troubles and pain and then faded into the darkness.

Chapter 36

August 29, 1985

Thursday

George pulled up into their home's driveway. "Wait for me, and I'll pop the trunk." It contained all of Amy's back-to-school purchases she needed to bring into the house. As usual, George opened the heavy car doors for Beatrice and Amy. As they approached the trunk to open it, a police cruiser pulled up in the driveway. Officer Gerard and Officer Randy Doyle, the Petersens' son-in-law, stepped out of the vehicle. Randy opened the rear door of the cruiser to let out a man wearing a dress shirt and striped tie. They quickly forgot about the school supplies in their curiosity.

"Hello, everyone!" Officer Gerard cheerfully said. "This is Alister Morgan, a private investigator from Toronto, Ontario." The man nodded in greeting but didn't say anything as Officer Gerard continued. "He has provided many clues to help solve these recent cases, including new information that led to someone else becoming a person of interest in the murder of Jeannie Young."

He pulled his notepad out of the breast pocket of his police uniform and flipped through a few pages. "First of all, you may have heard that Eddie Bates, who has changed his name to Bobby Wilham, is out on bail, pending the murder trial. Recently, he was shot in a drive-by shooting and he remains in critical condition in the Saskatoon Hospital. He's recently given us a full written, signed confession of his own actions since arriving in town and information we can use against a man named Charles Smith, also known as Charlie or Chuck Simmons. Does that name sound familiar to any of you?" They all shook their heads, and Amy asked who he was.

Officer Gerard turned the page on his notebook, continuing to read off information. "Charles Smith is in custody for the shooting of Bobby Wilham and Detective Kevin Calloway. When we ran his fingerprints, Smith's prints matched a set of fingerprints discovered on the murder weapon, a shovel found in the corner of the shop at the farmhouse. Other fingerprints collected on the scene and in the farmhouse matched Bobby Wilham's."

"So, which one killed my aunt Jeannie?" Amy crossed her arms to ward off the chill creeping over her. "Did they both handle the garden shovel? Did they both gang up on her?"

Clearing his throat, Officer Gerard continued. "We are still working on that piece of the puzzle. The point I'm trying to get across to you is that having now arrested another man whose fingerprints were found on the murder weapon; there is reasonable doubt as to Bobby's guilt in the killing of your aunt, which would likely allow him to go free, on that charge at least. Bobby claims that Chuck used the shovel to beat him after killing Jeannie. He says he may or may not have touched the shovel but that it was only in self-defence if he had. We're analyzing his statement and comparing it to our collected evidence. I just want you to know that we need to reinvestigate the farmhouse to make sure that no crucial pieces of evidence against the murderer, whoever it is, goes undiscovered."

"Are both of these guys going to walk away free if you can't pin it definitively on either of them?" George frowned. "It seems obvious that Eddie Bates, or Bobby whatever, was up to no good."

"George—" Officer Gerard paused, shaking his head. "Bobby can be tied to various break-ins and fraud against the Young Estate. He has already confessed to both. Chuck has confessed to the shooting and beating of Bobby with a garden shovel, which he claims was an act of self-defence. Both men have criminal records already. Rest assured that neither will walk free. However, both men could realistically prove reasonable doubt in regarding the murder of Jeannie. We are working on sorting out the details. The shovel in question has been sent to the lab to determine exactly how each man might have held it during the struggle. We already have enough forensic evidence to determine it as the weapon used to kill Jeannie Young, but which of them dealt the actual blows still needs to be determined."

"Why would Smith kill Jeannie?" Beatrice asked with her hands on her hips. "Did he even know her? Bobby seems more likely to have hurt her since she would have recognized him and could have exposed his scheme."

The private investigator stepped forward now to explain. "Eddie Bates, AKA Bobby Wilham, went to prison for a vicious assault on a teenager, Craig Simmons, back in 1978. Craig was simply in the wrong place at the wrong time, but he suffered a traumatic brain injury in the attack and has never been the same since that night. Chuck Smith is Craig Simmons' half-brother."

He let this sink in for a moment before continuing. "I sent a letter of warning that Chuck might be in town, which I understand now was given to Officer Gerard, alerting the police department that he could be headed to Glenmere in search of Bobby. Word on the street was that Bobby had been heading out this way to get revenge against John for ruining the high-stakes poker game that took place that same night in seventy-eight, which was what had led to his beating of Craig Simmons shortly thereafter, which in turn got sent him sent to prison for several years." The officers all nodded in confirmation.

"But how does my aunt fit into it? Why was she killed?" Amy needed to understand what had been happening in the whirlwind of the last two weeks—and why.

Then, Randy stepped forward to look Amy in the eyes. "Your aunt Jeannie probably went out to the farmhouse to confront her ex-husband, John, attempting to get some kind of settlement from him. Everyone knew that your Uncle John was a poker player. He was friends with Eddie. But Eddie had been posing as your uncle John to claim all of John's inheritance. It's probably a coincidence that Jeannie was at the farmhouse simultaneously as Bobby and Chuck. She may have been killed by either man, either by Bobby to keep her from revealing his true identity, or by Chuck to keep her from identifying him as Bobby's killer." He shrugged a bit at that statement as if the particulars didn't matter. "Though he didn't successfully manage to kill him that day. Still, it seems both men were at the farmhouse when someone killed your aunt Jeannie."

"Truthfully, it's my farmhouse now, but I don't want it anymore. It will never be the same. It used to feel like a safe place, but all I can see at the farm now is emptiness." Amy shook her head slowly while her eyes filled with tears. "I don't think I could ever go back, knowing all the violence that happened there. And I can't take care of it myself anyway. I don't know what to do with it, but please just finish your investigation. You must solve my aunt's murder."

Beatrice put her arms around her then, pulling her close. Amy buried herself in the ruffles of Beatrice's pink floral dress. The officers must have said their goodbyes and left in the cruiser, but Amy didn't even notice until she realized how quiet things had gotten. Slowly, she pulled out of the warm embrace, wiping her tears on her sleeves.

The silence suddenly seemed awkward. Beatrice cast her eyes over to George and looked at him for a long moment. He eventually shrugged in answer to whatever silent conversation had just occurred between them.

"Well," Beatrice said, leading them all towards the front steps but remaining outside, apparently taking a quiet moment to savour the day's beauty,

"I guess we know all that we're going to for the moment."

"Gerard didn't mention anything about that list of stolen items Amy dropped off at the police station," George pointed out with furrowed brows.

Beatrice pursed her lips, thinking for a moment before responding. "I think we can safely assume that Jeannie stole the missing items from the farmhouse." She started counting off points on her fingers. "There is no sign of a break-in of any kind. She had a key to get in and out whenever she wanted. Jeannie stocked her pantry with preserves I made for Dorothy. I certainly never gave any to Jeannie. Also, Amy found Dorothy's ring in Jeannie's dresser drawer!" She stood there with a smug smile as though she had just solved the mystery of the pyramids.

"Unfortunately, there is still one other mystery that remains unsolved," Amy said, wiping the back of her hand across one of her cheeks.

"And what's that?" Beatrice asked, handing her a hanky from her handbag. "I thought I'd figured it all out."

"The secret of my puzzle box!" Amy was exasperated as she wiped her face with the hanky. "I have been working so hard to try and open that box because my grandmother told me that whatever I'd find inside was super important, but I haven't even gotten close. I can hear something moving inside of it, but I can't get the little slide open enough to see it or get it out." She let out a sigh and then turned to George. "Do you still think you could break it open? At this point, I don't care about saving it anymore!"

"Sure, I can. Whenever you're ready to do it."

Amy went inside and retrieved the puzzle box off the top of her dresser. Slowly, she turned it around in her hands, looking at the few pieces she had managed to move. Discouraged, she carried it out of the house to let George help her break into it.

The sun was shining, and the air smelled fresh. George was in the front yard, discussing the flower beds with Beatrice. The lawnmower sat silently beside the sidewalk. It looked like George was preparing to start some yard work.

Beatrice interrupted whatever he was saying, looking at Amy, "What kind of flowers do you like, Amy?"

Amy shrugged. "Anything that smells nice, I suppose." She wasn't sure how to bring the puzzle box to him. He always seemed too busy with one thing or another, and Amy hated to interrupt whatever conversation they had been having.

George turned, facing Amy and looking at the puzzle box she had tucked under her arm. His face turned serious as he studied her face. "Do you want me to give it a go or just smash it open? It's very beautifully crafted. I wonder what's inside that's so important?"

Amy wasn't sure where to begin her request, so she blurted out her frustration. "I don't care anymore. I need some help. My grandma said it was important to open it, and that it would give me everything I wanted. Whatever that means. I have no idea why she couldn't just tell me what was inside it." She looked back and forth between George and his wife as she talked, feeling surprisingly nervous about the whole thing.

"How long did Dorothy have the puzzle box?" George asked.

She shrugged. "It's been around for as long as I can remember. I'm not sure if it belonged to my mom or my grandma. It was always sitting in the living room at the farmhouse, until someone stole it, at least."

George squinted his eyes, lifting his hat off his head to wipe sweat from his brow. "If someone stole it, how did you get it back?"

Amy's stomach flipped, realizing she had said too much. She swallowed hard before speaking. "Um ... It was in the pawnshop window. I confronted the guy at the pawnshop and asked for it back, but he said I'd have to pay him a hundred dollars for it!"

"Did you have a hundred dollars?" He looked at Amy warily.

Amy sighed. "No, ... I stole it from the pawnshop." She was ashamed, but admitting to what she had done was kind of a relief. "Sarah and I broke the window to get it."

Beatrice frowned worriedly. "I don't think the owner's replaced the window yet. Last time I was at the Family Grocers, there was still plywood over it." She looked at her husband for answers. "What should we do?"

"Well, I'll take Amy to the pawnshop to speak to Fred, the owner, about paying for the window repair. I think the first month's rent on the little house next door will cover the expenses, and we should have that money at the beginning of the month as soon as the new renters move in."

George rubbed his hands together in front of him as he continued. "You'll also pay for the puzzle box. Even though it belongs to you, you still need to be fair and pay whatever the pawnshop paid the person who brought it in there in the first place."

Amy nodded in agreement. It was only fair to the pawnshop owner that she would pay for the broken window. It didn't sit well with her that she had to pay for the puzzle box, too, though, since someone had stolen it from her grandma's farmhouse, but then again, it wasn't the pawnshop owner who had stolen it. Amy sighed, *It wouldn't be fair to make him lose money on it.*

Finally, she looked at George. "Can we open the puzzle box now, or will I have to wait until I pay for it?" She held her breath, waiting for his answer.

"Well, let me have a closer look at it. I've seen these Japanese puzzle boxes before. Nothing this intricate, mind you." George reached for the box and began silently turning it over and over. "Have you been opening each slide a tiny bit at a time in a certain order?"

"Yes." Amy pointed to the slides, explaining, "Each one moves a tiny bit at a time. There's a small gap on the bottom side now, but I can't seem to get it open."

He lifted the puzzle box near his ear, shaking it. "I can hear something. Bea, do you have a hairpin?"

"Yes, I think so," she said, running her hands under her straw hat. "Yes! Here you go!"

George used his teeth to bend it. Once he had it how he wanted it, he slid it into the small opening, digging around in the cavity beyond. A moment later, he smiled. "I think I've almost got it." He tilted the box above his head, letting the item inside slide toward the opening as he squinted at it.

Amy stepped in closer, trying to see what he was doing, her heart pounding loudly against her ribs. She tried licking her dry lips, but once again, her mouth felt as if it was full of cotton. "If you can't get it, we can smash it open. I'm tired of waiting at this point."

"Hold on," he whispered, concentrating on his task. "Patience can be very rewarding." He turned the puzzle box around, showing them that he'd caught the edge of a piece of paper with the hairpin. "Bea, see if you have another pin. If you can catch the fold of the paper, you can drag it out of the opening."

She did as he asked, finding another hairpin and stepping closer. "Here, George. Hold it facing the sun so I can see what I'm doing."

Once Beatrice had the proper light needed, she manoeuvred the hairpin, pulling more of the paper through the tiny opening. Finally, she had exposed enough paper to grab onto it with her fingers. Beatrice gently pulled it out of its hiding place and held it up, beaming from ear to ear as though she'd just uncovered a treasure chest full of jewels.

Amy reached out slowly to take the paper from her hands. Someone had neatly folded the paper, and it felt like a document. Taking a deep, shaking breath, she gently unfolded the paper and almost couldn't comprehend what she saw. It was another copy of her birth certificate, but this one had more information. The one she'd found in her grandmother's dresser had been wallet-sized, with only her name, birth date, and birthplace written on it. "It's another birth certificate, but bigger! I-I don't understand." Her eyes had started watering, making it impossible for her to read the words on the page.

Beatrice reached for the document, and Amy let her take it. "This must be the long-form birth certificate document." She read the document and then looked up at Amy with a shocked expression. Her hands shook when she handed the document to her husband to read for himself. "Amy ... the long form lists your parents' names. Did your mom or grandmother ever tell you your father's name?"

Amy shook her head. "No, no one ever told me, and it seemed like a sensitive subject for them, so I stopped asking a long time ago. Why?"

George smiled. "Because, according to this official document, your father is our oldest son. Gabe Petersen is your father, Amy. He was one of your Uncle John's best friends. I guess that explains why your mother was hanging around with their group. Gabe never told us about you, but maybe he didn't know either!"

Hot tears started to flow freely down Amy's face, off her chin, and onto her shirt. She swiped at them with the back of her hand. Beatrice stepped forward, wrapping her arms tightly around her again.

"I thought I was all alone," Amy said, sobbing into her warm embrace.

"There, there, girlie—you're with your family now. You belong to us," a teary-eyed Beatrice choked out, rubbing her hand up and down Amy's back. "Welcome to our family ... We will take good care of you, and I promise no one will ever abandon you again."

George wrapped his strong arms around the two of them. "Speaking of which, maybe you should stop calling us George and Beatrice. How about calling us Grandpa and—"

"Granny," Amy interrupted, squeezing a little bit tighter. Beatrice responded by putting her cheek down on the top of Amy's head to hold her even closer. Tears continued to run down Amy's face, now dampening the ruffles of her granny Beatrice's blouse.

After a prolonged and emotional hug, Amy took a deep breath, sniffing a bit. As she exhaled slowly, she released all of her pent-up tension and anxiety as well. She suddenly realized that she hadn't felt this good in a very long time—as though she were bursting with joy.

"Maybe we should call Gabe to hear his side of the story," George, Amy's Grandpa, mumbled with a chuckle. "Let's call the whole family to come home for a family barbecue to celebrate our new grandchild."

The group hug finally broke up, with a bit of laughter and all of them wiping away tears, and they headed inside together. Amy laughed as they climbed the front steps. "The neighbours are going to think we're crazy!"

"Life is crazy sometimes," Grandpa George said, "but somehow, it all works out in the end. The barbecue can wait. Right now, we should celebrate with pizza!"

Epilogue

6 months later

Chuck Simmons awoke in his new prison cell in the Saskatoon Penitentiary, looking forward to some yard time. He hoped that a little fresh air would give him the incentive he needed to start making alliances with other inmates. At the same time, he would serve his sentence for possession of a stolen vehicle, assault, attempted murder, and criminal negligence causing death. He had several years left on his sentence, but he hoped to be paroled early for good behaviour, assuming he could manage it.

The jury had found Chuck innocent of Jeannie's death because the prosecutor had been unable to provide definitive proof that Chuck had been the one to kill her. His lawyer argued that it was all circumstantial since the murder weapon had both Bobby's and Chuck's fingerprints on it. He argued that the shovel used as the murder weapon had been brought into the shop at the farmhouse by Bobby after he'd killed Jeannie and then used to attack Chuck in the shop, which had led to the men struggling for control over it, and the reason why Chuck's fingerprints were on it as well.

The argument cast reasonable doubt over the documented confession and accusations signed by Bobby Wilham. In his testimony, Chuck had claimed that when he saw Bobby standing on the steps of the apartment building, he had openly fired on him in a fit of rage over having been attacked by him at the farmhouse. He also testified that his shooting of the detective on the scene was an unfortunate accident.

The buzzer rang out in the corridor, automatically unlocking the door to the cells on his wing. He opened the door and stepped out into the hall with the rest of the inmates, preparing to go outside to the yard. Chuck was new to this cell block but had previously experienced prison life. He knew the guards could take away yard time on a whim, so he wanted to ensure he took advantage of the opportunity while it was available. Time spent outside was always the only thing that kept him from getting too claustrophobic while locked in a windowless prison.

An average-sized inmate with three large companions stopped in front of him. "I need to talk with you, Chuck." The leader smiled at him, immediately putting him on guard. "Step back into your cell so we have a bit of privacy."

Chuck backed slowly into his cell, keeping his eyes on the ring leader and his back to the wall. "I don't want any trouble. I might have just got here this week, but I've been in prison before." Chuck pushed up his sleeves, showing the prison tats on his forearms to prove his status. "Who are you?"

The ring leader and two of his men moved towards Chuck in the small cell, while the third man stayed outside to act as a lookout. "I'm the guy who's been eagerly waiting for you to get sent here so I could talk seriously with you. These are my boys. Their names don't matter, but you can call me Damien."

"What do you want, Damien? Another member of your gang?"

"That depends on your answers to my questions. Boys?" Damien nodded to his henchmen, and they rushed forward, restraining Chuck against the cold cement wall by his arms.

Damien started his interrogation and pulled out a sharpened metal shank, about six inches long, from behind his back. "If you are truthful with your answers and keep your voice down, this will all be over very quickly," Damien said, pressing the shank against Chuck's throat. "First, tell me about shooting the detective. Were you trying to shoot him, or was it an accident?"

"I recognized him as a detective. It was on purpose, but I didn't have a clean kill shot on the bastard, so he survived," Chuck answered, swallowing hard.

"No reason to try and sound tough," Damien said in an admonishing tone. "Stick to the basics. Anyway, that question was just out of my own curiosity, wanting to know what kind of man you are. Frankly, I just need to know about the other man, the one you beat up and then shot later. Tell me about him and what happened."

Feeling confident now that this was an interview to prove his worth, Chuck confessed to everything. "Yeah, well. I wish I could have done it sooner. Eddie deserved everything he got and more for what he did to my kid brother. I wanted him to die for what he did to him. It took me a long time to track the guy down to that little nothing of a town. When I finally caught up to him, he was about to kill some woman, and I would have just let him do it and rot in prison for it, but I figured prison was too good for that bastard. Plus, if he ended up on the inside, I wouldn't be able to get to him unless I went in, too. That woman almost messed everything up for me. She saw me sneak into the barn, and I knew she could identify me as Eddie's killer. So, after I knocked him out with a shovel, I had no choice but to kill her, too.

"I thought I heard a car slow down at the main road as if they would turn into the driveway. They didn't, but I figured it would be better not to take any chances. So, I carried Eddie's body and the shovel to the shop, hoping to steal his car, take off with him in the trunk and kill him later. He roused before I could put him in, and we fought over the shovel. I got it away from him and started beating him with it. When I figured he was dying, I took off in his car before anyone could spot me."

Chuck grimaced before continuing his confession. "However, he pulled through, so I just laid low and waited to see if he'd survive long enough for me to get another chance."

Damien held up his hand to stop him. "So—you killed the woman, managed to get off on that murder charge because his fingerprints were on the murder weapon, too, and then when Eddie got out on bail, you decided to shoot him and the cop? Do I have that right?"

Chuck figured Damien already knew everything he was telling him, but he played along, raising his chin and continuing in a boastful tone. "Yeah, I got my chance when the guy was standing on the steps of his apartment building. I shot him and the detective. Eddie died a few days later, though the newspaper called him 'Bobby.' I'm just sorry the gunshot didn't kill him instantly. Luckily, infection and internal bleeding did the job a few days later. Either way, though, he's finally dead, so it's all good for me."

Damien smirked. "Unfortunately, it's not good that he's dead."

"Uh … It's not?" Chuck's voice cracked nervously. "Why not?" What difference could Eddie's death possibly make to his chances of joining Damien's gang?

"The Big Boss is upset that you killed one of his favourite employees. He has no interest in you icing the woman or shooting the cop, but you ruined his big plans for Eddie. He would be his newest asset. For life." Damien leaned in closer then and whispered, "If he had lived, he might have just ordered a severe beating for you. But now, Chuck?"

The man pulled back a bit and stared into his eyes. "Now he's going to have to find some other talent to replace him, someone with a lifetime's worth of leverage against him. That won't be quick or easy."

Chuck started struggling against the henchmen now, panicking in their grip. "What about me? I'll do whatever he wants! For as long as he wants!"

Damien smiled at him almost sadly and shook his head. "You shot a cop, Chuck! Even if you survived long enough to get out of here, which, by the way—you aren't going to, you'd be useless to him."

There would be no escaping this; Chuck realized this now and felt a helpless rage break through his fear. "And who are you in all of this? Huh? His fucking lapdog?!"

Amusement lit up Damien's eyes. "I'm an employee, Chuck—a well-respected employee with exceptional talents for gathering information and removing the trash. In return for my loyalty to the Big Boss, I get all the contraband and female visitors I could ever want. What more can a lifer ask for? And do you know what the best part is? About being a lifer, I mean?"

He leaned closer once more, his breath tickling Chuck's ear as he whispered, "When I kill you, nothing will change for me at all."

Damien laughed then and stepped back a bit. "They can't exactly make me serve two life sentences without parole. The game is over, Chuck. And you lost."

Knowing he had fleeting moments left to live and that each would only become more torturous than the last, Chuck spat furiously at him. "Well then, just fucking do it!! What are you waiting for, chicken-shit?!"

One of the henchmen covered Chuck's mouth with his hand to quiet him as Damien slowly lowered the weapon until it was pointing at Chuck's abdomen, though he never broke eye contact. "What am I waiting for?" He chuckled humourlessly.

Suddenly, a cacophony of noise broke out further down the cell block, followed by blaring alarms. Chuck's eyes flicked over to the inmate standing watch in the doorway. He saw him turn towards Damien and nod.

"The distraction, of course." With that, Damien thrust the metal shiv into Chuck's abdomen three times, forcefully piercing his liver, pancreas, and intestines and breaking its tip against the wall on his final, skewering blow.

When Damien stepped back, Chuck watched through eyes that had already begun to blur as the man wiped the blade on the nearby bed sheet and tucked it back into his waistband.

Chuck's vision quickly narrowed to a single pinpoint of light, even as the two henchmen finally released his arms. As an eerie silence consumed him amidst the surrounding chaos, and his vision faded finally to black, his body started its slow descent to the cold, hard floor of his open prison cell, coming to rest at last in a darl red pool of blood.

The End.

The Ice Box

Sneak Peek

#1stdraftglimpse

The Glenmere Box Mysteries, Book #2

By Lisa Adair

Saturday, September 21, 1985
Amy yawned as she prepared the store for opening. It was early Saturday morning at the Family Grocers; her body was tired from working the close shift the night before for Brenda. Amy began to feel that trading the Friday shift wasn't getting her the best deal; maybe being this tired wasn't worth it. Longing for her warm bed, Amy shuffled her feet, pushing the mop bucket with her as she tracked water on the floor from the front area to the freezer aisle. Discovering a leaking freezer, Amy glided her hand across the cold water running down the front of the glass doors. Someone had left the door to the third freezer slightly ajar, frosting up the inside of the

glass. Grabbing the handle to open the freezer door and seeing what was interfering, Amy blinked a few times before her brain registered the frosty hand sticking out from under the frozen bags of peas. Amy's jaw dropped open, releasing a gut-wrenching scream from somewhere deep within.

Suddenly, two hands grasped her upper arms, pulling her away from the freezer door and turning her away from the scene before her. "Amy! Stop screaming! What is wrong?"

Amy closed her mouth, unmoving from her place before looking up at the tall stock boy who was holding both of her arms. "S-Shane," Amy stuttered. "I-I-I am alright. Go call the police station immediately! Someone has put a dead body in the freezer!"

Shane's eyes widened behind his thick glasses and moved slowly up and over Amy's head at the scene behind her. "Holy shit! I'll be right back. Don't go anywhere!" he growled, pushing his wire-rim glasses up and turning away. He inhaled deeply, walking purposefully towards the front of the store to use the phone next to the registers.

Amy's legs buckled beneath her as she sank to the floor. She doubted she could go anywhere even if she wanted to; her legs felt like heavy lead weights. Her eyes stayed fixed on the hand with dark pink nail polish holding the freezer door slightly ajar. Amy did not know if she was brave enough to look at the person, obscured by condensation, but morbid curiosity drove her. She mechanically crawled across the aisle, as if pulled by a wire, towards the dead body. Her brain barely registered her blue uniform pants getting wet, dragging through the water as she crossed the cold floor on her knees. Amy slowly placed her hand on the door panel, holding her breath. She jolted back to awareness suddenly when she kneed the freezer's kickplate, feeling a sharp prick. Looking down, Amy found a gold earring stuck into her right knee. She gingerly pulled it out, placing it in the small pocket of her uniform vest, with fleeting thoughts of depositing it later into the lost and found.

Amy slowly opened the freezer door, her eyes travelling from the pink-nailed fingertips up the arm of the body and over to the victim's face. Someone had carefully buried the girl's body up to her chest in bags of frozen vegetables. Whoever put her there had spent a lot of time packing frozen goods around the body. Somehow, Amy's hands gently cradled the girl's chin and lifted her face upwards. Amy gasped, snatching her hands away. *Anna! What are you even doing here? Sarah worked last night's close shift for you,* she thought.

Amy reached up to the freezer door's handle, using it to pull herself off the floor. She gently moved Anna's hand out of the way, setting it inside the freezer so that she could close the door, almost as if she was tucking her in for bed.

Standing two feet away from the freezer door, staring at the frosty glass and waiting for Shane to come rushing around the corner into the aisle. "The police will be here shortly. Stay clear of the freezer so you don't disturb anything while we wait for them."

Looking down at her hands, Amy realized she had touched the freezer door and the body. "Uh-oh! Too late. I just closed the freezer door."

Shane frowned. "Why would you do that?"

"I don't know! This is kind of, like, my first dead body!"

"I am going to go stand by the front doors to watch for the police," he paused, watching Amy nervously twirl her hair with her fingers. "You should probably come stand by the front doors, too. The rest of the staff will be wandering into work soon. We should probably keep the customers out. I'm sure old man Brookes will show up and want to roam around the store, complaining about the cost of groceries. Today is not a good day to entertain him."

Amy numbly followed Shane to the glass doors of the main entrance. As fellow employees walked up to the doors, Shane let them in, telling them to stay near the front of the store while waiting for the police. Amy ignored the questions being asked around her, trying to remember every detail of the night before. Still, she could not erase the vision of Anna lying in the freezer under frozen vegetables. Shifting her tired body, Amy leaned against a glass window. She closed her eyes, allowing her weight to pull her down to a cold spot on the floor.

Replaying this morning's events in her mind like a horror movie, Amy felt stuck in a continuous, terrifying loop that she didn't want to watch or star in as a main character. How did she get herself mixed up in another murder investigation? Amy hoped to give her statement soon so she could put everything behind her and return to her warm bed. She was still exhausted from working the late shift last night.

What could she do to help? She shook her head, desperately trying to focus, when she realized that Dan, the store manager, had just arrived. His usual ruddy complexion turned white when he was told why the staff were gathered around the front doors, waiting for the police to arrive. Someone said something to him that made him turn and look at Amy. She looked away, avoiding the accusing look in his eyes. Amy suspected the gossip would travel among the employees and be all over town within a few hours. She shuddered, remembering how hurtful words had stung her during her last time in the spotlight.

It didn't take long before the parking lot was lit up, red and blue flashing lights bouncing off the icy snow from yesterday's storm. Officer Gerard and several uniformed police officers pushed through the front doors, followed by young Officer Randy Doyle.

***

The Ice Box, book #2: This will continue in the next publication by Lisa Adair!

If you enjoyed "The Puzzle Box," please leave a review! See the author's website for details.

To connect with the author, visit:
https://www.booksbylisaadair.com
http://www.linktr.ee/booksbylisaadair

About the Author

Lisa Adair

Lisa Adair is a mystery and fantasy author known for her descriptive, immersive storytelling and richly developed characters. She writes *The Glenmere Box Mysteries*, a suspenseful series set in 1980s Saskatchewan, and *The Blaze Peppergrove Adventures*, a fantasy series where urban fairies navigate myths and modern challenges.

Her debut novel, *The Puzzle Box* (2023), launched her mystery series. Drawing on her love of crime fiction and her experiences growing up in northern Saskatchewan, she enjoys crafting atmospheric mysteries with positive role models, self-discovery, and characters who grow through adversity.

Beyond mysteries, Lisa brings her vivid imagination to juvenile fantasy. *Blaze Peppergrove and the Big Race* (2023) introduced young readers to Evergreen Park's lush, magical world, which was later expanded upon in the prequel *Blaze Peppergrove to the Rescue* (2023).

When she's not writing, Lisa enjoys scrapbooking, playing guitar, and exploring Saskatchewan's great outdoors with her husband, children, and beloved rescue dog.

Stay connected! Sign up for her monthly newsletter or follow her on social media:

BooksbyLisaAdair.com.

Also by Lisa Adair

<u>Juvenile Fiction: Fantasy-Adventure</u>

Blaze Peppergrove to the Rescue, Blaze Peppergrove Adventures, #0 (2023)
Blaze Peppergrove and the Big Race, Blaze Peppergrove Adventures, #1 (2023)
The Blaze Peppergrove Adventures, Blaze Peppergrove Adventures, #0 (prequel) & 1 (2025)
Blaze Peppergrove and the Web of Lies, Blaze Peppergrove Adventures, #2 (2025)

A Guide, the First Night of Camp (2023)

Adult Fiction: Mystery

The Puzzle Box, The Glenmere Box Mysteries, #1 (2023)

The Ice Box, The Glenmere Box Mysteries, #2 (2024)

Connect with the Author!

To connect with the author, follow her on social media:
www.BooksByLisaAdair.com

or subscribe to a monthly newsletter.

Reviews for a self-published author are very much appreciated. It encourages continued writing and helps other readers take notice of the stories. Please consider leaving a review where you purchased the book or submit it through the author's website. Thank you.